The Ghosts of Inchmery Road

The Ghosts of Inchmery Road

Mat Guy

1889 books

www.1889books.co.uk

ISBN: 978-1-915045-19-5

Chapter One

Me and Stacey start every shift the same way. I take off my coat, stretch, and look about our gloomy little office. Then I smile.

'My name is Charlie Truckle,' I say, 'and I have the best job in the world.'

Stacey always smiles back, dropping her bag by the side of the large old desk that dominates the room.

'Muh-my nuh-name is Stacey muh-Marsh,' she says, 'and I have the buh-best job in the wuh-world.' Her stutter less pronounced in the safe, familiar surroundings deep in the bowels of our little, lower league football ground

It is something we remind ourselves during more tedious, mundane moments clearing away litter, emptying bins, unblocking sinks. Looking up to the heavens, we repeat our little mantra, with plunger or broom in hand. Because we do: have the best job in the world.

At least, we think so.

It may not pay very much, but for those who love our little football club, it would be their dream job; though, in truth, precious few people even know that it exists – Nightwatchman at Inchmery Road.

There are more important jobs at our club on the road to nowhere, at the foot of the professional game – such as the manager.

His eighteen-hour days help sculpt the fortunes of our team, that in turn forge the moods and disposition of the few thousand supporters that call Inchmery Road their second home, and the Town, as we call our little club, the beating heart of who they are.

Lives mapped out across decades of loyal devotion and little matchday rituals, from that first game as a young child that had them spellbound, through adolescence and adulthood. Success and failure on the pitch becoming their own successes and failures to bear through life.

Successes and failures created, designed, mapped by our manager across countless Saturday afternoons at Inchmery Road, watching the red and yellow shirts of the Town as our latest eleven heroes trot out onto the pitch ready to do battle for us.

The world is ever-changing, but the familiar dimensions of the East and West Stands, the rows of benches along the lower tier, wooden flip-back seats on the upper – the sweeping Inchmery Road Terrace, and the paddocks of its counterpart away on Victoria Road beyond the far goal that separate away fan from home – meeting up with the same people, on the same corner, having the usual at the pub, filtering through the same turnstile, standing at the same spot, for all time – they are the anchor about which memories snag and drag. Memories the manager moulds across training sessions, team talks, and summer signings.

The decades come and go. Fortunes rise and fall. But so long as we have our little club. Our little ground. Our rituals, and friendships, surrounded by the warren of little terraced streets in which we live. Everything else is manageable.

We are anchored. Secure. Safe.

And at the centre of it all, with the weight of our lower league souls on his shoulders, our hopes and dreams – sometimes our only hopes and dreams in what can be an otherwise unforgiving world – piggybacking for extra burden, there is the manager.

He stays long into the night, studying formations, line-ups for the next game. Trying to mould his band of journeymen Fourth Division pros into something bigger, better than the sum of their parts.

Leaning in beneath an anglepoise lamp in his cramped, box of an office, he scans pages of players available for transfer. Heart rising at a particular name, then sinking again at the asking price attached – any fee being too great a fee for the Town, and its life on the footballing breadline.

The manager, haggard, tired, is often the last person we see every night on our rounds. All the other offices long since fallen silent, dark. He will be the first at the training ground in the morning too. Without fail.

Like I said, there are more important jobs than Nightwatchman at our little club on the road to nowhere. General managers who come and go and help keep the operation running smoothly. Keep the turnstiles operated with willing gate people collecting entrance fees on match day. Keep the club shop stocked. The ticket office ticking along. The match programmes delivered on time. Tea urns in tea huts beneath the stands, primed. Stewards decked in bright jackets, at the right spot in the stands or pitchside at the right time.

There are groundsmen who tend the pitch, scale the floodlights to change out failing bulbs, fix broken seats, taps, doors, anything and everything. Secretaries who register players, organise travel to away games, help re-arrange postponed matches, fix-up apprentices with digs.

Accountants who juggle bills and wages against the humble takings every other Saturday.

A laundry ensures kits are washed and ready. A canteen keeps everyone fed and watered. A tea lady with her trolley does her rounds of the offices, the changing rooms, offering out brews and biscuits to all and sundry. Volunteers doing anything and everything to supplement the work of this threadbare staff, where there is always one more job than willing pair of hands.

All vital, sometimes unassuming cogs in our little footballing institution.

And then there is us.

The Nightwatchmen. Or in Stacey's case: Nightwatchwoman.

If players and managers, and those busy worker bees behind the scenes who often stay in post for decades on end, as devoted as the supporters, are the heart of the football club – the very blood that pumps about this old and fading little ground that has stood for more than a century, holding it together with ingenuity and love, then the nightwatchman is the soul.

Detached in many ways from the rest of the team – coming in to work as most are leaving for the day – the Nightwatchmen of Inchmery Road have had the time, the space, the quiet to see beyond the hurly burly of the nine to five, or the match day. To see the sum of all the hard work, love and sacrifice. The sum of all the devotion poured into this creaking little football stadium. Time to see the lives lived, the friendships borne, triumph and tragedy, both on and off the pitch. And the little, everyday acts of belonging that enrich everyday lives in extraordinary ways.

We Nightwatchmen, we have seen it all. And we curate it – the stories that can't easily be found in match reports and the statistics of a season. Moments and events in the lives of those that have made Inchmery Road the special place that it is. That have poured their heart and soul into our humble club. Beautiful stories of friendship and hope that deserve to be remembered.

We see, we watch, we chronicle, the ghosts of Inchmery Road.

There have only been five permanent Nightwatchmen since the position was created in 1907. And I am the fifth. All being well, Stacey will become the sixth, when my time comes.

I come in a little before five p.m, wandering up through the dusky tangle of tight-knit streets of terraced houses, tiny backyards and alleyways criss-crossed with lines of limp washing, lamps in front rooms sending slivers of light across the pavement from cracks in curtains drawn to keep out the night. I walk and watch as the floodlights anchored in each corner of Inchmery Road begin to rise up above the rooftops.

Then I turn into Inchmery Road, the street, to find Inchmery Road, the football ground, the main stand looking out and across at the pub nestled in the middle of the run of houses lining the road.

It is where some of the office staff head after work on a Friday, waving goodbye to me as they cheerily celebrate the end of another working week; on a still night the faint sound of jukebox and laughter as the door opens. It is where generation after generation of supporter goes before a match, often spilling out onto the street, leaning against the wall outside. It is where they return at a quarter to five to commiserate, sometimes even cheer a Town win.

To me the football starts the moment you spy those floodlights, turn that corner into Inchmery Road. As soon as you can see the West Stand, the wall of the terracing backing up over the road, the pub, the main gates, the ring of the club shop bell. The football begins at that corner. And so too my job.

First things first, we drop our bags off, Stacey and I, in the Nightwatchman's office, say our little saying, then we make a tea for the general manager and ourselves, spending a few minutes catching up while everything begins to wind down for the evening, staff finally able to relax as shutters come down on club shop and ticket office, phones switched to answerphone, desks darkened, vacated. A few hours respite before the plate spinning begins again, with too few hands, money, resources. Straining every sinew to maintain and preserve our peeling, creaking little club at the foot of the Fourth Division.

Sarah is our current general manager. Young, barely into her thirties, she has an infectious smile and her eyes sparkle behind square-rimmed glasses. Auburn hair styled into a bob, she has long since dispensed with smart shoes and trouser suits, finding trainers and stretch-fabric attire more suited to crawling beneath concessions stands to try and source a problem with the beer lines. Or dismantling ticket printers to try and eke out a few more months, years, from tired, failing machinery. Or helping to bring in deliveries for the club shop in the pouring rain. Or anything else that may need attending to.

She always smiles when we appear at her door, flopping down into her chair and blowing out her cheeks. She pulls out a biscuit tin from her drawer and sits it on her desk, and we have a cup of tea, a biscuit or two, and she tells us about the day. All the spinning plates that will just about wait until the morning before potential catastrophe.

Although Nightwatchman is a monitoring brief, ensuring Inchmery Road is secure and safe, doing rounds of all the locked doors and shuttered turnstiles, the large iron gates in the car park, making sure its precious contents remain so, there is also plenty of time for other things. And so, over the years, I have learnt where deliveries go, and what jobs need doing. And in the long, still hours of night, we do our bit.

Sarah has never asked, and I have never offered. But jobs just get done. Shirts are unpacked and placed on hangers in the club shop. Crates of drinks are lugged up into the players' lounge, the supporters bar. Damaged seats in the East and West Stand are oiled, dismantled, fudged back together with parts salvaged from long-broken cousins gathering dust in storerooms.

It is nice, in the hush, the dark, fixing this and that. The sweep of car lights in the streets beyond. The laughter of friends after turning-out time at the pub. All observed from our quiet, shadowy spot.

We do it slowly, in our own time. And, one by one, they get crossed off Sarah's list on her desk.

In return we get that warm smile, I get a hug, Stacey settling for a few of Sarah's best biscuits from her special tin. An often cripplingly awkward shyness making her shrink away from any physical contact. And we have a nice chat on the day. On this and that.

Tea drunk, biscuits eaten, we wave Sarah off, then do a sweep of the labyrinthine corridors beneath the West Stand to see where we are at. And who is left.

Almost always Sarah is the last one out, bar one. And at the end of the top corridor, beyond the players' lounge and the little conference room that has seen every one of his predecessors hired and fired, the manager sits in his little office. The creeping dread of a losing run closing in on him, bearing down out of the shadow that deepens and sneaks out of the corners toward him. The light of his little lamp illuminating pages of potential saviours available for loan, the only thing saving him from his own nagging doubt.

If he is in his office, I always knock politely, wish him a good evening. And despite the pressure, the fear of failure, the cold hard black and white of the league table printed in the local paper, the Town's endeavours for the season tabulated dangerously near the bottom and highlighted in a darker print to add extra resonance, he always looks up and smiles. Gives us a few moments.

'How are you doing, Charlie? Stacey? Are you well? I don't suppose you know of any twenty goal a season strikers' looking for a club, do you?'

Stacey always giggles, shakes her head as she peers round the door like an inquisitive, but uncertain kitten. I will shake my head, sometimes mention a young lad who had been performing well for the reserves in the Combination League.

'Thank you, Charlie, I will give him a look. Have a good night now.'

The Nightwatchman's office has two doors. One leads off the main entrance, and if propped open can offer up a decent view of the foyer and the reception desk.

The second is at the end of a corridor lined with old black and white photographs of past teams, individuals, groups of proud, smiling folks pitchside, a few pennants gifted the club by visiting teams in town for a friendly, their colours faded over time. At the far end, a locked door opens out onto the concourse of the lower tier of the West Stand.

Beyond, a rake of benches sweep down to the pitch and a narrow track of red grit, the colour and texture of an old athletics track, that sometimes kicks up and over the few front rows if a player slides into it after a lunging tackle. An occupational hazard down among the cheap seats.

The Nightwatchman's office is naturally cold. A chill draft along the corridor from frigid winters swirling about still, silent blocks of benches and seating beyond would keep it unappealing if not tended to. The single bulb in the ceiling of this windowless room would make it seem stark, clinical, if not tempered.

But the lamp on the desk, with its shade that always tilts over to one side, even when corrected, and the three-bar heater on the floor that glows a soothing orange when lit, softens the edges and illuminates enough of the room to dispense with the ceiling light. And in time the Nightwatchman's office becomes warm enough, even cosy.

The walls of this little office, the corridor, slip back through the ages. Old photographs of my predecessors stand with nameless backroom staff, and long-gone players and managers. Friends, family all. Washed-out pictures of people, faces fading, some images water-damaged from when the visiting changing rooms above flooded in nineteen fifty-nine. Streaks bleaching some parts of the images to a sepia-tinged fog of faint outlines. Features, smiles lost. Only memory putting a name to blurred, dappled bodies.

No matter their state, they remain on the walls. Names are handed down from one generation of Nightwatchman to the next. Maintaining the meaning of those ghosted faces.

Gerald Mackie was the first. Appointed in the summer of 1907. You can find him right the way down the end of the corridor, by the door to the West Stand. A broad-shouldered, barrel-chested man in his late fifties, his face in shadow from the peak of his flat cap, flanked by two young lads in football kit, arms folded, beaming smiles as all three stood out on the Inchmery Road pitch. Behind them, through a haze of time, dust, and a bright, sunny day, the faint outline of the little box stand, a sweep of terracing in a paddock in front of it that used to stand where the East Stand is now. It is a photograph that conjures up the rich smell of fresh cut grass, the soothing warmth of a hot summer sun on your face. Unrefined happiness.

Gerald Mackie, standing proudly between these two young apprentices on 6th of August 1913, set the tone for all the Nightwatchmen to come.

He first saw the romance of this fledgling club. What it meant to all those who couldn't help but gravitate toward it on a match day. Their souls, their very identity caught in a tide of intoxicating play, and the hope that it would bring.

In standing shoulder to shoulder on the terraces with best friend and stranger alike, all would be united in the cause. All captivated, whisked away from the tribulations of everyday life. Elevated above it all on darting wing-play, barnstorming shots into the roof of the net, swaying, baying as one on the cramped terraces behind the goal.

Gerald Mackie saw what it meant, our little club away out on the road to nowhere. He saw the pride, the passion. The joy at victory. The sorrow in defeat. The mood, the hope of a few thousand followers of the boys in red and yellow, dependent on the fortunes of a Saturday afternoon.

Mackie first saw the reverence, the near religious devotion, the importance of belonging, of feeling like you belonged. He had, after all, been an ever-present behind the Inchmery Road goal since the club's inception back in 1885.

He set the tone. And as the very first Nightwatchman, he started collecting memories. Stories. Ghosts. Tales of love, devotion, friendship, and belonging through good times and bad, through everyday triumphs and tragedies. He started collecting tales, the soul of Inchmery Road.

It sits in the drawer of the Nightwatchman's desk. In the Nightwatchman's office – Mackie's ledger.

It is a heavy, over-sized, leatherbound book. Like one of those large bibles that you see in a church pulpit. And when it is opened the spine groans and creaks, the brittle pages warped through time crinkle and chatter like a muffled rattle when flicked through. It is a very satisfying sound: spine and page – when the book is opened. It sounds grand, important, its contents precious, which of course it is to those of us that know of its existence. To those of us who care about the Town.

Mackie's handwriting is large, slow, deliberate but flourishing. As if every word written took some real thought, to ensure it was just the right word for the moment, for the story it was telling.

Intercut with diagrams, sketches, little maps with arrows, asterisks, footnotes, Mackie's script lasts for thirty pages or so before a different hand takes over. Then a fair number of pages on and a third hand appears. Then a fourth. Finally, well over two thirds of the way in, comes me.

My handwriting is terrible. So, I print in capitals. It has a certain charm to it. It doesn't look aggressive. More like those ancient runic symbols of civilisations lost. Some letters larger than others. The arms of my t's sweeping across the whole word. D'o and w's always more prominent. I don't know why. It is legible. Different. As all the hands in Mackie's book are. Sketches and blocks of text in varying degrees of detail and accomplishment.

From the nineteen-tens, cuttings from the local paper appear. Little columns of print. The odd grainy picture.

From the mid-twenties black and white photographs are found glued in place to accompany the writing. From the seventies a few colour Polaroids have been fastened, written around. Absorbed into the text.

At the end of the book there is a swathe of smooth, untouched pages. Ready and waiting for Stacey.

Pages for after I am gone. Which is not just yet. I'm not quite done. But enough of that. Back to the beginning.

It is ironic that, by and large, the Nightwatchman's job misses out on the moments that matter the most – the matches themselves.

By the terms of the job, the Nightwatchman isn't required on Saturday afternoons until just after the final whistle. Wading against the tide of souls draining away from Inchmery Road and into the warren of cramped terrace streets that hem it in. The electricity of a feisty encounter diffusing among the gloom of the evening as stewards sweep discarded newspapers from the terracing, walk the rows of the stands to make sure all are gone. The chatter from the players' lounge obscured by the opaque glass in the doors, gauging moods and the result by the ferocity, or absence of laughter within.

General rule of thumb – if the manager's office door is closed, you can be sure that it is to hide the dismay within.

The rhythmic roll of tumble dryers on timers, laundering freshly washed match kit, coming to a standstill in the darkened kit room long after everyone has gone home. The idling of the away team's coach by the entrance, ready to spirit them away on long, tiring trips back home to far flung points of the country and Division Four. The slow drain of the car park as players and directors drift away. Taillights turning out the main gates. The mood in which all are conducted can be an indicator to an absent Nightwatchman as to the result of the afternoon's match.

Though, of course, the Nightwatchman never needs these clues.

The Nightwatchman is never absent. Despite neither being required to be there or being paid for the privilege.

The Nightwatchman never misses a game. First team or reserve.

We are there, watching the Town from behind the benches of the lower tier of the West Stand. Getting lost in the mood of the crowd caught up in the game. Monitoring the roars of encouragement, groans of disappointment. Cheers at a goal. Derision at an opposition miss. Mutters of discontent and misery at a costly defeat. Doubling over to try and keep the flight of a high ball in view as it sails up into the sky, lost behind the upper tier above and its creaking wooden seats – you can tell if an obscured ball is a good one by the clatter of seats flipping up, boots scuffing on the boards above, their occupants rising to their feet as one, in anticipation at a Town striker through on goal – markers for those of us in the cheaper seats until the ball falls back into view.

At reserve team games, where those few supporters wanting to see Combination League football are housed in the upper tier of the

West Stand, we Nightwatchmen have the benches to ourselves. Listening to the shouts of the players echoing about empty stands, the sounds of buses drifting past outside. We wait anxiously for the half-time score of the first team to be put up on the scoreboard above the away fans paddock, wandering down to the front few rows of benches to get a clear view of the Town's fortune, or otherwise, at some distant away fixture.

We are always there.

At the final whistle, after the post-match routines are observed and the stadium falls silent, then Inchmery Road becomes ours.

The Nightwatchman walks the perimeter. Checks the turnstiles are shuttered. Rattles the exit gates. Every door. Checks the padlock on the club shop shutter, the main gates.

Then we walk the interior. Rattling those same doors and gates from the inside. Walking the red grit pitch side. We head past the tunnel beneath the corner of the Inchmery Road terrace with wooden gates at the far end that open out onto the street, where on Saturdays an ambulance would back into it, just in case it was needed by player or supporter alike.

On match days the ambulance driver, the attendant, the ground staff with long pitchforks who tend to the pitch at half time, bedding back in sods of turf kicked up from ferocious tackling, would huddle together on a little wooden bench pressed up against the wall, cowering from the howling winds that could whistle through the gates and cut you clean in half at the height of winter.

On cold windy nights we hurry down to check the padlock, then back again before the chill could get into your bones.

Then it would be on across the terraces to the East Stand and its cloistered turnstiles, then down to the Victoria Road end. The pitch, a brilliant green beneath the floodlights, snaps into darkness in quarters as floodlight breakers are tripped, and one by one, four great banks of bulbs atop their pylons snuff out. The remainder of my rounds completed by torchlight.

Inchmery Road secured, we tend to odd chores that might help put a smile on Sarah's face. We make a cup of tea. Sip it on the benches of the West Stand, taking in the beauty of this grand old ground, shadowed, silent.

Then, as night falls, and the living rest, we warm ourselves in front of the little three-bar fire in our office and turn our attention to Gerald Mackie's ledger. We turn our attention to those chronicled within. We check in on the ghosts of Inchmery Road.

Stories. Lower league legend. Tales of wonder and sorrow. Oddities. Peculiarities. Humour. Tragedy. Gerald Mackie began collecting the tales of the everyday, the extraordinary, and everything in between that was of interest.

Tales of the people that made Inchmery Road what it was, often through no heroics out on the pitch, but simple acts of humanity, moments on the terraces and in the stands, in the streets outside.

It was a heady mix. Stories compiled so as they could never fade or slip completely from the unofficial history of our club that is handed down from generation to generation over pints in the pub, or a fish and chip supper on the way home from a game. On the terraces in absent moments at half time, or before kick-off.

Mackie's ledger attempted to save all of note from falling between the cracks, and into eternal shadow. A social history of our little club.

There was always something new to discover among the pages of dense scrawl. Stories somehow overlooked on the countless previous perusals. Little footnotes or asides not previously noticed that add extra meaning, extra resonance.

The ledger has also been how one Nightwatchman has educated their successor on the unwritten job specifications of the post – keeping history, memories, people alive, keeping them safe. Tending to the ghosts of Inchmery Road is as much a part of it as any job in the present.

The ledger was how I taught young Stacey, though she would become the first in our role to have been a part of the ledger long before she even knew of its existence. Her family having been an integral part of the fabric of this club for almost as long as it has existed.

Even so, I shared the ledger with her, as it had been shared with me. Warped and Crinkling pages between those old grubbed and weathered covers sitting on the desk in our office, like the cliffs of the Jurassic Coast, layers of stories, people, moments, stacked up over time, waiting to be explored.

And just like the other Nightwatchmen, in reading the ledger, she has taken it to heart, and those contained within. And, in time, she has begun to contribute. Adding colour, depth to the stories of our little club.

Stories like the tale of Jon 'Blitz' Sugg. It was one of the first ones I ever showed Stacey, being one of my favourites. A little piece of Town magic. And a decent enough introduction to our work in caring for these ghosts of Inchmery Road.

Mary Sugg worked in the fish market down by the harbour, where a small fishing fleet would off-load their catch after a night's work out at sea, trailing nets back and forth for Turbot, Plaice, and Haddock.

After a half day on Saturdays, she would walk up to Inchmery Road to watch the Town. Without fail.

By September 1940 Mary was heavily pregnant with her first child, which in her own mind was no way near a good enough reason to miss her beloved Town play. Illness, inclement weather or injury had never stopped her before. Nor would an imminent baby, or the very real threat of air raids and falling bombs that were becoming commonplace across the town during the Blitz.

She would half-walk, half-waddle with her arm supporting the crook of her back up through town and take her spot on the benches of the East Stand and continue to watch her team – a rag-tag band of professionals not yet conscripted to the front line, decent amateurs whose jobs were necessary for the war-effort, and promising youngsters drafted into the War League to help keep some semblance of normality in a world blighted with the creeping dread of invasion.

To Mary it didn't matter that it wasn't the Football League side of a couple of years previous. It didn't matter that matches were often abandoned long before full time due to air raids. It didn't matter that games were played in front of a fraction of the crowds.

It was still the Town. Her team. She would go.

On Saturday the 21st of September 1940, a War League fixture against Newport County barely lasted twenty minutes before the air raid sirens sounded and were almost immediately drowned out by the opening up of flack guns on the edge of town. Greats balls of black smoke bursting in the air, choking the sky as the dread drone of bombers overhead, somewhere above the sea of barrage balloons grew louder and louder.

Players ran for the cover of the West Stand, the designated air raid shelter of Inchmery Road. It was no safer than any other spot around the ground. But a place had to be designated, and the depths of the West Stand was chosen, even though a direct hit would have been catastrophic to anyone hiding out there. Supporters skittered down the terraces and vaulted down into the benches of the lower tier. Those in the East Stand streamed across the pitch to shelter, then looked back in horror at Mary, tottering painfully slowly with the burden of her load, not yet at the centre circle as the bombs began to fall somewhere close by, the ground shaking, a deafening roar as bricks and mortar dissolved in an instant. Somewhere among the knit of streets beyond, lives were changed forever, lives were lost.

Harry Bell, the Town centre half, a young lad brought up from the local junior leagues to bolster a threadbare squad, leapt back out onto the pitch. Head down, the thrumming of terrible engines above, the sickening boom of dropped ordnance, he ran to Mary along with a supporter, a young man by the name of Danny Stokes. Isolated, exposed out on the pitch, one stood each side of her, and they scooped her up and carried her across, where others helped lift her down and across the benches to relative safety.

It was only then that Mary, Harry, Danny and the rest discovered that her waters had broken. The violence, the noise of the bomb, the fear had combined to induce labour. And before a midwife, a doctor, could be safely called, Mary gave birth to Jonathan Sugg, right there in the bowels of the West Stand as the bombs fell, ably assisted by Harry Bell in his Town kit, and Danny Stokes – who wrapped up the newborn in his Town scarf to keep him warm.

When the raiders past was sounded, after more than an hour, an ambulance was fetched, and mother and child were taken off to safety, while Bell trotted back out onto the pitch, Stokes clambered back up into the East Stand benches, and a further twenty minutes' play was completed before the referee called time with the failing light.

In the margins of the ledger, as an aside to the block of handwritten notes on the events, Stanley Peters, Nightwatchman during the war, scribbled down the result, a three-one win for Newport County. Attendance three hundred and eighty-nine.

For their bravery, Mary made Bell and Stokes Godparents to baby Jonathan. A photograph had been fastened in the ledger of the three of them standing pitchside, with Stokes gingerly holding a swaddled baby hidden by folds of blanket. The empty West Stand rising up behind them. Both men in their best suits. Hair slicked back. Bell holding his flat cap to his chest, they flanked Mary, who stood with the scarf used to keep her baby warm draped over her shoulders.

Broad smiles on a sunny autumn day.

Beneath the photograph, taken by a staff photographer of the local paper, and printed in the following Wednesday's edition, two asterisks. The first followed by a note to turn the page. The second, written in blue rather than the black that chronicled Mary's birthing adventure requested the reader to turn a number of pages further on.

The first asterisk I will leave for now, for another time. I will move right on to the second, and a page littered with a newspaper advertisement, a photograph, and a folded sheet of grainy heavy bond, tactile paper fastened in place about columns of Stanley Peter's handwriting.

The advertisement was from the local paper, dated Thursday the 21st of November 1957 and detailed that Saturday's fixture at Inchmery Road – a third team match, known as the 'A' team, in the county league.

With the first and reserve teams taking precedence it was rare for the thirds to play at Inchmery Road. Their humble endeavour, where apprentices learnt their trade, and local amateurs who played for expenses only and the pride of being able to say that they once played for the Town, were often to be found at a roped off pitch up on the common overlooking the sea.

They sometimes played on the Football League ground once or twice a season. And Saturday the 23rd of November, at quarter past two, against Hythe & Power United in a County League Division Three fixture would be their first of that 57/58 season.

The story was an anonymous one. A footnote, even in the Town's modest history. Missed by many, if not all. Save for the Nightwatchmen. And those involved.

Carefully unfolding that piece of paper, which was a team sheet from the County League match against Hythe & Power, you might still miss it, if you didn't read the blocks of writing about the ad, the photograph, the team sheet, properly. Follow the asterisks' trail right back to the twenty first of September, nineteen forty.

There, in the line-up, at number seven for the Town, a seventeen-year-old by the name of Jon 'Blitz' Sugg, playing his first ever match at the place of his birth.

The photograph, taken by Peters, showed a mud-spattered young man in a Town kit, a proud looking Mary, and the recently retired Harry Bell, who had made it as a professional for the Town after the war, playing for ten seasons in their backline. All three stood beneath the floodlights at the side of the pitch. Game done. Celebrating the moment, their unlikely connection to one another, and life come about full circle.

Jon 'Blitz' Sugg, as he would forever be known, induced into this world by the Luftwaffe, didn't quite reach the heights of his mother's saviour. He played three seasons as a regular for the thirds in the amateur County League, before one season on non-contract forms for the reserves in the professional Combination League.

He managed five games. All away. At the grand old grounds of Bristol Rovers, Charlton Athletic, Shrewsbury Town, Walsall, and Newport County – where he was named, nickname and all, on the team sheet at Somerton Park. All completely unaware as to why he was called that, and the unique bond he had with their club, that eighteen years earlier, a wide-eyed Newport side in their amber shirts had cowered beneath falling bombs and had prayed for his safe delivery into this world.

It was an unassuming Town career, but one that Blitz's mum held so very dear. Her lad playing in the precious red and yellow strip that had long since captivated her. A dream come true for mother and child – stepping out at Inchmery Road the icing on the cake. Being able to tell anyone that would listen that her lad was born up at Inchmery Road, during a bombing raid in the war, and then he went on to play there, for the Town.

It was everything, you could tell from their expressions in the photograph. That Town shirt captured forever on the shoulders of her lad.

Released by the reserves, Jon would play a few more years back in the County League for a few local teams before a knee injury ended his football pursuits. After that 'Blitz' would join his mum on the walk up from the fish market to see the Town every other Saturday. Just two of the sea of faces looking out on the play from the shadowy rows of benches of the East Stand. Jon wearing the scarf he had been born into at every home game until Mary's passing aged seventy-one in 1992, then he would sit alone until his death in 2010.

Both services were sparsely populated, Mary's attended by Bob Andrews – Nightwatchman number four. I went to Jon's, though I was only a lad at the time of his Inchmery Road playing debut. Though I felt like I knew him, his mum, through Mackie's ledger. And like Bob in nineteen ninety-two, I pasted the order of service into the Nightwatchman's book.

Their remarkable story, from first to last, safe, for all time, in the pages of Gerald Mackie's ledger.

The very first shift of Stacey's as a trainee Nightwatchwoman, after I had shown her how to do our rounds, I showed her the ledger, the tale of Jon 'Blitz' Sugg, and we sat on the benches of the West Stand, Stacey looking out at the pitch, the ground that had changed very little since that day, imagining the scene of falling bombs, deafening explosions, Mary Sugg trying to reach safety.

'Huh-how brave were they, Chu-Charlie, running out luh-like that?'

And a day or so later she brought with her a sheet of paper, stowed carefully in an envelope.

'The luh-library has all the old puh-papers, guh-going back, well, all the way. On muh-microfilm. I found thu-this. From the duh-day Juh-Jon was born.'

It was a dark and muddy reproduction of a photograph sat in a sea of text from the local paper, dated Monday the 23rd of September 1940.

It was of a non-descript residential street. Terraced houses either side. The street deserted. Normal, and yet odd at the same time. Tape criss-crossing windows. Sandbag emplacements on a corner. And above, in the sky, dark clouds of smoke, making it seem like dusk, partially obscuring a scene of tracer fire flailing up into the gloom, silhouettes of two bombers above a sea of tethered barrage balloons. Beyond the rooftops, the glow of burning, from a direct hit.

'Wuh-what they must have suh-seen, eh, chu-Charlie? I can't tell wuh-what street this is. Buh-but it muh-must be close by. To Inchmery ruh-Road. Don't you thu-think?'

I did think. It reminded me of the warren of streets that enclosed our old football ground. Fanning out in every direction. All familiar, yet unique in their own way. To those who lived there.

We sat quietly for a time, staring into that terrible scene, then I took it up.

'Can we have this? For the ledger?' I asked her. She smiled, nodded, proud that I thought her work worthy of being included in it. Becoming a part of the story itself, for the next person to discover. She carefully slipped it between the pages holding 'Blitz' and Mary's story. Another layer. More context for those to come.

Stacey is a perfect fit for Nightwatchman, or the very first Nightwatchwoman. It seems like the job selects you, rather than you discover it. At just the right time. When you need it the most.

It happened that way for Stacey. It happened that way for me. And we weren't the first. Here's hoping we won't be the last.

When I first met Stacey, she was six years old and she helped her mother on match days at the family pitch by the main gates, where the Marsh family going back generations had sold match programmes for close to a century.

Layla would keep shooing her from out behind her legs, and hand her a little pile of programmes, and she would stand awkwardly, a little bobble hat pulled down as far as it would go in the hope that it might swallow her up entirely, and whenever a customer bent down and asked her how much she would blush:

'A puh. A puh. A puh-pound please.'

After a few warm smiles and sales, she would relax a little, so as it would only be 'a puh-pound please.' But as soon as she saw a funny look, or a raised eyebrow from those less sensitive to a little girl's stammer, she would fall mute with frustration, shame, and sidle back behind her Mum for a time, for as long as she could before she was coaxed back out.

I would always stop by to say hello to them both, pour Layla a warm mug of tea from the programme sellers' flask, have a chat. And when asked if Stacey would like to accompany me on the rest of my rounds delivering tea to the other pitches, she would look up at her Mum imploringly, skipping in alongside me when Layla had smiled, nodded her approval.

She would hold my hand through the busiest crowds outside the Inchmery Road terrace, then I would hand her a little chocolate bar from my pocket, and we would wander on our rounds while she ate it, along Lepe Road, up onto Victoria Road, finally back across the car park into Inchmery Road, handing out tin mugs of tea to all the sellers.

We would do it slowly, dawdling wherever we could, to save Stacey from having to face more customers, getting back to Layla with just enough time to pack everything up and get them to their seats in the East Stand not long after kick-off.

It was nice, our little friendship. I would chunter on for the both of us, and Stacey would laugh at my terrible jokes – those piercing blue eyes sparkling; an adorable smile. And in time, as we went round, she would snap off a square of chocolate and hand it to me:

'Chuh-chocolate, chuh-Charlie?'

It would melt my heart. Stacey choosing to talk to you was an honour. Or it felt like it to me. Her exposing herself like that. A precious trust built.

I would cherish it. Still do. Me and my little mate.

At the age of thirteen she was given a pitch of her own beneath the poplars on Victoria Road. It was the most sedate pitch, mostly serving the old-timers of the Upper East Stand.

She hated it. She would smile weakly as she set off with her box of programmes, visibly shaking with nerves. And while some sellers shouted out their wares, Stacey shrunk up against the wall by the Upper East Stand turnstiles, a small bundle of programmes in her arms, bobble hat pulled down so low over her eyes in the hope that she would become invisible.

It didn't work. People would stop off to buy a copy, most waiting patiently as she tried to spell out the one pound fifty asking price. And when it got so bad, she would just point at the top corner of the cover, where the price was listed.

Layla never knew, but I would often wander round to find young Stacey and stand with her to keep her company. Having seen her struggle I made her a rosette in the Town colours, with the price of the programmes in the middle in large black numbers that no one could miss. She would keep it in her pocket until she was out of sight of the other sellers, then she would pop it on her coat, and it would help keep the questions down.

I think that Stacey appreciated my company, and how I would chat to the buyers so as she didn't need to. And as soon as you had one or two stop off, you would be surprised how many more fell in line behind them, until you had a little queue form.

I would shout out the price, and young Stacey would hand out the programmes and take the money, and everyone would be happy.

She would still be the lowest performing seller when all the money had been counted up, but it would boost her little pay packet every Saturday night, where a basic hourly rate was topped up with a ten pence commission for every issue sold.

She would always buy me a chocolate bar with hers and leave it on my desk. A little thank you for my company and help. I would have it with a tea late at night, and I would think of that little girl, and my heart would break picturing the abject fear in her eyes as she set off round to her pitch.

It never seemed to get any easier for her. She was just a girl lacking in any kind of self-confidence, self-belief.

Which was not born out of any lack of love. Her mum doted on her and worried about her endlessly.

She did her schoolwork, and did well enough, but she made no friends, never went to the school discos. She was never invited to sleep-overs. To birthday parties. She never joined any of the sports teams, despite her clear passion for the Town. She ghosted through school, through life on the periphery. Withdrawn to the edges of the playground, often finding a quiet set of steps on the far side of school to pass lunchtime.

And when school was up, and others headed off to college, or elsewhere, Stacey remained a part-time programme seller. A volunteer at the local library. The rest of the time spent reading in her bedroom.

A life seemingly stalled. For a time, at least. Though she never seemed unhappy.

And then the Nightwatchman job came up. Or, at least, relief nightwatchman, two to three nights a week.

Stacey's bobble hat is as much a fixture as her dark hair, those crystal blue eyes, her smile that can warm the coldest day. From the first onset of autumn through to the last days of spring, that hat of hers in the Town colours goes with her everywhere.

Inside, where it is warmer, she pulls the hat back a little to expose her forehead so as she doesn't get hot, letting the hat flop back on itself like an old-fashioned nightcap. She does it instinctively, in one sweeping motion, pulling it back to her hairline, where on occasion a lock of jet-black hair can fall loose and frame her face.

She did so those first few shifts of her new job, where I first showed her how we tended to the bricks and mortar of Inchmery Road, and then, back inside the Nightwatchman's office, how we tended to its ghosts.

And that is our routine still, we walk our rounds, we do our chores, and then we lean in towards Gerald Mackie's ledger, and I watch Stacey scour through the stories collected there.

Learning the mostly forgotten tales of our football club's soul. That we are tasked with keeping safe. Handing them down from Nightwatchman to Nightwatchman.

Stories of her beloved Town. Of the people who have loved this club just as she does.

Mostly hidden people, just like her. People possibly lost for ever, had it not been for Gerald Mackie.

And his ghost.

Chapter Two

It seems certain that Mackie's ledger would never have existed, had it not been for chance, and an unlikely friendship. That all those stories and people collected within would have become lost to time, if not for that bleached out old photograph at the end of the Nightwatchman's corridor. And the story of one of those young apprentices standing proudly next to Mackie out on the pitch one summer's day in 1913.

Without him, that young lad making his way in the world, his story, how many more may have faded away to nothing with the passing of time? Without him inspiring Gerald to start his book, would anyone else have ever noticed Mackie's ghosts? Would anyone have known that they were there? Would anyone have bothered to chronicle them, keep them safe?

As it is, it is just us Nightwatchmen, who keep an eye out for them. Who tend to them, just as Mackie had hoped that we would. It is just us who acknowledge them. Remember them. Help them, as best as we can. We keep them safe. We do what we can for them. Just as Mackie did for the very first, for young Peter Wright.

And as soon as I shared his story with young Stacey, she too became as enraptured with him, with his tale, as the rest of us had.

I remember it was a cold winter's night. Howling gales whistling through the main stand, driving rain pounding on the roof, falling in cascades down onto the grit track.

We sat, mugs of tea in hand, and leant over the ledger. And I turned back to the very front, to that first story of Mackie's. And I told the tale, as it had been told me. As Mackie had wanted it told, from his own hand, stretched across those old brittle pages before us.

Peter Wright signed for the Town as a fresh faced sixteen-year-old, straight from school in the summer of 1913. He moved down from Newcastle after a successful trial, and lodged with Gerald Mackie for the whole season, along with the other fresh face in that photograph at the end of the corridor, the eighteen-year-old Michael Trim, from Aberystwyth, Wales.

Wingers Wright and Trim had both been considered prospects for the future, but after a horrendous start by the Town to the

1913/14 season, both found themselves plucked from the reserves and into first team action.

Peter Wright was a slight lad with gangly limbs, a shock of blond hair, and sharp blue eyes bristling with the excitement of a debut season as a professional footballer. In Mackie's photograph he stood proud, beaming, yet swamped in the Town kit that he would never grow into.

He made his first team debut a week after his seventeenth birthday and set up a goal in a three-two defeat to Swansea in December 1913.

He had arrived for the game on his bicycle that had been gifted him by Gerald Mackie for his seventeenth. And, unsure where to stow it, he picked an old oak tree at the edge of the club's car park to rest his precious gift, fastening it with a length of chain and a lock that he wore like a Bandolero's bullet belt, from shoulder to opposing hip, whilst riding.

It was a nice, safe spot, and from then on, for every training session, every game, it would be that tree he would trust to tend to it.

It was not a new bike, far from it. Mackie had discovered it in a scrapper's yard and had spent time making it as new after a series of botched attempts by Wright to use the buses to get home from training to his lodgings. He could never seem to use the right combination and would often trudge in long after he should have, having been round the houses. He would shake his head, slump into an armchair in the front room, and over a cup of tea and a biscuit he would bemoan his own failings, looking down with consternation at his pocket timetable and the myriad bus numbers and tortuous routes.

Gerald Mackie had never married. Courting had never been his strong suit. A shyness and awkwardness blighted any attempt at it. As well as a job, working such antisocial hours limited opportunities to visit the pictures, or local dances.

He had come to terms with bachelorhood. He didn't mind his own company. But to fend off any potential feelings of isolation and loneliness, he had answered the Town's call for lodgings for their young apprentice players, stepping out away from home for the first time.

It worked well for both parties. It helped the club out, providing a safe and warm environment for a couple of lads each season. Company and home comforts helping to stave off homesickness, keeping their minds on their football.

And it also helped Mackie out, and his own wellbeing, animating his otherwise suffocatingly still and silent little house with life and laughter – and though he had put up young prospects before, and enjoyed it thoroughly, he enjoyed the company of Wright and Trim like no other.

They got along well and could spend many an afternoon telling stories and laughing over a pot of tea.

Conversation came easily. Silences were comfortable. And Christmas became a special time – he would cook dinner while they trained ahead of their match on Boxing Day. Then they would sit around a little tree, that they would all help to decorate, and exchange presents. Afterwards Mackie would wash up and sit quietly, while Peter and Michael went back to the club, who would let the young players away from home use the office telephone to call home – or wherever proud parents had found a line. For Peter Wright's parents, that had been the local rectory. There would be a glass of sherry waiting for them when done. A warm smile. Idle chat to help ease the nagging melancholy of missed loved ones

Of all who had passed through his little terraced house, it was Peter and Michael who became most like surrogate sons to Mackie.

He collected team sheets and programmes from their reserve and first team endeavours, proudly tucking clippings from the local paper inside them when they mentioned Wright or Trim. He stored them in the top left drawer in the Nightwatchman's desk – where they sit to this day.

He loved their company during the season and felt their absence keenly during the summer. He circled the first day of pre-season on his calendar, waiting for their return.

Because of his affection for them both, Mackie would spend some of his shift as Nightwatchman oiling the cogs and chain on the reclaimed scrappers bicycle, fitting a set of second-hand inner tubes that he had patched up to make good, dismantling and cleaning pedals that had frozen solid, rubbing down rust spots and daubing them with a preservative treatment. Finally, he painted the bicycle a dark racing green, and presented it to Peter on the morning of his birthday, hoping that it would help him find his way.

Peter adored it. He had never owned a bicycle before. And he would care for it like he was caring for a precious jewel, wiping the frame down after every trip, cleaning mud from the tyres with a damp cloth before towelling it down and storing it in the little shed in Mackie's cramped backyard.

And he would always be sure to don his chain and lock whenever he set out in the morning. To keep her safe.

From that day on everyone at the club would know when Peter had arrived or was leaving. The ring of his bell as he entered and exited through the main gates of Inchmery Road, the rattling and chinking of his chain as he wrestled with his favourite oak tree, securing bike to trunk.

He was such a softly spoken young lad, his lilting Geordie accent never carrying far in the changing rooms or players' lounge, in Mackie's lodgings. It was his bell as he waved to the ladies in the ticket office, and his stirring runs down the wing on match days that did Wright's talking, the rattling of his chain, a cacophony as he tried to get to grips with it, spilling through his hands like a nest of snakes.

By the end of his debut season, young Peter Wright had amassed twenty-five first team appearances and had become a fans' favourite in a team that had struggled to keep in touch with the rest of the sides at the foot of the league. A youthful antidote to a winter of struggle and disappointment.

Pre-season of 1914 came with much enthusiasm, Peter returning from the North-East to continue his lower league football odyssey with the Town. Unpacking his mothballed bicycle from Mackie's shed, the familiar sound of bell and chain at Inchmery Road began to herald the start of training, the end of play as he set off for home once more.

It was a hot, breathless, lazy summer of sighing net curtains, basking cats in patches of dappled sun. It was a time to dream of the new season ahead. A fresh set of fixtures promising who knew what. Fixtures that would never come.

Instead, it would be war.

Like so many of the teams of the time, when the call to arms came, the Town players marched down to register as one, gathering outside the club before heading down to the recruitment office. And with that, in next to no time, they would be gone, whisked away to prepare for their fate in the trenches of Flanders, the Somme.

And while players shook hands with the manager, the secretary, hugged some of the girls from the office, Peter sought out Gerald Mackie, to say goodbye on their day of enlistment. He had chained up his bike at his usual spot, and with no time to return it home, he asked Mackie to keep an eye on it for him. To keep it safe until he returned.

A hug, a gushing thanks for all Gerald had done for him, a lingering look up at the West Stand, a glance back at his bike, then, with a wave of his hand, Peter Wright jogged through the gates of Inchmery Road after his team-mates and was gone.

Mackie was good to his word. Every day he would check Peter's bicycle was safe, still secured against that old oak tree. If it rained, or snowed, he would wipe it down as Peter had done. He would use a rag to brush away fallen leaves. Pump up the tyres when they became doughy. Oil the chain and the cog to keep them turning over smoothly. He would ring the bell, for old time's sake, before heading back in to continue on his rounds of Inchmery Road.

He would get letters, from time to time. They talked about the Town, asking after the ladies of the ticket office, the manager, if there was any news about his team-mates.

They talked of memories of matches, and how he longed to run back out onto that pitch, share tea and biscuits in the front room. Mackie would slip them back in their envelopes, holding them in his hands, imagining what these sheets of papers had seen, heard, away on the frontline. Then he would store them in the Nightwatchman's desk, on top of Peter and Michael's programmes and clippings, where they remain to this day.

Peter would not speak of the horrors he saw. Only that there were horrors. Writing to Gerald he wanted to think about home, his football life, the future. So that is what he did. Enquiring about the works on the West Stand, the new terracing that was being put in place behind the Victoria Road goal.

It was his escape, and Mackie let him have it, writing back long letters about the place, the people behind the scenes that Peter had seen every day, how the new sod of grass was looking good. Ready for Peter's darting plays down the touchline. Just as soon as he came back. Back home.

But Peter would not return.

He would fall in the frigid, barren trenches of the front line in 1916. Among huge muddy craters and splintered trees, amidst runs of clawing barbed wire and the bodies of long fallen comrades. In the dark, beneath sickly flares and falling bombs, beneath jaundiced clouds of mustard gas, the softly spoken Peter Wright slipped away.

One of five Town players to be lost within months of seeing action.

Mackie was inconsolable.

He wrote as much. Just that one word. Beneath the tribute in the local paper that he had kept, then pasted onto the first page of his ledger, bought a short while after.

He would be forever changed after Peter's death. Insular. Quiet. As he wrote in the ledger, it was as if he couldn't quite find himself anymore. Like he was forever just round the corner. Just out of reach.

Time passed. Mackie kept up his rounds of Inchmery Road. He kept tending to Peter's bicycle, warning any off who sought to remove it. He had been tasked with looking after it, he would say, and by God he would do so. The bicycle would remain. And so, it did.

The ladies of the ticket office would look out solemnly at Mackie tending to it in all weather, in failing light. Oiling the bell, ringing it. Standing quietly. Head bowed. Those broad shoulders of his, sagging, hitching for a moment or two, that would bring tears to the eyes of the ticket office, before Mackie would retreat to his office for a quiet cup of tea.

Not long after, Mackie began the ledger with the line 'A note to those who would listen.'

He told Peter's story, his life, who he was, his death, the position of his bicycle, and how it must remain.

'We are to look after it for him. I promised him that we would, keep it safe until he came home. And now that he isn't coming back, we need to keep it safe anyway, in his memory. Because he loved his bike. We need to do it for our Peter. For his ultimate sacrifice, we owe him that much.'

It would be the first thing that Mackie would show Tanner Rowe, Nightwatchman number two, when he started as relief Nightwatchman in nineteen twenty-two. Reading the ledger would be a part of Rowe's induction to the job. Mackie's words convincing him that one man's promise should become another's. Out of respect, a quick wander across the car park to check in on the bicycle of a fallen Town player was the very least that Tanner felt he should do.

Reading Mackie's ledger would also be the way Tanner discovered what Gerald couldn't express out loud, for fear of what he was saying would have him in the asylum before too long.

That bicycle bell, those chains. They could ring, could rattle. All by themselves.

Mackie noticed it one night not long after Peter's passing, while on his last sweep of the ground, a little after one a.m.

The ledger read: 'I had just reached the main entrance. I had paused to take in the night air, which was fresh and filled the lungs, when I heard the rattle of chains, then a few moments later the ring of Peter's bell, growing faint, just as it used to when Peter turned out into Inchmery Road for home. Ringing and waving behind him as he went.

'I had a good view of the main gates, the car park, my eyes grown accustomed to the dark after my rounds across the East Stand, checking the shutters along Victoria Road, wandering round to my spot by the players' door.

'I ran across the car park to the main gates, expecting to see the thief away past the pub, turning into the tangle of streets beyond. Away scot-free. But there was nothing. No one. I ran fast. They couldn't possibly have reached the end of the street in that time. But there was no one. Inchmery Road was still, empty.'

'Sick to my stomach, convinced the bicycle had been stolen, I turned back, not wanting to look out at Peter's tree, knowing that I had failed him. That his precious bike had been lost.

'But there, leaning against that old oak, Peter's pride and joy in racing green. Chains secure. Waiting patiently. I was astonished.'

'It was Peter's chains I heard, just as I had heard them countless times before, chiming against the frame as Peter came to grips with them, an unmistakable sound. It was Peter's bell. The exact same pitch. His trademark pattern of ring, ring-ring. Ring, ring-ring. Fading away onto Inchmery Road.

'I heard it. Clear as can be. Just like before the war. I swear I heard it.'

'I kept closer attention after that. Doubling my rounds. Taking my tea outside, just in case. If there had been a would-be thief, I would make sure that they wouldn't try again.

'A few days later, I heard them again, those chains, Peter's bell. I rushed to his old oak, and there it was. His bicycle. Untouched. Safe and sound.

'A day or two later I heard it again. Always a little after one am. Seven minutes past to be exact. Rattling chains. Ringing bell. Fading away down Inchmery Road.

'After that I would make sure that I was there, every night. To see. To hear.

'I have to be losing my mind, no? But I hear it. Seven minutes past one. Peter's bell.'

'I have to reconcile myself that it is the grief. In the cold light of day, what else can it be? But late at night, in the dark, I hear it. We never knew when Peter fell. His mother's letter simply stated that it had been during a night raid. He had gone over the top, and never came back.

'Maybe it was at seven minutes past one?

'Maybe free from the horror of it all, released in death, he found himself back here, at a place he had come to love very much. And he would take his beloved bicycle, sail out through the gates, waving at the shuttered ticket office, ringing his bell. Heading for home and a second season of professional football. A season that never came for him. For so many.'

'But at seven minutes past one, every night, freed from his fate, he finds himself here. Where he can hope, dream once more. For a time.

'The thought soothes me. Brings me some kind of peace. That maybe Peter has found his.

'Maybe the bell, the chains, they are in my head, so as I can cope? I don't know. They sound so vivid, right here in the moment, in the quiet dark of seven minutes past one. They sound so real.'

Gerald Mackie retired in 1925 aged seventy-two. He died three years later, peacefully in his sleep in his armchair.

Tanner Rowe, his successor, dutifully continued with his ledger, that Mackie had used to chronicle other little stories of interest, about the people of Inchmery Road. Though none quite as heart-wrenching as young Peter Wright.

And as with all the Nightwatchmen that have come since, Mackie's notes – telling tales, capturing observations – left more than a little piece of himself behind. A character unwittingly captured by his own hand, through a warmth and compassion when describing others. Preserved within his ledger.

The pages of Mackie's handwriting ended with a wonderful tribute that was included in a match day programme after his passing, carefully cut out and pasted into his ledger by Tanner Rowe.

Among those collected tributes, a recollection from Michael Trim – Peter Wright's friend who also lodged with Mackie the season before the great war – telling of Mackie's warmth and generosity, and how both he and Peter saw him as a father figure. Without whom neither would have been able to achieve such heights in the first team.

Trim had survived the war relatively unscathed, physically at least. He never returned to professional football. Instead, seeing out his playing days with his hometown team Aberystwyth.

He made the trip down for Mackie's funeral, and afterwards Tanner Rowe showed him round Inchmery Road for old time's sake. Trim placed flowers at the foot of his old pal's bicycle and is captured in a grainy picture taken by Rowe, holding his cap in one hand, the other rested on Peter's saddle. It is pasted safely in the ledger.

By all accounts Tanner Rowe was a man of few words, borne out by the ledger. Entries in his staccato hand are short, precise, and few in number. But that only seems to give them greater meaning, greater significance.

Including one. A short footnote at the bottom the page containing Mackie's story of Peter Wright. A neat asterisk at the end of Mackie's writing, in blue, not black.

And then, at the foot of the page, another neat blue asterisk, and in his juddering, spiky script the note:

'I have heard it too. 1.07. Tanner Rowe.'

From 1925 to 1938, Tanner Rowe would dutifully look in on the bike in the corner of the car park. Making sure it was safe.

Though the years were not kind to it.

Racing green paint faded and peeled. Patches of rust scarred the frame, froze the chain solid, eroded the pedals. Rubber grips on the handlebars perished and fell into the weeds and scrub that wound between the spokes.

The bell's mechanism grew heavy and dull, though it was still heard, as if new, through the years.

Stanley Peters, Nightwatchman through World War II mentioned hearing it from time to time, just past one in the morning, as did Bob Andrews when he took over in nineteen seventy. Little asterisks at the end of Mackie's story in different coloured pens, added decades apart, page numbers next to them, had Stacey flicking through the ledger to the appropriate spot. To testimonies of rattling chains, ringing bells. In the dead of night. Out the main gates and away. Relief Nightwatchmen adding their names – sometimes their only act during what could be a relatively brief stint as relief – a few words, an initial, a first name, sometimes both

I have heard it too. I am sure I have. Though it comes and goes so quickly it is hard to know for sure what you have heard. Whether it is your mind playing tricks.

I hope that it isn't. I really do.

I have written as much: what I have heard. My own little asterisk added. And when Stacey read my little affirmation, she stared at me wide-eyed.

'Buh-blimey, Charlie,' she said, and nothing more. Lost in thought. In possibilities. And as she sat there, on one of her first shifts, I carried on with the story.

For thirteen years Tanner Rowe looked after Peter's bicycle. Made sure that it stayed put. Stayed safe. When he took over so too did Stanley Peters. Then Bob Andrews after him. And I do to this day, more than a century after young Peter left it there. All inspired by their predecessor when handing the story down, by Gerald Mackie's original heartfelt testimony.

And now I have the help of young Stacey, who tends to it lovingly, as if she knew Peter Wright personally.

'I fuh-feel as if I do. Suh-somehow, Charlie,' she said to me once, 'when I ruh-read the story, touch the pages. When I huh-hold onto the handlebars.'

Though the bicycle Stacey now tends to looks nothing like the bicycle Gerald Mackie fixed and gave to Peter.

Because over that time, though the ledger doesn't say when exactly, something strange, something remarkable happened.

As the seasons, both meteorological and sporting came and went, as the snows fell, rainstorms pounded, harsh frosts froze, heaps of brown, autumnal leaves gathered, and long sunny summers nurtured. As excitable crowds gathered on match day. As roars echoed through that old oak tree's boughs. As floodlights were erected, and night games lit up the sky. As crowds drained away into the weave of streets, every other Saturday. Season after season. Decade after decade – the old oak tree in the corner of the car park grew. Imperceptibly slowly.

Peter's bicycle was heavy, leant against the tree. A primitive thing by today's standards.

The tree adapted. Growing out round it. Fraction by fraction, unnoticed by the human eye. The gnarled bark joining back together once the tubular frame had been circumnavigated – decades of interminably slow endeavour.

Year on year, more of the frame assimilated into the tree as it grew out. As did the saddle. The right arm of the handlebars. The uppermost curve of the rear tyre. Rusted chain disappearing into trunk, as if it had always been that way. Peter's bicycle, his old oak tree, fused together over more than fifty years, until they were one. Bound together for all time.

Front wheel and bell. Part of the handlebars and frame. A crescent of dulled and buckling rear wheel remains. The rest preserved, cocooned. Hidden.

So that is what we clean, that is what we tend to. Stacey has a polish that she gently rubs into what is left of the metalwork. A cloth to treat spokes that grow ever more brittle and fragile. She does it with great care, oiling the bell with a little can, though it is so stiff these days she can barely get a sound out of it. It doesn't stop her from trying, every time, pausing for a moment. Lost in her thoughts.

I think old Mackie would approve. Peter's bicycle frozen in place like that, frozen in time among the whorls and knots, the rings of that oak. His Nightwatchmen protecting it, even though it was beyond the reach of opportunistic thieves.

Instead, their endeavours turned to preventing the felling of the tree when its deep roots started to buckle the macadam of the car park.

Bob Andrews in 1974, then myself in two thousand and five both pleaded with the general manager to leave it be. Mackie's old ledger brought out to tell the tale of it and young Peter Wright. How this old oak, and its precious contents were a part of the club's history and should be preserved as much as we preserve and maintain the East and West Stands – that are but juveniles compared to the age of the oak.

So far, the ledger has worked. Peter's story, heart-breaking, compelling enough to tolerate an uneven surface. The affected areas are blocked off on match days, leaving that old oak be, clutching Peter's bike to its body. As if it too missed Peter, holding on tightly to all that we had left of him.

And every now and then, carrying on the breeze late at night, at a little after one a.m, the rattling of chains, the ringing of a bell. Out and away through the main gates. Out onto Inchmery Road.

I don't know exactly when it was added. I don't know when I noticed it – Stacey's very first annotation in Mackie's ledger.

I found it as I flicked through the pages one day. A new asterisk at the foot of Mackie's story. A page number. And on that page, in neat handwriting:

'I have heard it too. Peter's bicycle. Stacey Marsh.'

Peter Wright was the first ghost of Inchmery Road, without whom Mackie's ledger would not exist. And if the ledger had never existed, then it is quite possible that Peter's story would have simply faded away with Mackie, the ladies of the ticket office. His bike removed, that oak felled long, long ago. Our little club diminished in meaning, in memory, letting such a precious little moment slip into obscurity. And all the others that have been kept safe since.

Even so, I wonder how many others might have been lost over the years, that deserved their spot in Mackie's book.

Not many, I hope. I hope that the Nightwatchmen haven't let too many drift away over the years. Because that would be a terrible shame.

Chapter Three

Not much is known about Tanner Rowe, Mackie's replacement. There had been no pictures of him in the Nightwatchman's office, the corridor down to the West Stand, like there are of Gerald and most of those that came after him.

He was a man of few words. He preferred to be stood behind a camera rather than in front of it. It had clearly been a passion of his.

Indeed, the majority of the pictures in the ledger were taken by him.

He may have been a faceless name. He may have been hard to fathom through his limited entries. But through his photographs of everyday life at the club he caught Inchmery Road in the twenties and thirties in all its glory. All framed in a beautiful sepia-tinged black and white, and pasted carefully into the ledger. A sea of mostly anonymous faces, whose names had long since been lost to time – that once helped keep our little club on track.

Images of mundane office work – men in suits and slicked-back hair, women with natty reading glasses perched on noses lost in the task at hand. A face to rear of the office pool looking up from her desk while all others carried on oblivious. A solitary, knowing, beaming grin to camera. Sparkling eyes captured for all time. Nameless maybe, but vibrant, full of life, kept so within the ledger.

Images of training sessions silhouetted against the sun. Rows of shadowy figures in the middle of running drills across the Inchmery Road pitch. The groundsman standing proudly next to his machine while his picture was taken.

Office parties and gatherings. Grins and laughter. Paper hats, streamers frozen in the air. Great smiles, laughter, arms raised to meet them.

One of my favourites is a picture of the ticket office booths – three in a row next to the club shop. A head protruding out from each. Smiles and laughing. One looking at her colleagues, the other two at the camera.

There are images of great lines of people snaking away down Inchmery Road, queuing for tickets to special cup games. Flat caps, head scarves, children waving.

Others of queues at the turnstiles when those big games came around.

Boys and girls decked out in scarves, flailing rattles above their heads at the front of the terrace. A sea of faces behind them waiting for kick-off.

A strange one of an old man caught with an over-exaggerated gait, striding along the grit track by the side of the pitch, gurning at rows of laughing faces in the benches beyond.

The coach driver who took the team to all away games pausing from polishing large headlamps, looking up, nodding seriously, a bucket of suds from wiping down the chrome wheel arches. The shadow of his green bus stretching across the car park.

Pictures of children playing football in the street beneath the looming Inchmery Road terrace.

Men outside the pub across from the main gates, beer in hand.

Terraced houses laden with snow, the picture virtually bleached out as a flurry swirled down from leaden skies. The world outside Inchmery road dissolving away.

Apprentices in the boot room, knee high in dirty boots.

The kit lady pegging out shirts on a line hoisted between the goalposts.

Beneath them, the odd name, or nickname: 'Alice and Netty,' 'Smudge.'

He didn't use words like Mackie, he didn't tell stories that way, but he still brought a richness to Gerald's ledger. He understood what Mackie had attempted, in preserving the little stories that brought our club to life. Elevated it in people's souls. And he gladly contributed. And if not with photographs, then sometimes with snippets from the local paper. Little oddities that would have been lost, if not pasted away into Mackie's book of memories.

Such as a small obituary, for a young lad called David Smith. 'Died suddenly on the 20th of October 1934, age seventeen, from complications with an incurable tumour of the brain, on the way to see his beloved Town.'

He had felt compelled to salvage it, this little cutting that, to most, was nothing more than a sad marker of a life cut much too short. But to Tanner Rowe, it spoke of love and friendship, the special bonds between people that Inchmery Road helped create. That Mackie had first chronicled

Young David's life was worth more than this little official notice, which is why, pasted beneath it, he had saved a letter from the same edition of the paper, a letter written by a Thomas Coneelly, the last ever doorman at Inchmery Road.

Thomas Coneelly had stood, immaculately dressed in his navy suit, at the doors to the main entrance to Inchmery Road for more years than anyone could remember. He would be the first face anyone would see, and as such, Thomas took it upon himself to be warm, welcoming, and as helpful as he could be to whoever came his way. Ushering newly signed players up to the manager's office, taking in deliveries, giving the odd impromptu treat to awestruck children looking up at the main stand – sneaking them through and down the players tunnel to the pitch for a few moments.

He saw what Inchmery Road meant to people. And he had seen young David Smith. And had been compelled to write a letter to the paper on David's passing. Saved from obscurity by Tanner Rowe.

'He may have just been another face in the crowd, another body at the turnstiles, but to me, young David Smith was a friend.

I first met him at the door to Inchmery Road when he was barely eight years old. Full of life, energy, and dreams, he would wait to greet the players on a match day as they arrived. He would always arrive hours too early "just in case," so as not to miss a single-one, and would wait until he had greeted them all, his excitement as they wandered across from the car park turned to slack-jawed, wide-eyed wonder when they were upon him. He would shake their hand, wish them luck, tell them that he would play for the Town, when he grew up. I had my doubts, given that I had seen him play with a ball I kept behind the doors, to help him while away the hours. He wasn't very good. But that didn't stop him believing, hoping.

I had survived the trenches of the Great War. I had seen a world without hope. David's beaming grin, his faith in a future that, in truth, he knew he was never likely to see due to his condition. That he would play for the Town one day, alongside his heroes. It saved me from myself so many times.

He must have shaken the hand of some of our longer-serving players more than a hundred times, as dumb-struck with awe on the one-hundredth as he had been the first. Mumbling "I will play for the Town, one day, just you wait and see" to kindly, humouring professionals. Who mourn his loss. I see them, looking for him, just as I still do on match days.

They say that it was quick. That he would have felt nothing. It is a small comfort.

I will miss you young David Smith. Forever the first name on the Town team sheet.'

The first time Stacey read it she wiped away tears at such a tender eulogy. Peering into the little sepia photograph pasted beneath the newspaper clippings. The middle-aged Thomas Coneelly in a smart blazer with the club badge embossed on the breast, smiling at the camera in front of the mains doors to Inchmery Road. He is standing next to a young man with slick-backed hair, a sharp suit, also smiling at the picture-taker while shaking the hand of a young boy. The young boy, David Smith, was oblivious to Tanner and his camera, to everything else, staring open-mouthed, with awestruck eyes up at Town centre forward, Alf Horton, neck craning up, lost in his moment of wonder. His little arm straining up to hold the hand of his hero.

Beneath it, in Tanner's hand: '*Thomas, Alf Horton, young David Smith.*'

Safe in Mackie's ledger.

Stacey read Coneelly's letter, indeed all the ledger, over and over again during quiet moments. Until I imagine that she may now be able to read the passages from memory.

She got it. The stories within.

We later learnt more of David's story, Stacey and I, from a diary of Thomas Coneelly, donated by his family to the club when they discovered it in some old boxes – full of little snippets of his life as doorman at Inchmery Road. Some as mundane as remembering to get milk for tea, promises to bring in the paper for Alice in the office, or flowers on someone's birthday, or a part he had found for one of the players ailing cars. And among it all, we found David.

And Stacey carefully drew an asterisk next to his obituary letter from the local paper, Tanner Rowe's picture, and dutifully transcribed Coneelly's take of young David Smith into the ledger. Wanting it to be known. Young David kept safe, with all the rest.

And from Coneelly, decades after his passing, we got to hear him talk, and tell his tale of David Smith.

He wrote of a "fragile looking lad, with gangly arms and legs that he never seemed to be fully in control of." He wrote of a boy who appeared in a perpetual state of excitement, his eyes wide, glassy with the opportunity of a new day.

As soon as he was old enough, he would be a fixture at the players' entrance on match days, arriving mid-morning, hours before any player would be expected, clutching a paper bag with his lunch in. He would stand, in readiness to meet his heroes, craning his neck with every movement through the gates to Inchmery Road. Standing down if it was just ticket office workers, turnstile operators, programme sellers arriving for work.

He couldn't have been more than eight or nine at the start, when he first began to assemble outside club doors. And while he was waiting, through rainstorms and snow flurries, beneath cold, leaden skies, and the baking sun of early season, he would tell Coneelly as he tended the players' entrance, the postman dropping off the morning's correspondence, delivery men – anyone that would acknowledge him – that it would be him one day, stepping through that door – a player of his beloved Town.

He would be full of beans, hour after hour, eating his sandwiches whilst walking back and forth outside the entrance. Sometimes, on particularly cold days, Coneelly would fetch him a mug of tea, and David Smith would warm his hands, chatter excitedly. The magic and opportunity of match day, and what 3 p.m. might bring, the anticipation of goals and great saves, thundering tackles and pinpoint passes fuelled his energy, and he would wait, a coiled spring, for his Town heroes.

And as soon as they arrived, the players, he would fall silent. In awe. Young men in cheap suits, with slicked-back hair, faces solemn, focused on the job ahead, would file in in ones and twos. And young David Smith would ensure that he was the first person they would encounter.

He would stand silently, looking up at his heroes. And shake their hands as they filed past. Week after week. Without fail. Mouth open, eyes wide, he would watch them in through the door, disappearing into the corridors beneath the West Stand, his heroes in red and yellow.

Only once they were all accounted for and through would David head round to the turnstiles and wait for them to open, where he would be the first in, making it down behind the goal, to the best spot, to watch his heroes that he had shaken hands with, warm up. Crowds slowly filling up around him as kick-off approached.

Eight years of standing outside the players' entrance at Inchmery Road, in all weathers, wanting nothing more than to shake the hands of the Town players, who would reduce him to a stunned silence.

He would look out for Coneelly when he first arrived, and wave, go say hello, and Thomas would look out for him, this little dynamo of Town passion. And he would enjoy watching the young lad dream, meeting his heroes. The hope was infectious. The happiness too.

And they would pass their Saturdays together, such an odd couple, outside the main doors to Inchmery Road.

And it would be David's infectious hope, his warm smile, that innocent youthful excitement that inspired Coneelly to do what he did as the season wound down in late spring of 1932.

On the last day of the 1931/32 season – another where the Town spent most of its time looking nervously over its shoulder at last place, something that did nothing to dim the awe and excitement of young David, just shy of his 16th birthday – came the news that he had always yearned to hear. Coneelly had beckoned him over, handed him an envelope that bright, warm Saturday morning in May of 1932.

'I was asked to give you this,' he had said, shrugging his shoulders with a false innocence, pretending not to know of its contents.

Inside, a letter, inviting him, David Smith, to pre-season trials on the 15th of July.

That he must report to the players' entrance at 11 a.m. sharp.

Kit would be provided.

He had held his letter tightly in his hands. His eyes turning glassy. Looking down at the club crest embossed at the top of the page. His address typed out neatly below. A young life's ambition one step closer to reality. It was a strangely subdued, distant young lad who greeted his heroes that day. Lost somewhere in a fog of daydream and disbelief.

By all accounts, young David Smith was a willing, enthusiastic footballer at school, sadly lacking the talent required to be competent, let alone stand out.

He played for his school's third XI – a side known for their heavy defeats in the lower reaches of the town's school leagues. A side made up of similarly enthusiastic players lacking in the mastery of dribbling, positional sense, and passing, it was an exercise in romantic notion, sustaining fanciful ambitions of being a professional footballer in the face of regular, thumping defeats. While there was another 90 minutes to look forward to, there was hope. Time enough to dream. As young children do.

Coneelly had been doorman on match days for all of David's acts of dedication. Had seen him grow from a gangly, frail eight-year-old into a gangly, frail school leaver – enthusiasm undimmed. Age had not brought perspective, reality. He still dreamed of making it with the Town.

He was a dreamer, and the world needed dreamers.

Thomas had fought in World War I as he had written in his obituary of David. He had seen a world without dreams, and had returned on a stretcher, having lost more than a right foot and ankle. He topped up his army pension by taking the job as doorman at Inchmery Road, to help ends meet. It had also helped with so much more – the isolation, the night terrors – holding doors open, watching people come and go. Cups of tea and a natter with the receptionists, with Tanner, with Gerald Mackie before him. Watching young David, smiling and nodding at his assertion that it would be him one day through the door Coneelly guarded. And he would shake his head at him tripping over an old football that Coneelly used to stow inside reception and roll to him to help him pass the time until his players arrived.

He would chat excitedly about his last game for the school as he clumsily dribbled, chased wayward touches up and back outside the entrance. Kicking it against the wall and cheering an imagined rocket shot of a goal for the young Town striker, David Smith. He would raise his arms to the sky, and Thomas would smile, nod.

It hadn't been as hard as Coneelly had imagined, arranging for young David to attend trials. The first week of pre-season would include a couple of days where drills tested invited triallists – young local prospects and seasoned pro's looking for a new contract.

The operation was overseen every year by the club's trainer, Alf Horton, who had been a player for the Town for eight seasons before retiring into his backroom position.

He must have shaken young David's hand on match day more than a hundred times over the years.

Their young super-supporter was well known to him, and his dream of making it for the Town. And when Thomas approached him, rather sheepishly, knowing how ridiculous his request to a serious, professional football club trainer sounded, Horton listened, smiled, nodded, and arranged for the letter. He would turn sixteen during the summer. He would be old enough to take part. In body, if not ability. And Horton hadn't been averse to a simple act of kindness. In fact, he relished it.

The serious task of looking over new prospects for the season could also accommodate making the day of a young lad who had been dedicated to the Town cause for more than half of his young life.

When the day came, Coneelly had nodded, winked, opened the door to a saucer-eyed young David, and ushered him inside. He watched him trail away with the other prospects into the warren of corridors, letter clutched tightly to his chest.

Due to the number of trialists, young David had to change on a bench that hugged the wall of a tunnel between the West Stand and the Inchmery Road terrace. At the far end of the tunnel were wooden gates that opened out onto the street, and on Saturdays an ambulance would back into the tunnel, just in case it was needed by player or supporter alike.

On match days the ambulance driver, the attendant, the ground staff with long pitchforks used to tend to the pitch at half time, bedding back in sods of turf kicked up from ferocious tackling. They would sit on that bench. Huddling together from the howling winds that could whistle through the gates and cut you clean in half at the height of winter.

But this benign summer's day, changing on the bench was no great hardship, other than the bruising of the egos of some of the out of contract professionals, who were used to better.

David found himself a spot at the far end of the bench, and a spare set of kit laid out. On top were a set of tie-ups in the club colours. One red, one yellow. He held them up, unsure what to do with them.

Horton pointed to his socks.

'No professional should step out onto the pitch without them,' he was told. A true professional always ties his socks up, to look the part. No one takes to the Inchmery Road grass without them. We only want professionals here – in mind as well as body.'

He nodded as David knelt down, pulled up his socks, tied them neatly.

'Good lad,' he said 'a model professional. Now out onto the pitch with you. Join in the warm-ups.'

Horton told Thomas afterwards that he fared about as well as they thought he would. He ran about willingly, mostly chasing shadows. When he did get the ball, he was tackled quickly or hit a misplaced pass. The fitter professionals would streak past him during the drills.

Coneelly had told him that he didn't think that it had mattered. Young David had left beaming from ear to ear, Horton's words repeated for anyone who would listen.

'Alf Horton said that he didn't think I was quite ready. But that I should keep practising, keep working. Maybe next year, he said. Imagine that. From the great Alf Horton. And look – he let me keep my tie-ups. Only the professionals of Inchmery Road wear these. He said that I had earned them. That I could count myself among them. Imagine!'

Thomas thanked Horton for his kindness with a bottle of scotch. He had made this young lad's year.

Enthusiasm undimmed by the kindest of rejections, young David would keep his letter, his tie-ups safely tucked away in their envelope in his pocket and would show anyone who would look that he had had trials with the Town. That only professionals got these tie-ups. That next year he would make it. That he would work and work down the park, every hour that God sent.

And in between, he would be there on match days, first thing. And he would smile, and wait, shake hands and dream.

And Horton made sure that, on the last home game of the 1932/33 season, Coneelly had another letter inviting David for trials that summer. And the summer after that.

He ran the trials. It was no imposition to anyone but him. And when he had been a player, he had appreciated David's awe at shaking his heroes' hands, shaking Alf's hand. This young lad, gobsmacked, every other Saturday, making a lower league journeyman like himself feel First Division.

His enthusiasm, his optimism, his lust for life and all its potential opportunities, was infectious. It was nice to be around. And worth the drafting of an extra letter.

That summer, and the summer after that, David arrived at the players' entrance with his letter in his hands, and Thomas would watch him off into the corridors of Inchmery Road.

Young David would make for the bench in the tunnel without prompting, change into a strip of Town kit, and be sure to show Horton his socks tied up smartly with a new set of red and yellow ties before jogging out onto the pitch.

He would play his hardest, chasing after his wayward ball during drills, chasing shadows in practice matches. He would nod earnestly and listen to every word of Horton's coaching during the sessions, his kind rejection speeches, beaming when he was told to keep his tie-ups, that he had earned them, that his attitude was that of a first-class professional. That he must keep going, keep dreaming.

His first letter from the Town, his tie-ups tucked inside, that had become a permanent fixture in his trouser pockets, was joined by a second, then a third letter. Precious treasure containing the clubs crest, the signature of Alf Horton himself, ties only professionals at the Town used. Tales of the time that he, David Smith, had trials with the Town. That next year would be his year. That he had been training extra hard.

David died in October of 1934, aged just 18. Early one Saturday morning as he was walking up to Inchmery Road for a match against Exeter City.

A young girl who had been walking her dog said that one moment he was passing them with a smile, ruffling her dogs head, the next he just fell to the floor. Motionless. Gone.

Thomas knew that something was wrong when young David didn't materialise. He remembered glancing up toward the gates, wondering where he could be. He had never missed a game, after all. In ten years.

Thomas and Alf Horton attended young David's funeral, met his inconsolable mother, who clutched David's letters to her chest. She had bound them together with a red ribbon, and thanked them for their kindness, their friendship with young David. It had meant everything to him, she had said. The letters, the trials, mugs of warm tea on cold, wet Saturday mornings.

He had a tumour on the brain from birth, she had said, that couldn't be reached. Found when he was no more than five. It would grow, the doctors had said, slowly, painlessly, until it met a critical part of the brain, which would take young David in a heartbeat.

He could have lived his life in fear, she had said. Instead, he embraced every day, dreamed big. He knew of his fate. He made every moment count. An extraordinary life hidden within an unassuming looking little boy. He had wanted to be a professional footballer for his beloved Town, and with these letters he was, just for the briefest of moments.

'And who truly gets to live out their wildest dreams? Well, my little David did. He lived a life,' she said, and squeezed my hand and Alf's. 'A lovely little life.'

Tanner Rowe, for the most part, played his role in David's story from the sidelines. Coneelly mentioned in his diary that Rowe would come in hours before his shift on match days to watch the game from his door in the West Stand.

He would share some tea with Coneelly and David, sometimes having a kickabout with him while he waited for his players. He would nod seriously at David's assertions that he would make it as a player one day, and smile and celebrate every trial letter David received.

On the occasion of his second trial, Rowe took a picture of young David, socks pulled up tight, fastened with his new ties, stood next to Coneelly in a strip of Town kit – who had stolen a few minutes to see young David out on the Inchmery Road pitch.

The smiles, the pride captured within, chests puffed out, reminds me of Gerald Mackie's picture with Peter Wright and Michael Trim. A simple joy at another's fortune – the pride of finding yourself in a position you had dreamed of your whole life. Unlikely friendships for all time. Captured on a warm summer's day, a brilliant sun beaming down on the players on the pitch behind them, the shadow of the East Stand. Cut grass and happiness rich in the air.

A blissful moment in time.

The photograph, the notice for David's funeral had been pasted carefully in Mackie's ledger. Rowe's notes on poor David and his brief life.

He had also attached a pair of tie-ups next to David's photograph. The red and yellow laces never seeming to fade. A shot of colour among Rowe's black and white pictures, his blocks of notes and newspaper clippings.

And at the foot of David's page, he had drawn a large oblong, highlighting its border with a thick, black pen.

Young David had clearly moved Rowe as much as he had Coneelly and Horton. His optimism inspirational, in the face of impending, certain tragedy. Grasping life in the here and now with both hands. His bravery in the moment, it was motivation enough for Tanner Rowe to draw his oblong, fill it with instructions, in the hope that future Nightwatchmen may continue the little tribute to David that he instigated.

The summer after David's passing, on the day of the Town's first pre-season session, the day of Horton's trials, Tanner Rowe found Coneelly, beckoned him pitchside. And at the bench where young David used to change, in the tunnel beneath the Inchmery Road terrace, he fished out of his pocket a pair of tie-ups, red and yellow in the Town's colours, and gently placed them on the bench. For young David, he had said.

Coneelly had smiled, put his hand on Tanner's shoulder, thanked him warmly, then they looked out at the session on the pitch, where David would have been rushing enthusiastically here, there, and everywhere, before they wandered round to the players' entrance for tea and stories of David that had them both chuckling. His effervescent smile despite a wayward dribble sending his ball bobbling into the car park.

They would hold their little memorial every year, on the first day of trials, up until Rowe left in 1938 to join the navy. Coneelly would have a quiet moment on his own the following year, placing down a set of ties for David, before the war called time on the position of doorman at Inchmery Road.

From 1946, the receptionist would keep an eye on the door, and it has been the way ever since. Coneelly, with his one good foot, joined the home guard, before a well-deserved retirement spent every other Saturday on the benches of the East Stand, and a season ticket for life gifted him by the club.

The night after those trials in the summer of 1935, Tanner wrote, while on his rounds of Inchmery Road, he noticed young David's tie-ups had disappeared. They could not be found. Not under the bench. Not slipped down the back.

They could have been cleared away. Maybe the wind had taken them, though it had been a still, breathless summer's day. Maybe an opportunist had pocketed them.

Or, maybe, Tanner wondered, nothing quite so mundane, so depressing, had happened to them?

It was wishful thinking, he knew. Making the unpalatable a little less so. Easing the sadness. Giving life once more to such a sweet soul. But maybe young David had them?

Maybe, on his big day, the first day of pre-season, he had picked them up, tied up his socks with them. Like he had in years gone by. Readying himself for his big trial. Jogging out onto the pitch, for one more crack at making it for the Town?

He liked that idea. It brought with it a comfort of sorts. Made more tangible over time because, after all, every year it would be the same. Rowe and Coneelly would place some ties on David's bench.

And every night on his rounds, Rowe would discover them gone. And he would wonder.

He would hope, spending a few minutes looking out across the darkened pitch, remembering young David, borrowing a little of that hope that had defined him.

He knew it sounded ridiculous, his notes said, but then again, the tie-ups would always be gone, sometime during his rounds.

They had to have gone somewhere. And with no better, or obvious hypothesis forthcoming, why not think it was young David?

Why not find some comfort in that?

Either way, whatever you believe, Tanner stashed a carton of tie-ups in the drawer of the Nightwatchman's desk. And in the ledger, he left a note, to all that would come after him, asking that, on the first day of pre-season, they might find a moment to place a pair on the bench in the tunnel where David used to change. Just in case.

At the very least it would be a small memorial to a young lad taken too soon. And if they could take the time, then it would be very much appreciated.

So we do, find the time, Stacey and I. We lay down a set of tie-ups from Tanner's box - that is still going strong all this time later, so stuffed full it had been - on the bench in the tunnel on the first day of pre-season, just as Tanner and Thomas did. And when we return a day or so later, they are gone.

We know it is most likely the wind, it is always blowing down that tunnel. But we do it anyway. And every now and then, we can't help but wonder.

Ours may just be a small club, from a small town. The small-time played out to a few thousand in the lower reaches of the football league. But our stories, the stories in Mackie's ledger, they are important. The people contained within them, their friendships, their actions, and interactions, they are important. They are the soul which knits our little club together, keeping it vibrant. Even here, all the way out on the outskirts of the game. Random acts of friendship, passion, devotion. Making our little club, and our little ground, precious. To some, everything.

People like me, and Stacey. Gerald Mackie and David Smith. Jon 'Blitz' Sugg and his mother Mary.

Small voices, with precious stories of lives lived. Some everyday, some not so.

And here we are. Keeping them safe.

It is the best job in the world.

Although the position of doorman was never filled again thankfully for Stacey and me, and those in between, the position of Nightwatchman was retained when Tanner Rowe left. And it was his successor, a Stanley Peters, who performed the sombre task of pasting in Tanner's small obituary from the local paper in 1942 when Rowe was lost, along with his entire ship in the deep waters of the

Atlantic from a torpedo strike, trying to defend a convoy from New York, bound for Southampton.

It affected Stacey deeply when she first came across it, this yellowed and brittle square of newsprint, no more than a couple of inches across, a couple of inches deep.

'Suh-so sad,' she said quietly as she read it again, wiping away a tear. 'He muh-must have been so scuh-scared.'

I think it hit her hard, this news a full eight decades old, because in Tanner Rowe she had found a fellow wallflower – to all intents and purposes a mute, all but invisible to the outside world. In him I think she saw herself.

And in his work in the ledger, that she went back to time and again, nearly every shift, she realised that, just as he had found a voice, a way to contribute, to belong, so could she.

Without words, or precious few at least, he had helped to create what Gerald Mackie had dreamed of when he started his book. And Tanner Rowe's photographs created a backbone, a foundation, both physically and emotionally, through his pictures of life at Inchmery Road.

The brittle pages of pasted photo paper, stiff, immovable almost, they felt weighty, powerful – all those people long-gone, kept vibrant, here, right now, with the turn of a page.

It was as if you could almost hear them, the whirring typewriters, the chatter and laughter from along the corridors and offices that hadn't changed a bit since their time.

Rooms and walkways that were so familiar from our rounds, it was as if we had just missed them – those sepia faces from another time – that they had just clocked off and slipped away only moments earlier. Farewells drifting and echoing away out the door. All thanks to Rowe, and his ability with his camera to find the right moment. The exact moment.

We came to know them well, his subjects, through Tanner's pictures. Or so it felt to me. And Stacey.

She would flick through them slowly, those first few shifts of hers.

'It is suh-such a shame. We duh-don't even know what he luh-looked like. Tanner Rowe. He is lost. Buh-but at the same time nuh-not. Because of thuh-these,' she said, always pausing on that one isolated picture of young David Smith, Thomas Coneelly, and centre-forward Alf Horton.

'And I don't know why, buh-but I feel like I have suh-seen this photo before. Somehow. I duh-don't know,' she would trail off into silence, deep in thought, looking at that young boy staring up at one of his heroes.

'It seems fuh-familiar. Somehow,' and she would sigh, frustrated, at a scrap of memory, of something, just too distant, too foggy to come into focus. At least, not right away.

I can't remember exactly when it came to her. How many weeks, or maybe even months, but I remember her flushed face, a look of excitement at secrets discovered, worlds opened, things for the ledger.

Once she had calmed down, and caught her breath, she flicked through Mackie's book to that picture that had felt known to her before she had seen it among Tanner's pages.

'You know that I vuh-volunteer at the luh-library. A couple of days? Wuh-well, one day, quite a while ago now, they had me down in the vaults suh-sorting out storage boxes. One had lots of old playbills from local thuh-theatre productions going all the way back to the nuh-nineteenth century, pamphlets from exhibitions held at the town hall, puh-posters from fairs and circuses, programmes from athletic meets at the old ruh-running track. Postcards of the suh-seafront. All suh-sorts of things.

'I wuh-was walking to the shuh-shops for muh-mum, and it came to me.' She rummaged around in her bag and brought out a folder.

'I knuh-know where I've suh-seen Tanner's picture before.'

She opened the folder and pulled out an old, battered, fragile booklet with a threadbare spine. On its cover the title:

Impressions – an exhibition of contemporary photography. 7 – 23 September 1927. Town Hall Gallery.'

Beneath it, right there on the cover, was Tanner's photograph. And on the inside:

'Overleaf – David, Thomas, and Alf, by Tanner Rowe.'

'And there's more,' she said, flicking gently through the pages to a spread of four pictures towards the end of the booklet. One was *'David, Thomas, and Alf'* reproduced. Beneath it was a picture of a fog bound Inchmery Road on a match day. In the foreground a silhouette of a goalkeeper peering into a thick sea of fog. In the distance, among the near impenetrable blanket, the faintest impressions of players, maybe racing toward him, maybe slipping further away, we would never know. Vague apparitions.

In the gloom to his left, looming like a monstrous cresting wave, the body of the West Stand, dark, brooding, black among the dense greys and whites of the fog.

Beneath it, the unnamed goalkeeper looked small, lost, terribly alone. As if he were the only person for miles around, when, in truth, he would have been surrounded by thousands of spectators if it were a first team game. Hundreds, if the image had been captured at a reserve team match. All made remote, subdued beneath a supernatural pea-soup pall. Leaving just him. Like he was the last man left on Earth. The rest rubbed out. Gone. The fog so heavy it seemed impossible that it could ever lift again. That this was it.

Beneath it, the title *Fog.'*

It was a beautiful, atmospheric picture. One that Tanner hadn't pasted into the ledger and had remained unseen by all except those who attended the exhibition, close to a century ago, all this time. Stacey pulled out a photocopy of it.

'Fuh-for the book,' she said and handed it to me. Another heartbeat of Inchmery Road, a blink of an eye, reclaimed, made safe. Added to the rest.

On the opposite page two more images. One of two faces, heads pitched back in laughter. Around them the blur of neons and lights intercut with night. A young man and woman. They are at a fair, huddled together in the cab of a dodgem. Both are holding the steering wheel, laughing.

Fairground.'

The last image took my breath away. Unmistakeable as it was of the old façade of the cinema that used to be on the seafront.

A young woman, all smiles, dressed up in a smart usherette uniform, stood outside, beneath the canopy that displayed all the names of the movies on show. She stood with her tray of ices and sweets hooked around her neck, resting against her stomach. Two children were on tiptoes to try and see what was on offer, while their parents stood at the ticket booth. Beyond, and the backs of two people were slipping behind a thick curtain, and on into the pictures.

But the usher. She looked so familiar. So much like my Evie. The uniform, the smile, the way her hair was tied up. Her position by the ticket booth.

It took my breath away – *The Pictures.'*

But before I could let myself feel anything more, Stacey pulled out two more photocopies of the fairground, the cinema, from her folder.

'I knuh-know they aren't football, buh-but they are beautiful pictures. And they are tuh-Tanner. Maybe they could guh-go in the ledger too? I nodded. They must, I told her, and she dutifully slipped them into the pages of his photographs.

I watched that scene of the cinema slip away, though I would linger on it in absent moments from time to time, in the years after it came into our possession. But right then, it was gone in Stacey's excitement.

'Thuh-there's still muh-more,' she said, turning the page of the booklet gingerly. 'Thuh-there's this.'

On the next page, his name, a few lines:

'Tanner Rowe works as Nightwatchman at Inchmery Road. This is his first photographical exhibition. Indeed, his first exhibition of any kind. His work is a study of the everyday, captured with a beautiful, intimate precision.'

Alongside, a small photograph: Tanner Rowe. Standing out on the steps of the Town Hall. He stood, a little embarrassed, out there on his own, his hands clutching his flat cap to his chest, an awkward smile. Neatly combed and slicked hair. His suit, too short for him in the leg and arms by an inch or so, looked borrowed for the occasion.

Dark hair, dark eyes, a tall man with gangly arms and legs. A soft, kindly face. Tanner Rowe. Finally.

A mystery of the ledger had been solved. Not the last that she would fix.

She had a knack. A passion, for these people she had never met, save through the pages of Mackie's book. She was touched by the stories, the people.

But she had the ability to find a way to reach back, across time, to some of them. Finding new insight. Adding something to their story.

Like Tanner Rowe.

Just like that, after all those years, Stacey found him a face. A smile. Warm, kind eyes. And a few more of his wonderful pictures.

And she would find a way, in time, to reach more.

Chapter Four

When Tanner Rowe left to join the navy, he handed over Nightwatchman duties to Stanley Peters, showed him the ledger, the photographs and clippings of the people that made Inchmery Road. He told him Mackie's tale of Peter Wright.

Though a man of few words, his earnest, heartfelt retelling of Mackie's story of young Peter clearly did more than enough to convince Stanley that his chores extended beyond the simple guardianship of the bricks and mortar of Inchmery Road.

His faithful, emotional testimony, as handed down to him by Gerald Mackie in person, and written down for those that came after set the tone. And ever since, it has been Tanner's respect of another man's story, another man's beliefs and hopes that has set the benchmark for all the Nightwatchmen that have followed him.

Rowe's words, these little acts of remembrance and kindness, the handing down of the stories from one Nightwatchman to the other has kept Peter's memory alive all these years, where maybe it would have faded into obscurity, lost to time without the ledger keeping it safe. Which would have been tragedy all over again.

A snippet of this little football club's heart and soul gone. Never to return.

So, the occasional visit to check in on Peter Wright's bicycle has become a part of the Nightwatchman's routine,

Thanks to Mackie's notes, Tanner's retelling, and the emotion in both.

In the photograph of young David Smith, staring up in awe at his hero, Alf Horton, Tanner captured David's passion for our little club. It is a passion we can all relate to.

Because David's Inchmery Road is our Inchmery Road. His heroes in red and yellow, are our heroes.

Time is the only difference.

And even that seems to pause, overlap, from one generation to another. Our feeling of belonging that we have through our little club, the meaning we find in it, the pages of Mackie's ledger are like a mirror – in them we have all seen our own passions, played out through others, from another time.

Time is the only difference. And so, the tending of a young lad's bicycle, from a century past, a lad who pulled on the Town shirt – something all of us who care have dreamed of, but never achieved – it almost comes naturally, the respect, the connection, the friendship almost, to those we have never met. At least in a physical, flesh and blood sense.

Thanks to that book, most of the time, it feels very different.

I feel it most keenly on my rounds at night. On Stacey's nights off, when it is just me, Mackie's ledger, and all those memories. All those ghosts.

I always wander round to Peter Wright's bicycle, mostly concealed now by a row of shrubs that hide it to all but the precious few who know it is there – and why it remains. Then I come inside and scuff round the grit track pitchside and up onto the Inchmery Road terrace, heading down the steps to the shuttered turnstiles, and along the concourse where moonlight sends faint beams of silvery light down the stairwells that lead back up pitchside. I walk from one patch of moonlight to the other, sometimes listening to footsteps on the pavement beyond, the rumble of a car engine, a muffled conversation just out of reach.

Then I walk back up onto the terrace, climb over into the benches of the lower East Stand, weaving my way up to the little kiosks at the back that serve hot tea and pies; their custodians reduced to following the game from the thin sliver of pitch available beneath the beams of the upper stand. A scuffle of football boots and legs, mostly, the ball dancing here and there before the camber of the pitch rises up to snuff out the play, crushing the match between the advertising hoardings hanging from the upper tier. The game gone once more, gauging the mood of their half-time customers by the cheers and groans in the air.

I wander along, climbing up the steps to the upper tier and rows of old, wooden flip-down seats. From here you can see the rooftops of tightly knit houses beyond the Victoria Road terrace. Streetlights casting an orange halo above if it is a cloudy night.

I carry on for a block or two, before slipping back down into the cheaper benches.

I cannot help myself.

I always look.

Just a quick glance mostly, at the benches in line with the Victoria Road penalty area.

Where the remaining asterisk from the rescue of Mary Sugg marks the sad tale of Danny Stokes.

Life can come down to a matter of fractions. Seconds. Moments of instinct that seem to come before rational thought. Doing, rather than being.

That is what propelled Harry Bell and Danny Stokes back over the benches of the West Stand to rush to the aid of heavily pregnant Mary Sugg on the twenty-first of September, nineteen forty.

No matter that bombs had started to fall, and the terrifying, deafening drone of bombers had frozen others to the spot.

One a player who had been out on the pitch moments before, the other a young factory worker on a break from manufacturing parts for the war effort, who had been sitting a few benches away from Mary Sugg in the East Stand, losing himself from the troubles of the time with a game of football.

Having both scattered across the pitch with the air raid siren, the opening up of the flak guns, both ran back out to Mary's aid. And both were rightly celebrated for their bravery – for facing down the Luftwaffe, and then for helping to deliver baby Jon 'Blitz' Sugg.

Both returned to pitch and stand once raiders past had sounded, and Mary had been safely sent off to hospital. Taking in what was left of that War League fixture with Newport County.

Both stood proud as punch as Stanley Peters took their picture with Mary and baby Jon, out on the pitch at Inchmery Road – Godparents to baby 'Blitz.'

Both had been at Inchmery Road two months later, on the thirtieth of November, for a War League match against Bournemouth & Boscombe.

Fractions. Seconds. Moments. The air raid siren. Flak guns and that sickening drone, somewhere up among the darkening cloud.

One, Harry Bell, took for cover right away. The other, Danny Stokes, for some reason unknown, fatally paused, waited, before contemplating his dash across the pitch.

Stanley Peters, Harry Bell, all that were there, heard the dread rasping whistle that signified a bomb was on top of them. All in attendance, players and supporters alike that had huddled together along the concourse outside the Nightwatchman's door, dived for cover.

At twenty minutes past four, the one and only bomb that singled out Inchmery Road directly during the war splintered the section of the East Stand closest to Victoria Road as if it had been made of matchsticks. Fire, iron girders, wooden beams and stone pillars exploded up and out across the pitch with an ungodly roar. Smoke, dust, and flame raced across the pitch toward them, the shockwaves of the blast hitting like a punch to the face, Peters describing it in the ledger with a clarity of vision that suggested that the trauma could never be forgotten, no matter how much he might want it to be.

In failing light made worse by the thick, acrid smoke choking the sky, players from both teams in their kits, supporters who had only moments before been enjoying their endeavour, rushed across to the wreckage to look for survivors. The distant peal of fire engine bells among the firing flak guns, and the terrifying drone above.

It was Stanley Peters who found Danny Stokes, while the Bournemouth player Chambers pulled a lifeless lad by the name of Arthur Thompson, just fifteen years old, out of the wreckage, laying him gently on the pitch littered with smoking debris.

Stokes couldn't be moved. He had been crushed by the falling timbers and iron of the Upper East Stand. His face strangely peaceful among the chaos and destruction. Not knowing what to do, Peters held Danny's hand, watched him sleeping, and listened to the clatter and clamour of ambulances and fire engines growing closer; the heat from fires that had grown up all about them singeing his eyebrows, the hair on his arms, causing minor burns to his face and neck.

Smoke choking him, he held Danny Stokes' hand. And didn't let go of the lad whose photograph he had taken not eight weeks earlier holding little baby Suggs.

And when he was finally pulled away by the firemen, Danny's little four-page match programme that he had been nervously clutching in his hand when the bomb fell came away with Stanley's.

As people worked to free Stokes, Peters sat in a daze on the pitch and gently flattened out Danny's programme against his leg, absently looking through it like he had so many in his time; Danny's friend Harry Bell listed at Eight for the Town. Chambers of Bournemouth at Five. A league table, results and fixtures all forging a sporting path through the horrors of war, the future mapped out. A future that Danny, young Arthur Thompson had been clinging to, every other Saturday, to help get through them.

When free, they gently placed Danny down on the pitch next to young Thompson and looked down at them solemnly and waited for the ambulance. Only two months earlier he had stood not far from where he lay, cradling baby Joe, smiling from ear to ear.

The attack had been so severe there had been no photographs for Stacey to find in the micro-film at the library. Those tasked with capturing life in our small town for the local paper were as terrified, as hopelessly pinned down as everyone else beneath the heaviest bombing raid the town would endure. All they could do was document the aftermath in bombed out streets, entire rows disappeared. Stone splinters of fallen churches jutting up into the cloud-choked sky. The East Stand, or what was left of it, cut completely in two. One part imploded down into a ragged crater, the rest teetering over it so fragile it seemed as though a puff of wind might send it crashing down.

She printed that one out. For the book.

It would be testimonies such as Stanley Peters,' written down in the Nightwatchman's ledger, that would accompany the articles in the paper the following Monday. Piecing together the horror. The terror. You can see the tremor in his hand as he wrote, those pages a little more scattergun than his otherwise neat and precise efforts elsewhere.

What he saw. What they all saw, it is hard to imagine. Yet Stanley helps you to, his private testimony for the Nightwatchmen of Inchmery Road.

After the war, the club planted five trees on the pavement by the East Stand turnstiles on Victoria Road. One for Danny, one for Thompson, and one each for Charles Manning, his wife Anne, and their seven-year-old daughter Alice, all of whom had been rushing along the street for shelter when the bomb hit, the Victoria Road end wall exploding outwards, killing an entire family in an instant.

Eighty years on, this little row of Poplar trees has grown up above the rebuilt walls of the Victoria Road terrace, looking down at the pitch. An uninterrupted view for young Thompson, for Danny Stokes on match day. Some welcome shade for those queuing at the turnstiles on a hot, sunny early season Saturday.

Poplars that had been companions to Stacey as a little girl during her first solo pitch, selling match programmes. She would sometimes back herself up against one of their trunks if her usual spot by the East Stand turnstile was occupied by enthusiastic children waiting for the gates to open.

Feeling them at her back had been a comfort.

'I huh-had no idea. Wuh-what they represented. Who they ruh-represented. That they were suh-special trees. Just like Peter wuh-Wright's.'

And just like Peter Wright's tree, Stacey took it upon herself to look after those poplars, as best she could. On first reading the story, we not long after headed out one of the exit gates onto Victoria Road, and we weeded out the little borders around each trunk. Eight or nine inches before they were hemmed in by paving slabs. She gently made them neat and free from litter, discovering that beneath the scrub each had a little plaque that clearly hadn't seen the light of day for who knew how long, based on the grimy, rusty patina that had obscured them.

It took her a while, but with some effort and polish, they became clear enough to read again, each bearing the name of one of the fallen – Danny, Arthur, Charles, Anne, Alice – and the date – 30.11.40.

We would pay them a visit, every now and then, Stacey laying flowers on the anniversary, clearing them away again when they grew tatty.

Peters didn't go home for days after the bombing. In shock, he stayed in post. He helped remove the debris from the pitch, dragging it back over and into the ruined East Stand. Often pausing at the spot where Danny and Arthur had been laid. Breaking from his task to shelter when the sirens began to wail.

For the rest of that season the Town had to play all their games away from home, until the East Stand was made safe, finally being built back up in peace time. Even so, Peters would keep on with his rounds, tending to the ruins of Inchmery Road, sitting at night at the back of the West Stand, watching the lights and flashes away down the coast at some distant town being hit. Watching the gutted shell of the East Stand, and where Danny and Arthur had been rested, just shy of the penalty area.

He would do what he could, to keep Inchmery Road together. For Danny. For Arthur. For everyone who needed it, and the hope, the escape it represented, kept safe within.

And he wrote their stories – Danny and Arthur – their final moments. He wrote of Danny's bravery alongside Harry Bell, just a young lad trying to do right by another, with an infectious laugh and self-effacing manner at the praise heaped his way. He wrote about them, their ordeal in Mackie's ledger, so as they would be rightly remembered. Honour in memory, their maintaining of tradition, their passion, a little normality in going to the football beneath the devastating skies, Peters described with a horrifying accuracy.

Now, eighty years after the fact, it is hard to see where the old section of the East Stand that survived the blast meets the 'new' – decades of weathering binding one to the other seamlessly.

But I always stop where I think it is and look down at the benches where Stokes and Thompson could have been sitting, where Mary and Jon Sugg sat after he stopped playing. Where countless others have hunched forward, following the play intently. Generation after generation. For well over one hundred and twenty-five years.

Sometimes I see them, or I feel that I do, on my night rounds, figures materialising out of the shadows. Those lost to time squashed up, shoulder to shoulder along the benches like they used to, swaddled beneath heavy winter coats and flat caps. Rows and rows. Looking away out onto the pitch at some long gone ninety minutes. Decades of faithful devotion earning them the right to linger on. To inhabit the place that had meant so much to them, had animated, inspired them like no other.

I feel them. I feel that they are there. At their spot. Where they found peace, friendship, escape every other Saturday. I hope they still have it now. Danny Stokes, Arthur Thompson, all of them.

I feel them, whether they are there or not. I feel the weight of history. Their history. I remember those I know about. I imagine those I don't. All those people who cared, who lived for the Town on a Saturday afternoon.

After the East Stand, I clamber back down onto the red grit track around the pitch, then transfer across onto the Victoria Road terrace, watch fallen leaves from the row of poplars skitter and tumble across the steps. Listen to their boughs and branches whispering on the wind. Voices for the voiceless.

Sometimes after my rounds I find myself absently turning to the page in Mackie's ledger where Stanley Peters wrote the sad tale of Danny Stokes. An old, yellowing envelope, fastened by a fragile old paper clip, clings to the top of the page.

Inside is Danny's programme, from the day he died, that he held tightly in his hand until the very last.

A memorial to its owner, this dog-eared relic with failing folds. The creases caused by Danny's terrified hand forever etched into it.

I look at it with a tender reverence, like those Nightwatchmen who have gone before me. Then I slip it back into its envelope, to keep it safe. Just as those before me did. Safe inside Gerald Mackie's ledger.

It is hard to conceive of the horror it saw, this sheet of foolscap folded once by design, then again by hand to fit inside Danny's pocket as he passed through the turnstiles.

Flak guns and sirens, falling bombs and the deep rumble of wave after wave of bombers. The dread whistle of a falling bomb, the deafening roar of a direct hit. It experienced it all, saved from destruction in Danny's hand. I turn its pages slowly, carefully, with the respect it deserves. So much more than a little football programme.

Stanley Peters' tenure as Nightwatchman was not only the most eventful – nursing Inchmery Road through five years of war, among other things – but it is, to date, also the longest run any Nightwatchman has put in. Thirty-two years as full-time custodian, plus a couple of years right at the start as a relief, covering days off and Tanner Rowe's holiday, learning the ins and outs.

He saw Jon 'Blitz' Sugg grow up, turn into a footballer, then a devotee with his mother on the benches of the East Stand. He saw Danny Stokes' and Arthur Thompson's, the Manning family's poplar trees grow up and peek over the top of the Victoria Road terrace.

He saw the Town's one and only promotion in the Football League in 1955, up into the dizzying heights of the Second Division for two seasons of struggle – back when Division Three was the basement, split into two regional leagues – before an almost inevitable relegation, gate receipts being a fraction of those clubs about them.

He saw players and managers come and go. Backroom staff too. Friends, friendly workmates, and those restricted to smiles, nods in passing. He saw crowds gather, then slip away again, every other Saturday. Hopes raised and dashed. Only to be raised once more. Decade after decade.

He watched the erection of the first ever set of floodlights at Inchmery Road in October 1953. He watched from the Nightwatchman's door in the West Stand at a friendly match against First Division Arsenal that christened them before more than eight thousand supporters.

A photograph from the local paper, with Inchmery Road all lit up, was pasted into the ledger, along with a programme from the match – the centre pages housing the team line-ups covered in Arsenal autographs of international players, FA Cup winners, and First Division champions.

He had waited outside the changing rooms and had politely asked every one of them to sign above their names on the page. Welsh International goalkeeper Jack Kelsey, and his national team compatriot Walley Barnes. Joe Mercer, Bill Dodgin, Don Roper, and

Doug Lishman. England international Lionel Smith, and Scottish national team winger Alex Forbes. All of them.

He did the same with the promotion winning Town team of 1955 – autographs across the team sheet, the front page, the programme carefully affixed into the ledger alongside black and white photographs of celebrating players and backroom staff up in the players' lounge. Smiling faces holding up glasses of beer.

In one, a beaming, middle-aged Stanley Peters. Balding hair and thick-rimmed prescription glasses. The programme destined for Mackie's ledger tucked inside the pocket of his cardigan, flanked either side by two of the girls from the ticket office.

By the time he retired in 1970 aged sixty-five, he had seen triumph and tragedy. Footballing status earned and lost, careers launched and failed. Lives coming, and sadly going. The minutiae of all life and endeavour at Inchmery Road, no matter how mundane. All working for one cause, all a part of preserving this beloved little institution.

Everything he had seen, it consumed him, and he consumed it. To the point that he would often join his replacement Bob Andrews, for a few hours into the night, long after he had officially retired. 'For old times' sake,' he would say, holding out a tin of biscuits to go with the tea, and wander around with Andrews with a heavy, arthritic limp.

Letting go of your life as a Nightwatchman, and all the pride, all the meaning it instilled, was easier said than done for Stanley. And he would prolong his little visits by telling tales from his time as Nightwatchman. Tales that had become a part of his life, preserving them, and the people they homed as best he could. Tales that touched Bob Andrews, who took to caretaking the ghosts of Mackie, Rowe, and Peters as if they were his own. Which they soon became.

Stanley always had a story for Andrews – happy, sad, funny, tragic, whatever best suited the moment – though there was one particular story that Andrews liked the most. He would happily listen to Peters when he told it, no matter how many times he had heard it before.

More ghosts at Inchmery Road.

Chapter Five

George Chester remains the most successful manager in the Town's history, and one of the longest serving.

A large bull of a man, who seemed to fill the entire door frame when passing from room to room, he came to Inchmery Road in the summer of 1952 after a promising spell as manager of non-league Whitby Town in the Northern League.

He had played as a professional for his home-town team Hartlepools United for seven seasons, before a move to local rivals Darlington for a further four. He had dropped into non-league with Whitby Town when he was released by Darlington, and he had been player, then player-coach, player-assistant manager, assistant manager, and finally manager.

The club was in a bad state, he would tell anyone that would listen, when he took over. No money for good senior players, he had to build a side from youth prospects, collecting up young lads let go by Hartlepools' and Darlington's youth teams.

He did well, steering the team to back-to-back county cup final appearances, a string of promising finishes in the league, as well as a run through qualifying to the first round of the FA Cup – a feat that wouldn't be bettered until after Chester's passing in 1982.

His ability to make something from nothing did not go unnoticed. Along with his ability to build up, then secure the transfers of five of his young dropouts back into the Football League – all generating transfer fees that helped secure the future of Whitby Town – this new manager attracted the attention of a number of Football League clubs.

Why he chose the Town and Inchmery Road when better bets had offered him a contract, he would explain away on walks around the ground with Stanley Peters.

He had liked Stanley, and Stanley liked George – in Mackie's ledger, among the pasted photographs celebrating that promotion of 1955, there is a picture of Stanley and George, arm in arm, looking at each other and beaming, as only people with genuine affection for each other can – and when Peters came on shift and popped his head round the manager's door, George would often get up, and join him as he checked the doors and shutters of Inchmery Road, walking with him across the stands and over the terraces.

It was, and is to this day, an unlikely friendship – manager and Nightwatchman. But it seems to happen more times than not, that the Nightwatchman becomes a shoulder to lean on for the manager. A sounding board with someone who only has the best intentions of the manager, the club, at heart. A sporting confessional, someone to express fears, concerns, ideas and the like to, without fear of being undermined in his position.

Some friendships are bigger than others. My relationship with our current manager is more distant than Stanley and George's. Me and Stacey pop our heads in to say good evening. We have a quick chat, giving him a break from the stresses strewn across his desk. A couple of friendly faces on a cold, dark night.

But Stanley and George, they were genuine, warm, heartfelt friends, both of whom loved a good yarn, and they would swap tales as they wandered on their rounds around Inchmery Road.

George Chester was a born storyteller. He loved a story. And more importantly, he had the intelligence and timing to weight a tale perfectly, so as people would stay engaged right to the end.

'Coming here was an easy choice,' he would always say. 'This club was in the biggest mess. In the worst trouble. I knew they would give me the most time to do my work.

'If you were to get just the one chance at managing in the Football League, then you would want that to be at a place where they really needed you. Where they would let you build up your master plan. And well, a few years down the line, and it hasn't worked out too badly for either party I would say.'

A modest claim from the only manager to turn a bottom four Town side into a promotion winning team in three seasons. Swapping trips to Shrewsbury and Southend with fixtures at Anfield to face Liverpool, Hillsborough to play Sheffield Wednesday, and Elland Road to go up against Leeds United. Two seasons in the rarefied air of Division Two before the almost inevitable relegation back down again into the basement.

No matter George's ability, simple economics dictated that playing against sides with crowds ten times larger, with budgets ten times greater than your own would mean struggle. But it was a struggle the supporters delighted in. Every Saturday a David versus Goliath encounter that felt all the sweeter when David won out.

George Chester quickly became a living legend at Inchmery Road. Tales of his boys taming Liverpool, Nottingham Forest, West Ham United, Blackburn Rovers and the like on home turf are still talked about to this day. He had only ever been brought in to steady a sinking ship, to lift them up into mid-table mediocrity in the Third Division South.

A Championship season, then two up in the Second Division, with crowds growing through the turnstiles, and handsome transfer fees for his young charges – George Chester exceeded his brief, and then some, effectively giving him a job for life at Inchmery Road.

After relegation Chester kept his team there or thereabouts, ensuring there was never a pointless, mid-table end of season run in, or worse a scrap, to avoid last place. There was always something to play for, though the Town never made it again to the promised land.

He kept finding and churning out young new talent, bringing through local lads that the crowd loved him for. The club was in rude health. Everyone was happy.

Even now, some sixty-five years on, people still look back to George's time as the best of times. They wouldn't be wrong.

He would never restrict his activities to the training pitch or his office. You could find George everywhere and anywhere about the club.

He would often stop by to say hello to the girls in the ticket office, in the club shop, where he would wander about looking at all the scarves and pennants. He would chat laundry powder with the kit man, watching the rows of tumblers spinning.

He would wander up and back with the groundsman as he mowed the pitch, talking different seed combinations and grass length. He would hold ladders and watch as maintenance people climbed up onto the floodlights to change out snuffed bulbs. And he would have a story for everyone. A funny little line or two to raise spirits. A soothing anecdote for someone having a bad day. Inspiration when it was needed. A course limerick if required to bring a smile. Tales of changing room bust-ups and pranks pulled on bus rides, training pitch altercations and side-splitting gaffes behind the scenes. Always engaging. Always eagerly anticipated. One for anyone that needed it, be it the tea lady or the chairman.

He knew them all, by first name. He knew the names of their children. He knew when it was someone's birthday or anniversary, and he would find them out, have a tale that seemed fitting for the occasion.

Though Bob Andrews' favourite George Chester story, as told him by Stanley Peters, happened to be Peters' favourite as well. A story Chester would reserve for Christmas time, when it had grown dark and wintry outside. A tale told over a glass of whisky, looking across his office at the Christmas tree in the corner.

After hearing it multiple times, Stanley wrote it in Mackie's ledger, transcribing Chester from memory. It is there for anyone to see, but it is better being told it, by someone who had been captivated, when it was first told to them.

Just as Stacey had been when I told her.

Chester used take the first team, the apprentices, and any triallists making a serious case for being signed up, up to Whitby for a week during pre-season.

One of his old team-mates ran a dated holiday park that opened out right on the beach, and every year, from the summer of 1952, all the way to 1968 when he finally retired, George Chester took his team for a week of intense training and three friendly matches against his old teams Hartlepools, Darlington, and Whitby Town.

The holiday park was basic, as any of the players would tell you. They slept in a large dormitory once reserved for live-in staff when the camp was busy enough to need them. Rows of bunk beds like a military dorm, with a washroom at the far end.

Every morning at seven they would jog through the park past bemused campers and down onto the beach for sprint and stamina drills on the sand. Brutal, energy-sapping runs across the dunes before breakfast were concluded with the player deemed most sluggish being carried by the rest and thrown into the surf.

The poor unfortunate would then have just enough time to race across to the dormitory for some dry kit and make it back to the canteen before the team ate all the breakfast buffet laid out for them. Fuelling themselves for the double training sessions awaiting them.

Chester believed the week helped greatly to bond the team together for the coming season, contributing to their successes, and made it happen even though the club had no money for such things.

Chester's team-mate had turned a field that had once been an overspill for campers, when the park had been booming, into a football pitch – complete with a small stand, a perimeter barrier, and a manicured pitch that looked more like a bowling green.

During the summer he would run football sessions for the kids in camp, and referee chaotic, joyous twenty a side matches where the little tykes swarmed about after the ball like a plague of locusts.

And when George inquired about his Town team coming up to stay, they found an ingenious way to make the trip free.

The pitch would be mown and marked out until everything was in pristine condition, and on the first Saturday of the Town's stay it would host a friendly match between them and Hartlepools, and on the following Saturday, just before the bus ride home the Town would play another against Darlington.

George's friend would position himself and a few of his staff at the gate to the pitch and charge a small fee for any campers or supporters who wanted to watch a professional football match. He even printed up a team sheet and charged a penny a time.

The matches would draw hundreds of people. Seven or eight at least. Many from Whitby, a town who had never had the Football League on their doorstep, but also a good number of campers would go – the kids readying themselves to duck under the barrier and storm the pitch at full time to get their team sheet signed by as many players as they could.

Topping up the crowd would be die-hard Hartlepools and Darlington supporters, who would come down to cast an eye over their beloved sides. A long summer without football blissfully ended with this low-key friendly.

And from gate fees, team sheet sales, and the kiosk selling fizzy pop, sweets, and bottles of beer a tidy profit was made. Enough to cover the Town's stay and make a handsome profit for the holiday park.

Everyone won.

Wednesday during these weeks in Whitby would be free from early morning beach runs and double sessions. They would play Whitby Town in the evening, and George would let the team relax during the day any way they saw fit, that didn't include alcohol or women.

Some would relax on the beach. Others would head into town to play on the arcades. A few of the more senior players would head up onto the East Cliff to look about the ruins of the gothic Whitby Abbey. It had been an inspiration for Bram Stoker when visualising his novel *Dracula* and was as atmospheric and spooky as any Transylvanian castle: gothic towers and grand ruined walls silhouetted against the sky above the town.

George Chester, on his day of leisure, also liked to wander up to the Abbey – he had read Stoker's book while living in the town, and he always felt the chills of that story when he first caught sight of it every year – before pottering about the shops, lingering in old haunts.

'Though my favourite shop,' he would continue to his Christmas audience, gathered round a desk in the main office, or in the foyer, sometimes sat in the directors' box in the West Stand, 'was a little off the beaten track. Where tourists rarely reached. An old parade of shops, most shuttered, long vacant. Among them, an old bric-a-brac shop.

'The window was full of shelves of old books, old typewriters, a couple of trumpets sat on top of their cases. Piles of records, papers, and journals. Wooden trinket boxes. All sorts.

'I am a sucker for places that like. I love to rummage through shelves of old books and magazines, boxes of this and that. Just in case. You never know what you might find.

'I used to pop in every now and then, to see what had washed up there, though the old man who ran the place would never remember me. I don't know why he should really. But I very much doubt he ever had many visitors. The shop always looked closed, dark and gloomy, as if someone had forgotten to shutter it like all the others when they abandoned it.

'But I would always make the trip, to see what there was. And he would never remember me.

'Inside, it was the trip of 1954, I recall, in one of the gloomier recesses of his shop on a dusty shelf bowing with the weight of piles of old magazines there was this old Christmas tree, carved intricately from wood, listing to one side on the failing shelf. Each limb looking so fragile, pine needles fashioned one by one, green paint faded with time.

'It was nice looking. A nice shape. Dense, with lots of branches so that there was lots of body. It looked very old, had lots of character. Like it had lived a life or two, before finding its way there.

'You know the Christmas tree in my office? In the corner next to Anne's desk? It is the very same. She had been going on at me since I came to the club that my office looked very depressing at Christmas, all undecorated.

'As your secretary, she would always say, you should want to make this little office as nice for us both as it can be. A little Christmas cheer wouldn't go amiss you know.

'So, when you think of my story after this, know that it is all Anne's fault.'

If she was present, he would always wink and smile at Anne – a young woman in her twenties, with long blonde hair always tied in a knot and sparkling green eyes – when she huffed her disapproval.

'What that old thing? the old man told me when I asked him about it. Yes. I suppose it is for sale, he had said with an element of surprise in his voice, as if it had been some time since someone had shown any interest in his treasures.

'I remember a long pause, the bell from the newsagent's door, two boarded-up units further along, breaking the silence.

'We both looked at the tree on the shelf, the swirling dust that had been disturbed by my arrival settling back onto the piles of books, magazines, records, boxes and cases, beneath this single, dimly lit bulb in the ceiling, that illuminated so little of the shop you wondered if there was really any point to it.

'He had kindly eyes, the old shopkeeper, eyes that betrayed his love for his little store and all its treasures, no matter its ramshackle state to the outside world. And he began moving a few boxes to reach the tree, pulling it carefully out and setting it on the floor next to a little bar fire by his cluttered desk.

'It was warm enough outside, but his shop, in the gloom, always seemed to miss out.

'It was cold enough for his fire. It was always cold in there. At the height of summer, or in deepest winter, he would have his little bar heater on, glowing orange in the gloom, whenever I came to visit.

'I remember the cold from when I used to visit him in the weeks leading up to Christmas, trudging through deep piles of snow that seemed to collect and drift up against the precinct of shops. As if trying to bury it. My nephew loves old *National Geographic* magazines. He loves to explore faraway lands with the large, detailed pull-out maps that used to accompany the stories. The old man always seemed to have a never-ending supply of old, brittle issues from a bygone time to fan a young boy's imagination – and I used to buy a bundle every Christmas for him, picking my way gingerly through whiteouts and swirling flurries to fetch them.

'The snow seemed to dampen down all sound outside. As if the whole world had stopped. Whitby silent in the eerie half-light of a heavy, snowbound winter's day. The ruins of the abbey, menacing up on the cliffs, in the gloom.

'Anyway, the old man stepped back so as we could take a closer look at the tree. About four feet in height, the trunk made from a dark, rich wood.

"The branches, they slot in, so it can be packed away," he said, "I just leave it up. It is no bother away over there."

"Believe it or not, but these trees were made over in Germany, in the Black Forest. I did some research on it, from the markings on the bottom." He leant it over to show a crudely etched run of unfamiliar symbols on the base that looked maybe like a capitalised word or two from an unknown language. Sharp, jagged strokes, that never joined up with each other, like capital letters do. Instead, they fell a little short, suspended in proximity, but never truly forming up. Almost letters, making up unknown words.

"It turns out that church congregations started making them in the mid seventeen-hundreds. Though there is no date on this one as far as I can see, so I can't say for sure how it is," the old man said as he brushed carefully at the dust on the branches. "But it feels old. If that makes any sense. The wood, it looks like it has some age to it, at least to me. It is amazing that none of the branches have been damaged. They look so fragile."

'I knelt in front of it and nodded.

"It is attractive," I said. "In a strange sort of way."

"Strange yes," he said, "I've not seen another like it. And strange in other ways too. You won't believe this, but this isn't the first time this tree has found its way to my shop."

'I looked up at the old shop keeper.

"Really?" I said.

"Really," the old man replied and beckoned for me to sit in a spare chair at his desk while he took his seat by the bar fire, turning it a little so as I would feel its warmth.

"I don't remember entirely how it first came here," he said. "People used to drop things off all the time, house clearances, that sort of thing. And among it all, that tree. I found a spot for it on that shelf and there it sat, for years. With no one so much as looking at it, let alone buying it."

"Then maybe five Christmases ago a local gent snapped it up. He had travelled a lot through Europe on some business or other that he didn't specify, or if he did, I don't remember what he said, and he recognised the tree immediately from his time in Germany. And he had a story to tell about them, or some of them at least. This one in particular," he thought.

"This gent said that it was true that church groups used to make them, to raise funds for their congregation. They would mark them on the base to show which group had produced them, where they came from."

"He said that he had been told one particular story, about an eccentric spiritualist group in the eighteenth Century, with a branding just like, or very similar to, the one here on this tree, who claimed that their pastor, a Tomas Dzvoric, instilled these Christmas trees that they carved with a power. To reach out to the dead. Opening a pathway between one world and another, at midnight on Christmas Eve.

"They attached candles among the branches – the first instance of lights being added to a Christmas tree, this gent had said. I'm not sure if that is where the tradition comes from or not. I suppose it must." The old man shrugged.

"Either way, they did it, and this gent explained that they had believed that from within the shadows of the branches that the candles cast, up against a wall behind it, a pathway would open up.

"The shadows would thicken, grow, begin to bristle and rustle on some chill wind, pine branches swaying gently away into the darkness.

A dim path just visible between them, trailing away…"

"Now, I thought that that would be the end of the story, but this gent had more. He had found the story fascinating when he came across it and had wanted to learn more. He studied it."

"He discovered that this congregation of Tomas Dzvoric lived in a small village, the name of which was so strange-sounding that I didn't catch it. Isolated deep within the Black Forest on the shores of a large lake."

"He said that he had taken a detour on his travels to visit the village, or the remnants of it; virtually lost amongst the forest that had grown up through it. Rubbled walls of old buildings suddenly looming out of the trees in front of him, the odd stone hearth, chimney breast, chimneys slipping up into the tangle of branches."

"It had lain untouched for two hundred years or more – this ghost village, after its entire population just disappeared, one Christmas."

"Neighbouring villages across the lake claimed that this thriving, if not quirky little community, with their Pastor Dzvoric, simply vanished."

"They were there in the days leading up to Christmas. They would row across the lake in little boats, materialising out of a thick mist that always hugged the water during winter, where they would sell their produce in the local markets. Their beautifully carved trees, trinkets, bowls, wind chimes, as well as preserves and stewed apple pastries, before dissolving away back across the lake. Faint twinkling lights of the village on the far shore, hemmed in by a near impenetrable forest."

"But then, after Christmas Day, nothing. They never crossed the lake again. They were never seen again.

"And when some traders crossed the water to check on them, they found the village devoid of all life. Each house empty – candles burnt down to the nub on each little beautifully carved Christmas tree in each front room."

"Their clothes still in cupboards. Books on shelves. Plates and cutlery stacked neatly in fully stocked pantries. Everything was as it always was. Only every living soul was missing. Gone. Like they had never been."

"And the pastor, the villagers, were never seen again."

'The old man had paused, shook his head.

"And that's the story this gent had to offer. He had said that the people back then had drawn their own conclusions."

"They had heard the pastor's claims, of pathways into the beyond. At midnight. On Christmas Eve. They had dismissed it as the ramblings of an eccentric. But now the pastor, the entire village had vanished. As if into thin air. Never to be seen again."

"The story of the missing village persisted, and was handed down from generation to generation, on Christmas Eve. People never went close to the abandoned village after that, excepting the odd gaggle of terrified, inquisitive children, daring each other on to row across the lake to peer into the ghost village."

'But they would never step foot on dry land, and they would steer well clear on Christmas Eve, preferring to listen to one of the elders tell the story round a log fire in the village square."

"And everyone, no matter their age, would always make sure to snuff out the candles on their Christmas trees long before midnight. If they had been brave enough to add them. Just in case. Not wanting to feel the chill breeze, hear the rustling of branches, coming from within."

"Many had bought these pretty Christmas trees from the village over the years. They were so beautifully made. So delicate and pleasing to look at. Magical by candlelight."

"Those that didn't move theirs on would pay extra care and attention to them on Christmas Eve."

'The old man stopped and looked down at the tree, faint silhouettes of the lowest branches cast by his fire stretched out across the floor, dissolving away back into shadow. It was a captivating story, I told him. And I had very much enjoyed it. He shrugged his shoulders.

"That's not quite the end of it," he said, "At least, I don't think it is."

'I remember looking across the desk at the old man, staring down at the tree, his face barely lit by the glow of the fire.

"Why?" I said, "What happened then?"

'The old man had shifted in his seat.

"Well," he said, "the gent bought the tree. To remind him of his travels, he had said. And that story he hadn't thought about for more than forty years. He paid more than I asked for. Saying that it was such an intriguing little thing."

"We carefully wrapped it up, and off he went. And that was that. Or so I thought."

"I didn't make the connection. Not for a little while, because it must have been Spring the next year when the tree came back to me, as part of the leftovers from a house clearance."

"The man who I hire to collect and drop off house clearances had got talking to the solicitor overseeing it all. And when he got to me, he had a story to tell."

"The gent, that had brought the tree from me – he disappeared, over Christmas."

"No note, no signs of a disturbance, or anything out of the ordinary. Just an empty house – the lights still on in the kitchen. Wax from candles he had fixed to this tree melted down into the carpet of his living room."

"He was gone. It made the local paper. And

to my knowledge he has never been seen since."

"I put the tree back on that shelf, and there it has stayed, for a good-few-years now. I look up at it from time to time and think of that gent and his story. Especially at Christmas. I can't help but wonder. I wonder what became of him. What he may have seen, by candlelight, in the shadow of his tree. And where he might be now."

'He remained lost for a moment, deep in thought before he snapped out of it and looked at me and smiled.

"Look at me," he said, "getting caught up in an old yarn like that. All manner of things could have happened to that gent, to that village all those years ago. Anything really. I'm sure I don't know what can go on in the minds of others. But with people, I have learnt, anything is possible."

'He stood up and shifted the tree with his foot gently.

"It is a strange old thing though, this tree, and no mistake. But it is just that, an old wooden ornament." He looked up at me and smiled.

"But, if you buy it, maybe lay off on the lights, eh! Just in case!" He winked and watched as I crouched down on my haunches in front of the tree, brushed my fingers gently against those fragile little carved pine needles.

'Well, I bought it. How could I not after a tale like that?

'Though sometimes I wonder if that old man just played me as a sucker for a good story. That he had a box full of those trees out the back that had been knocked up in some factory somewhere. That there had never been a mysterious Tomas Dzvoric, a lost village, or a missing gent in Whitby on Christmas Eve.

'I carefully took out each fragile branch and wrapped them in tissue paper, packed it all away safely, stowed it on the bus for the trip home. And when Anne went on her lunch one day in early December that year, I brought the tree out, tenderly put it back together, draped

it in a bit of tinsel and a few strings of coloured lights, and put it in
the corner of the office next to her desk.

'When she came back, we had a ceremonial turning on of the
lights, and that evening, after work, we snuffed everything else out
and sat in the darkness and looked at the lights and had a whisky. And
I told her the story the old man told me. About the tree.

'I don't mind telling you. She held her glass of whisky to her
chest and sat wide-eyed as I told the tale.'

Again, if Anne was present at George's retelling, she would
protest at this point, saying she did neither thing. But George would
carry on regardless.

'After that, we sat in the darkness and looked at the shadow of
the tree lit up across the wall, the reds and greens and blues and
yellows of the string of lights backlighting the fragile branches, casting
enlarged shadows. Frozen in silhouette. Both of us lost in our own
thoughts.

'Every day, after her lunch, as the light began to drain from the
cold winter skies, Anne would tuck her bag beneath her desk, then
turn on the Christmas tree lights. And for the rest of the day, she
would work at letters of invite for new triallists, letters of rejection for
unsuccessful prospects, and everything that needs to happen to keep
a club like ours ticking along – the lights a little cheer in an otherwise
drab outlook.

'Most of the time she would be working by herself, if I was out
conducting training, or away around the country with the team. Her
only interaction would be if any of the staff from the general office
needed her expertise on something. And it was them she first
confided in when she began to notice little things.

'A slight, chill breeze where there shouldn't be one. The faintest
sounds of hushing, rustling boughs, bristling pine needles. What
seemed like imperceptible movement among the shadows of the
Christmas tree, captured out the corner of her eye.

'She would stop her work, look, listen, before checking the latch
on the office window, feel for a breeze at the door. She would then
stand and look at the tree for a moment – still as can be, its shadows
deepening across the wall as darkness closed in outside – before
deciding that she needed a cup of tea and some company in the
general office.'

Once more, if Anne was present among Chester's audience, she
would protest foul play. That George had somehow rigged a fan or

something to spook her. To provoke her reaction. That he took some wicked pleasure in trying to unnerve his loyal assistant.

He would always hold his hands up and shake his head. Where, he would always say, could he do something like that in such a compact office? Anne would shrug her shoulders begrudgingly, in a tacit acknowledgement that George was probably right.

'And besides,' he would continue, 'I have felt it too. Late in the evening, while all of you are safely tucked up in your homes, with a cup of tea and a good book. I am still here, working away on formations and tactics to make the team successful. To make you all happy. And while I do, I hear things, I think I see things. Just like Anne. Enough to make me sit up in my chair, stock still. And watch, listen.

'Then, with the club silent and empty around me, I switch off the lights, and go and find Stanley our Nightwatchman, take in the night air on the pitch with him for a time, clear my head, regain my composure, before I head off for home. And I always make sure that the lights are switched off long before we leave on Christmas Eve.

'I have never been tempted to wait up, until midnight, to see what happens. And my advice to anyone that would listen – don't be tempted either. Some things are better left unknown. And I believe the story of our little Christmas tree is one of them.'

Then, without another word, he would nod and leave his audience to ponder what they had heard. And without fail, in the days after a famous retelling of the tale, people from the general office, the first and reserve team, the ticket office would find themselves knocking gingerly, popping their heads round the manager's door. "Just stopping by to say hello" – something no one ever did any other time of the year – offering cups of tea and vague questions as a pretence for a glimpse of the Christmas tree.

Chester would nod seriously and beckon them in, accepting the tea, while Anne would look at the scene from over the top of her cup and shake her head. At George playing up to those casting nervous glances into the corner and the shadows of the Christmas tree across the wall.

For a time, Chester's story became as much a part of Inchmery Road's Christmas calendar as Boxing Day fixtures and first team training on Christmas morning.

Christmas just wouldn't be complete without a telling of it at the office party, or in a doorway over a hot brew. People would seek him out – young apprentices who were in awe of him any other time of the year and would normally speak only when spoken too. New members of the ticket office staff, or admin trainees would be egged on to ask for it. Old heads such as Stanley Peters, Jim the groundsman, old Frank Marsh who organised the programme sellers on match days would also seek it out like others sought the nativity.

And every time Anne would shake her head, but find herself drawn in, again and again, looking deep into the tangle of branches and lights as George told his tale.

When George Chester finally retired in 1968, Anne went with him. His tall tales and ripping yarns of life in the lower leagues had long since become legendary, and he was offered a deal to write his autobiography.

Chester – The Life and Times of a Lower League Journeyman came out in 1970 to much acclaim, and had been transcribed in full by Anne, who went on to manage the many bookings for George as an after-dinner speaker at events up and down the country.

She would drive him, then be the butt of his jokes in the audience, shaking her head and protesting as she had always done at his recitals at Inchmery Road. Her "straight woman" role became an integral part of his act, and she took it with the good grace that all straight "men" in double acts did, knowing the affection George had for her.

It was a rich and rewarding life for the both of them.

When the book came out, a box of them arrived at Inchmery Road – each one personally transcribed to each individual member of staff that George had known and shared his life with while manager of the Town.

All bar one reached their recipient. Each personal note treasured by their owners. The affection for them detailed within the pages of the book worn with a badge of honour. At their contribution to such halcyon days.

The one rogue copy left without a home was for a young lad called Simon, who had been an assistant groundsman, but had left in early 1970, and no forwarding address could be found.

His copy sits in a drawer of the Nightwatchman's office, and has become a little dog-eared, having been read multiple times by all the Nightwatchmen. All pondering the inscription inside:

Dear Simon – Milk, three sugars, and a drop of engine oil. See, I remember! George

When Anne left with George she wasn't replaced. Any work the manager needed doing was, and still is to this day, done by someone in the general office. As a last of her kind, she was the perfect full stop. Deadpan, with a wicked sense of humour, she had a heart of gold, and a love for the Town that was more borne out of the camaraderie and friendship she found within, than from the exploits on the pitch. Her joy at promotion was more at the happiness it brought, the pride it instilled in those that went on to revel in Second Division acts of defiance against greater, more famous opposition. At a job well done, by good people.

When she left, she handed the box that housed the Christmas tree to Stanley Peters, knowing as custodian of all things Inchmery Road, that he would keep it and its story safe. And that he did.

'It has become like folklore here. It wouldn't seem right to take it away. Let everyone have their story at Christmas. And besides,' she had said to Stanley, ushering him in close to impart her secret, 'I have always thought that it is a rather ugly looking thing. But, God, please don't ever tell George that!'

Every Christmas after George and Anne left, Stanley, then Bob Andrews, then I, would carefully unwrap and put the tree together, standing it in the corner of the Nightwatchman's office by the door. And from there anyone that wanted to, could pop in and take a look at it.

With it being just off the main entrance that everyone passed through, their curiosity could be masked with a simple nod and a smile, and a wave of the hand. 'I was just passing through and I thought I'd put my head in,' was the common line. Newer staff members intrigued by the promise of a good, spooky story by the older heads, egged–on, back down the stairs to peer round the door.

They would congregate at the Nightwatchman's door and wait for Stanley, then Bob, and now me to arrive for my shift from out of the night, asking to be told the story of George Chester's tree. A cup of tea and a packet of biscuits in hand as inducement.

The junior staff would be put up front and made to ask. But you could be sure to see a number of familiar old heads behind them, Sarah our General Manager would always be one of them — a confirmed lover of a good old-fashioned Christmas ghost story.

We would – Stanley, Bob, and I – always try to carry the story as George had done, with a sombre tone and a serious look. We would pull out Gerald Mackie's ledger from the drawer and drop it onto the desk, beckoning people in, opening it up to the pages where Stanley Peters had transcribed Chester's story.

We didn't need it. We knew the story by heart. But Stanley said that it had always leant an extra element of drama to the proceedings, so Bob and I would use it as a prop too. Looking into the tree as we started in on the tale, knowing that everyone would soon be drawn into its shadows, frozen in relief across the wall by the lights draped around it.

The same story. Year after year. As important to some as midnight mass, mistletoe, advent calendars and carol singing.

The same story. Since 1954. Sending chills down the spines of generations of workers at Inchmery Road. For more than 65 years.

The same story. But for the last few years, with a postscript.

I went before work one cold, blustery day in late November to the library. I had been shifting things around in the office, getting the Christmas things out ready for the first of December, when they went up around the place. I had sat quietly in the dark, looking down at the old box containing George Chester's Christmas tree, turning the odd wooden branch over in my hands.

I don't know why I went. I guess I had become as possessed by his story as anyone else. And I wanted more. Of the story. Or, at the very least, I wanted to try to find out more. And the library was the only place I could think of to start.

Back then it had a wall of telephone directories, from ceiling to floor. Directories from the Scilly Isles all the way up to Lerwick and Shetland's outlying communities. A sturdy wall of knowledge, but the contents of those shelves would crumple and sag every time you took a volume or two out from it, the flimsy, tissue thin paper and covers bulging outwards.

I found the address for what seemed like the main library in Whitby and wrote them a letter. An extremely apologetic, vague letter. That I was looking for an article in the *Whitby Gazette*, about a man who disappeared from his home on Christmas, year unknown, but possibly late forties, early fifties. I wrote a little about the story, the Christmas tree. I thought they might appreciate a little mystery, to maybe entice some inquisitive soul to take my request seriously. Though in reality I didn't expect a response. People are busy, too busy for foolish old men and their wild goose chases.

But I sent it anyway. Expecting nothing. But a week later, I had my reply.

It was from a young library assistant called Beth, who explained that they had an archive of the local paper, in large, newspaper-sized bound books. That she had been intrigued by my spooky Christmas story and had spent a few lunchbreaks sifting through Christmas and New-Year editions, starting in 1946.

"And there it was," she wrote "in the January 11th edition, 1950. Please find a copy enclosed. And thank you, for this chilling mystery. I will think of you, and that tree this Christmas. And the shadows. Beth."

Folded neatly beneath her letter was a photocopy of a newspaper article.

"Whitby Man Discovered Missing."

Below the headline the article described the strange circumstances of fifty-three-year-old Whitby resident Jude Buckingham's disappearance.

A reclusive man: neighbours that had been canvassed by the article's author said they had last seen him on Christmas Eve at a carol recital put on at the end of their road every year. They had grown concerned for his wellbeing in the New Year, when the bottles of milk delivered by the milkman remained on his front step, building up, day after day.

Police jimmied his door to discover Buckingham missing, the kitchen light on, all windows latched tightly shut, all doors locked from the inside, with keys still in the lock.

In the living room a fire in the hearth that had long since burnt down to a cold, black ash, and a Christmas tree – the candles that had been fixed among its branches burnt down to their bases – solidified puddles of wax bonded to the carpet below.

And no sign whatsoever of one Jude Buckingham.

It was as if he had simply vanished…

I tucked Beth's letter, her research in Mackie's ledger, at the pages of Chester's story.

His old man in the bric-a-brac shop hadn't been pulling his leg. His gent did exist. He had bought the tree. Had gone missing on Christmas Eve night, or shortly after. The tree returned to the old bric-a-brac shop in a house clearance. Jude Buckingham's house clearance. Where it waited some four years. For George Chester.

And now, when I tell the tale at Christmas, I don't add what she found to the story. I finish the tale as George had told it. Leave a pregnant pause, then get up from my desk. Look at the tree, then point at the article resting on the open page of the ledger.

'Maybe you would like to read this,' I say, then wander out the door to fetch another cup of tea, leaving them in the gloom of the little bar heater, the twinkling lights of the tree casting long shadows.

An extra chill for them.

An extra chill for Stacey, who I clearly remember craning on tiptoe to see the article, the ledger one Christmas party – all the programme sellers were always invited – tucked into her mother's side as a young girl, wide eyes sparkling with the thrill of it all.

And I see that sparkle now, nearly twenty years on, as we silently, carefully unwrap the tree, build it up together every Christmas. I let her dress it with a string of lights, the bulbs chattering against the wood as she weaves them between the boughs. Standing back when done, she flicks the switch, and we stand in the darkness, watching it all lit up. Shadows splaying out across the wall behind it,

Stacey's face animated by the blue and green and red and white lights, lost in thought, eyes wide, like that little girl all those years before. And at the Christmas parties, those dark nights where we get the odd passer-by step in to take a look, she blends into the shadows, and listens to the story once more. Her gaze lost in the sea of reds, and greens, and blues.

It also never ceases to send a shiver down my spine.

And I am always certain to have those lights turned off at close of play on Christmas Eve.

That and Christmas Day are the only two days where the Nightwatchman isn't on duty. He is sent home by the General Manager after drinks in the office on Christmas Eve and is told not to come back before Boxing Day.

And while I sit at home on Christmas Eve night, with a glass of whisky in my armchair, looking at my own little plastic tree that sits on top a stool by the television, I can't help but wonder. What would I see if I were at work right then? Would I dare to turn the lights on? What could the walls of the Nightwatchman's office reveal, of things they may see at midnight on Christmas Eve, if only they could talk?

It is enough to make sure that the curtains are pulled tightly shut about my little house, the doors locked and checked, my blanket pulled that little bit further up underneath my chin.

The only thing that I know for sure – that George Chester would absolutely love that his story is still going strong, all these years later. God rest his soul. Safe and sound within the pages of Mackie's ledger.

Am I ever tempted? To see what those villagers, their pastor, Jude Buckingham, saw? To sit up and wait for midnight in the Nightwatchman's office? To see once and for all if the story is a load of old cobblers or not?

I am not.

I love the mystery.

I prefer the wonder, to have faith in the story, and those who told it. I prefer having it every Christmas, intact, spooky. A ripping old yarn. A ghost story for dark, wintry nights. And I hope it always stays that way.

All I can say is that, on the odd occasion, on long, dark nights leading up to Christmas. In idle moments before my next round of door rattling, in the gloom of the Nightwatchman's office, I have looked up from the warm little halo of the bar fire by my feet, the desk lamp by my side. At what sounded like the soft rustling of branches, from somewhere. And in the darkness, lit faintly by the string of lights, the shadows of branches from that Christmas tree shivering, swaying ever so slightly across the wall.

Whether it was my eyes playing a trick on me, the darkness in the dead of night getting to me where the slightest sound seems to amplify and appear sinister in the mind's eye. Whether a breeze from the corridor leading up from the benches of the West Stand has tickled the strings of lights without me noticing, sending shadows rippling across the wall. That door is loose in its frame after all. It rattles and shudders in a storm. There can be a breeze that whistles up that corridor.

Whether simply my own telling of George's story had got to me too – I don't know.

All I do know is that, at those moments, I would find myself shrinking behind the magazine that I was reading, looking out at the shadows across the wall, before taking up my torch, heading out early for another sweep of Inchmery Road.

And no matter how cold it was, I would take my time…

Chapter Six

When Bob Andrews took over as Nightwatchman in 1970, after Stanley Peters' well deserved retirement, he took on the burden of history willingly.

Although not a keen football fan himself, he felt the weight of reverence for our little football ground, our club, among the few thousand souls who would be drawn to it every other Saturday.

And while not enraptured with the cut and thrust out on the pitch, he felt the passion and meaning that ninety minutes' endeavour instilled in those on the Inchmery Road terrace, the benches of the lower West Stand that could be seen from the Nightwatchman's door.

When Peters showed him Gerald Mackie's ledger, and told the stories held within, Andrews took them on as if he had always been a life-long fan. The human element to each story, their passions and tragedies, they became his, and he would tend to Peter Wright's Bicycle.

He would take a moment to think about Danny Stokes, Arthur Thompson, and the Manning family.

He would always turn up long before his shift started on match days, to take in the spectacle. Watching the bustle of expectant faces outside the ticket office and club shop. Groups of old friends outside the pub on Inchmery Road, drinking and laughing. The sounds of the brass band that played and marched up and down the pitch before kick-off, drifting in bursts over the West Stand when the wind carried it.

Tobacco smoke, frying onions from the hot dog stand, Frank Marsh and his band of programme sellers dotted all around the ground barking out their never changing mantra:

'Programmes. Get your match day programme. Programmes'

He enjoyed it all. He felt the anticipation. The electricity that was generated, even at such a lowly Fourth Division fixture. He could tell that it meant the world, to this small band of brothers and sisters. And over time he even found himself instinctively cheering at a Town goal, punching the air, shouting 'YES' from his vantage point. If not for the build-up and wicked shot, the rasp of ball against net, then for the joy that it would bring. Hugs and handshakes on the benches, scarves flailing wildly on the terraces. Beaming grins. The twinkle of hope in the eye. A Saturday night, a whole week set up with three points safely in the bag. The fortunes of club and community intrinsically bound together. Ninety minutes on a Saturday afternoon the barometer.

And Bob Andrews bought into it completely. Custodian of the physical entity. But also, thanks to Mackie's ledger, of its soul. The little stories of love and living that knit team and town into one. He helped to preserve them, tended to them like the groundsman tended his turf.

He loved it all.

He read Mackie's ledger from cover to cover. Over and over. And he would dutifully add to it with little snippets of life at Inchmery Road: children poring over white paper bags of programmes and player pictures safely acquired from the club shop with pocket money, so eager to explore them that they would clog the doorway, all quiet, lost in their treasures.

He wrote about 'Crazy Mary,' a small, frail old woman who was so polite and timid if you met her in the street, but on match days she would become possessed in her love for the Town, banging her hand on the roof of the visiting dugout at every Town goal, not stopping until play had resumed. She would nod and smile at the stewards as they shuffled along the rows of benches, pleading with her to stop. Which she would. Until the next Town goal.

Bob Andrews would see these little moments around Inchmery Road: old men lingering outside the turnstiles on match day, waiting for them to open. The first in, they would find their usual spot, and stand, and look out at the scene, lost in their own thoughts, the place all to themselves. He would see the kids holding their parent's hand, weaving through the animation of a match day, looking up in wonder at the scene all saucer-eyed and smiles. He would see these little acts performed by mostly nameless protagonists, acts of devotion to our small-town team, and he would record them in the ledger. The odd line or two. No dates or names, just a sentence, a snapshot, a fragment in time.

Folks craning their necks, looking out for a friend, large grins when they spotted them. A hug, before slipping into the pub for a quick pint before kick-off. A young lad dribbling a tattered ball as a crowd drained away at full time, re-enacting what he had just seen away down the road. Heartbeats, no more, of life around Inchmery Road.

And in time, having let the place get under his skin, he began to become a part of it. Not just an observer. Just like all that went before him, he began to assimilate into the pages of that old ledger.

Assisted in the first instance by his friendship with Frank Marsh, Stacey's grandfather.

There are those who walk straight by. Who never engage their entire lives – decade upon decade of going to see the Town – with the programme sellers of Inchmery Road – their calls just a part of the cacophony of match day, and nothing more.

There are others, however, for whom the match day programme is everything. A precious little document of all things Town. Statistics, reports, interviews and images. Managers' notes, articles, opposition pen-pics, league tables and the all-important team sheet, detailing the eleven names from each club picked to do battle.

Precious information – every other Saturday – this thin journal added to boxes or shelves of programmes that had gone before it. A living, growing Encyclopaedia of the Town. A collection that can never be complete and is added to with a near religious dedication. Containing, as it does, all that information on their beloved team.

Match days cannot be considered a success until a copy is bought. Eyes darting through the crowd outside Inchmery Road, looking for their regular seller. Listening out for their siren song. The thrill of going to the game only truly unleashed once programme has been safely secured and tucked into a coat pocket. The more devout carefully placing it in a bag so as it can't get creased. Others still, buying two copies – one to be kept pristine, unopened, for the collection – the other to be read at the game, team changes jotted down when announced. Folded and placed in a back pocket for easy access during the match, so as the name of a visiting winger causing the Town defence all sorts of problems can be sought out.

And orchestrating this transaction between seller and supporter every home game was Frank Marsh – head programme seller. He would ensure there were the requisite number of sellers, with the right amount of stock, and an apron with a pocket in the front where change and takings were stowed. He would make sure each seller was at their pitch at the right time and returned the right amount of money into the club shop at the end of the game. Though discrepancies were rare – those offered the position had mostly been vouched for by another respected seller. Often mothers and fathers for their sons and daughters.

For the Marsh family, being a programme seller at Inchmery Road was a way of connecting to the club they loved in a deeper, more profound way. They were, after all, a part of the staff, albeit only at every home game.

No matter. They were a part of the family: they were on the same payroll as the players, the manager. They were invited to the Christmas party, rubbing shoulders with their heroes on the pitch, and all the other backroom staff. They received their little brown envelope of wages every week, just like all the full-time staff. They were thrilled at a little Christmas bonus, just like everyone, appearing in their envelopes. But most important of all, they carried the trust the club had in them like a badge of honour.

Their takings were always right. Or thereabouts. Only the odd ten pence lost here and there. And always willingly made up out of the seller's own pocket.

For his own part, Frank Marsh was a fourth-generation programme seller, following in the footsteps of his great grandmother, his grandmother, and his father. Each taking over the former's prestigious pitch outside the main gates when they retired. One family tending the one spot for more than sixty years, Frank Marsh told Bob Andrews when he became Nightwatchman in 1970.

'My family have been doing this longer than I have been alive,' he told Andrews when introduced to him by Stanley Peters 'And I am fifty-five going on fifty-six!'

He also had a daughter posted outside the away paddock up on Victoria Road, who would, in time, become Stacey's mother, and a nephew working the corner of Lepe Road, a narrow, terraced street whose small box gardens backed up against the wall of the East Stand.

All three would be at their posts, come rain, shine, howling winds, or heavy snowfall. Match after match. Season after season. And proud as punch, to boot.

If he knew the weather was going to be foul, he would employ his youngest daughter to ferry hot cups of tea in tin mugs round to each seller. She would dart and weave between the legs of the crowd without them even knowing that she had been there, keeping everyone topped up, before standing with her father handing out the programmes once Frank had taken the money.

Frank had inherited his father's programme collection when he passed away, who had inherited his mother's, who had inherited her mother's. Issues stretching back long before the outbreak of World

War I, all sold by the Marsh family, including a copy from that fateful day in November 1940, where Godfather to Jon 'Blitz' Sugg, Danny Stokes, lost his life.

It was widely understood to be the most comprehensive collection of Town programmes anywhere, though he wasn't as precious as some.

From the very first box to arrive from the printers, he would drop his money into his apron and take the very first copy off the top, just as his forebears had done, then he would fold it, and pop it in his back pocket, where it would stay while he tended his pitch. Only once his work was done, and he had climbed up to his seat in the East Stand would he pull it out and clutch it between his hands as he leant into the play.

'I like the folds in a programme,' he once told Bob Andrews. 'I like for them to be match worn. To have lived a life at the game. I like the fact that, even some fifty years later, I can pick up a programme of my grandmother's and see the fold where she had tucked it beneath her shawl. I like seeing the team changes scribbled out in her hand. Wrinkled pages where the rain got at it.

'They are perfectly fine. Perfectly readable. But they have taken on some of the personality of their owner. They have lived a life, been to the match, all those years ago. I like that. You can feel it, you can imagine the scene. Those that went before us. Just for the slightest of moments.'

In the weeks leading up to the hand-over of Nightwatchman duties from Stanley Peters to Bob, Peters passed down the stories of Inchmery Road, and the little things the Nightwatchman did, for the living, as well as the dead. Among them was the long-standing kindness afforded the Marsh family, to help with their programme collection.

It started in 1927 with Tanner Rowe, and an initial act of selflessness for Frank Marsh's grandmother, Betty.

Rowe would, after a kickabout with the excitable David Smith by the main entrance, help Betty to bring the boxes of programmes in, once delivered by the printers. He got to see first-hand that thrill in her eyes at opening the top box, dropping her two pence into her apron, picking up that first copy, losing herself in its contents for a few moments, before tucking it away safely for later.

She would proudly tell him every other Saturday how she and her mother had every programme from every Town home game stretching back to 1905, and that they were precious to them.

It was Rowe, seeing that passion, who spoke to the kit man for the first team.

Rowe would always come out to help the kit man bring everything in off the team bus after a long away trip, tired players drifting away to their beds as the town hall clock chimed ten, eleven, sometimes midnight or worse by the time they made it back to Inchmery Road, though the kit man still had more work to be done.

He would offload the bags of kit from the bus, so that the driver could be on his way, then he would drag them in to the laundry, sort it all out and put it into sinks to soak, ready for a proper cleaning on Monday morning.

He would have been the first person at the club in the morning, getting everything ready, and he would be the last person out sixteen or seventeen hours later. He was most welcoming of Tanner's kindness, who would carry in the worst of it, before offering the kit man a sandwich and a cup of tea.

Through Tanner, the closeness between Nightwatchman and kitman was forged. And lasts to this day.

I will always keep a look out for the lights of the team bus on a Saturday night, or the early hours of Wednesday after a midweek match. I will always be there as the bus pulls in, with a cup of tea for the kit man, and a spare pair of hands for carrying whatever needs it.

A simple act of kindness played out for the best part of a century now. Henry being the grateful recipient back then; Mark, a portly man in his fifties who used to play for the reserves many years ago, receives his mug of tea with a tired smile in the present.

Tanner Rowe, not knowing how things worked at other clubs, mentioned Betty and her love of programmes, and asked if they did them at other grounds. Henry nodded. There would be a small pile of them waiting for the team in the away changing room, every match, he said.

Tanner asked him, if he had the time, and it wasn't too much problem, if he could possibly pick one up for him, to give to Betty. 'I think she would really like it,' he had said.

'She has such a collection of home games, maybe she would like a collection of away ones as well?'

And every away game after that, if there were any spare, Henry would pick up a copy. And better yet, after he had cleaned up the changing room, and packed the kit back on the bus, while he was waiting for the team to leave the players' lounge, he would ask opposition players for their autograph, and they would happily sign beneath their names on the team sheet. Some weeks he would only get one or two if he had been especially tied up with clearing up and preparing for the journey home. Other matches he collected the entire starting eleven.

Betty was thrilled, by the programme, and the signatures, and the kindness of Tanner Rowe. She loved to flick to the pen pictures of her beloved Town team and pore over the autographs of the opposition. She would delight in all the different layouts, font types, and colours of each programme. Precious additions to their collection.

Tanner would leave whatever the kit man brought back on the corner of the Nightwatchman's desk. And whenever there was one to be picked up, he would nod and wink to Betty, who would beam and hurry in to take a look, thanking him profusely, turning straight to the team sheet to see the names and autographs. They were so special, she would tell Tanner, because they had been in the changing rooms, had been behind the scenes, had been handled by the players.

Precious, even among her collection of Town treasures.

And so, it went. Year after year. From Henry to Tanner to Betty. One kindness after another. From Nightwatchman to kit man to head programme seller. Another ritual for Mackie's ledger. Passed down through the generations.

And in time it would be a young lad known as 'Chuck,' with a terrible limp from a leg break suffered as a small child, who would bring back programmes for Stanley Peters, who would leave them safely on the corner of his desk for Betty's son, Don.

Later still, Colin would hand them over to Bob Andrews, who would leave them in their usual spot for Don's son, Frank.

Today Mark brings them back for me to give to Frank's granddaughter Stacey, who is not only the first Nightwatchwoman at Inchmery Road, but also the youngest ever head programme seller at Inchmery Road.

She has moved on from her spot by the poplars of Victoria Road, and now tends to her family's pitch outside the main gates, that familiar bobble hat pulled down over long, jet black hair and piercing blue eyes. Just it had been when she was a little girl all those years ago, hiding behind her mother's skirts.

She does it out of respect for those who went before, putting aside her awkwardness. People like her grandfather, Frank, a man she would never know, but she would come to know, thanks in part to Mackie's ledger.

Chapter Seven

It takes a little time for Nightwatchman to feel worthy of adding things to Mackie's ledger. Most do not consider themselves fit to just start in.

Bob Andrews was no exception. Preferring instead, for the first years of his stewardship, to maintain and preserve, rather than add.

It was Frank Marsh who compelled him to add his own voice.

Or rather, Frank Marsh's ghost.

Over a helping hand bringing in boxes of programmes, a cup of tea, Bob and Frank developed their own friendship – like all those who went before them. Andrews was tall and wiry, with blond hair that always seemed a bit of mess, even when he made an effort. So too his moustache, grown out of reverence for a hard-nosed television detective from his favourite show.

Frank Marsh was a good foot shorter, and a great many pounds heavier. A balding head almost always covered by his flat cap. They were a right odd couple, but they enjoyed each other's company.

Frank would always stay on after a game and they would chat on about nothing and everything, the game, the wellbeing of loved ones, the weather. Even Town's chances that season, though Andrews would be sure to qualify everything with a: 'But I don't know anything about football really.'

Marsh would always chastise him for that, replying that everything he ever said was always astute.

'You may not have lived your life in the game like some of us,' he would always reply, 'but you see things. You can judge the mood. You can see and feel Inchmery Road – falling for one player, turning on another. You know the state of play, if not the tiny silly minutiae of it all. I value your judgement over most of them spouting off down the pub.'

Twelve years of helping Frank with the boxes of programmes, a cup of tea in the Nightwatchman's office, watching the Inchmery Road faithful draining away into the night on the full-time whistle. Twelve years of watching Frank poring over away programmes brought back by the kitman, turning straight away to the team sheet to look at any autographs, just like his grandmother always had.

By the 1970s the team line-ups had mostly migrated to the back page, so Frank only needed to flip the programme over, where his grandmother had to turn to the centre pages.

Knowing how he loved to discover any autographs, Bob would ensure the programme was face up, so as Frank would have to flip it to see which lower league journeyman had neatly signed next to their name. Lost in the moment, he would smile this innocent, childlike smile of discovery at every reveal. A little boy once more, in awe of a journeyman footballer's autograph.

It was a simple friendship, with Christmas cards and bottles of scotch exchanged every year. Sweets always in the Nightwatchman's drawer for Frank's daughters and nephews, when they came back up to Inchmery Road to fetch Frank for his dinner.

Hours of idle chat, warm handshakes, and laughter. Two friends who would never have found each other if not for their vocations. Enjoying each other's company every other Saturday, and countless midweek matches. Regular as clockwork. Until it wasn't.

It was a non-descript Fourth Division fixture in November 1982. The kind of day that never really got going. Skies low and dusky, no better than that, so as the floodlights had to be switched on to banish the gloom. Though it couldn't do anything about the lowly position of both teams near the foot of the table – Scunthorpe United just two points worse off than the Town.

It was a statistic that stuck with Bob because Frank described the match as a 'six-pointer,' and he needed that explaining.

'Really?' he had said as they lugged the boxes of programmes into reception 'You've never heard that? Well, I suppose it is quite a new saying. It's only recently that you get three points for a win. So why should you? Basically, if both teams are in trouble at the bottom of the league, then if either wins not only do they get the three points, but they also help to bury their rivals deeper into the mire. They help themselves twice, hence a six-pointer.'

And as he left for his pitch that day – the rest of the programme selling team having been kitted out and sent out on their way – he turned and smiled at Bob

'I'll see you later, and we can have six sugars in our tea – one for every point the Town will get today!'

And with that he was gone.

Bob never saw him again.

The Town drew, conceding a last-minute equaliser, which had scuppered Bob's little display on the Nightwatchman's desk, of six sugar cubes lined up in front of both his and Frank's tea mugs.

He boiled the kettle, then stood by the door looking out on the benches of the West Stand, nodding and shrugging at heartbroken supporters bemoaning their bad fortune, and the Town's bad defending at a last-gasp corner kick.

After ten or fifteen minutes and the last stragglers had ebbed away into the night, the p.a. system piping tinny music cut out, leaving an eerie silence where there had been such animation and clamour just a short time earlier. He would begin his rounds to check all the turnstile shutters and exit gates once the kids had come for Frank.

Only they never came. And neither did Frank.

He sat at his desk, and waited, but Frank didn't show. He stood outside the main entrance and looked for him, but he was nowhere to be seen.

He waited, for an hour, idly flicking at the corners of the Hereford United programme from a midweek trip, that he had waiting for Frank in its usual spot on the desk. Looking down into the black and white photograph on the cover – a moment of action, frozen in time. A bank of supporters looking on expectantly at a player haring down the wing in front of them.

It was only by chance that he came across one of the ticket office staff while he was on his rounds, checking the door to the club shop.

The lad shook his head, said what a day he had had, that the programme seller by the main gates had had a massive heart attack a little before kick-off. He had been selling programmes once second, then the next. Gone. His young daughter in hysterics next to him.

The lad from the ticket office had seen it all, and it had really shaken him up. He knew a little first aid, so went to help. But there was nothing that could be done, though he tried, for the young girl who looked up at him imploringly. But when the ambulance arrived, well, they just tapped him gently on the shoulder, and he sat back, looked up at a sea of ashen faces, the sobbing little girl.

Bob Andrews went to the funeral. Laid flowers at Frank Marsh's pitch by the main gates. Brought out a cup of tea to Frank's young daughter Layla, who had bravely taken up her dad's spot for the next game. Selling programmes in front of the small display of fading flowers, where her dad had fallen.

Bob's first real entry into Mackie's ledger; where he left a piece of himself behind, detailed the man that was Frank Marsh. His dedication to the family tradition, and his friendship with Bob. He and his family were an Inchmery Road institution, and he described their family tree of programme sellers. And he hoped that Mackie's ledger would help preserve his name – a kindly man with a warm smile and a hearty laugh that couldn't help but make you laugh too.

His second entry most definitely would.

Sometimes it is the smallest things that cause the biggest stir. And that was the case for Bob Andrews. Something imperceptibly small, that would be overlooked by everyone else, that came to have such an effect on him, from the day of Frank Marsh's passing, and every night after, where there was a new away programme sat on the Nightwatchman's desk.

He didn't notice fully, that first night. At least, not enough to really interpret its meaning, lost as he was in a fog of sadness. He absentmindedly turned the Hereford United programme that he hadn't had the opportunity to give to Frank back over, resting as it was with the team sheet face up.

Lost in his thoughts, he instinctively turned it back to the cover, and that black and white image. Always face up, he left them. Ready for Frank.

A midweek away fixture the following week at Walsall came and went, and Bob helped travel weary kit man Colin lug in his heavy load of mud-covered shirts, shorts and socks a long way past midnight. Before he set off for home, Colin pulled out a programme from his back pocket and handed it to Bob. As he drifted off into the night, Bob looked down at the red cover – a large football dominating. Each hexagonal panel of the football replaced with a photo of a different Walsall player, all smiling benignly. On the team sheet, four signatures.

Bob flattened it out as best he could. A three-plus hour bus journey, crumpled in the back pocket of Colin's trousers, had left it in a sorry state. But Frank would have loved it all the same. He would have called it character, all those creases.

Waving off the bus, Bob locked the main door behind him, dropped the programme, cover up, on top of the Hereford one on his desk, and set off on his rounds.

In time it would be Layla who would come in for a cup of tea, pick up the programmes. The Town collection that had once been her great, great grandmother's, then her great grandmother Betty's, then grandfather Don's, and father Frank's, handed down to her to preserve, to continue.

She cherished it as much as all those who had gone before her did. And every new addition was very much welcomed.

In the early hours of that first midweek match after Frank's passing, Bob wandered the terraces, drifted through the rows of benches in the stands, kicked idly at a drift of poplar leaves gathered on the Victoria Road paddock. Checking shutters, gates and doors.

Back in the Nightwatchman's office, he switched on the kettle, waited for it to boil. And despite looking across at it for some time, it took him his second or third sip of hot tea before it dawned on him. The Walsall programme: it had been turned over. So as the team sheet, the autographs, were facing up.

Knowing he had definitely placed it cover up before his rounds and knowing that he was the only person left in Inchmery Road, he shot bolt upright. He did another sweep of the ground, the offices, checked every door. He was locked in. And on his own.

Gently, he turned the programme back over, and sat. And thought.

After Frank's death it happened, not every time, but sometimes, with a new programme brought back from around the country. It would be placed face up, like he had always done, for more than twelve years, in its spot on the corner of the Nightwatchman's desk. And sometimes Bob Andrews returned from his rounds to find that new programme, team sheet up. Autographs on display.

He would check the offices, the doors, just to be sure. Then he would sit down, make another brew, and leave a mug where Frank used to sit. And he would sit quietly, looking at the programme, the team sheet, and drink his tea.

He told Layla about it all. The whole story. How her dad used to love checking for autographs. That maybe, even now, he still came to take a look.

She liked that idea, Layla told him. He told her that he did too. It gave both of them some comfort, that little connection to Frank.

Whether it was a draught of some kind that was flipping the pages, or whether it was Frank, Bob Andrews would never fully commit one way or the other. He conceded that the Nightwatchman's office was susceptible to draughts rattling along the corridor from the

West Stand. It could be that that made the programmes move. It was, at least, possible.

He simply wrote in the ledger what he knew. Hinted at what he believed. Left enough room for what he hoped.

Now, so many years later, we still keep up the tradition. Mark, who is not only kit man, but runs the social media match updates, and is Assistant Manager of the Town Women's team, brings back programmes from away fixtures. I place them on the corner of the desk for Stacey, who took over from her mum Layla when her arthritis became too painful for her to stand for very long. Always cover up.

And every now and then I pause, look down at the programme flipped to the team sheet, and I sit, and I wonder.

You can read it any which way you like: Bob Andrews and those programmes. But me, I know which notion pleases me the most. I know which I prefer. Stacey too.

I watch her, reading about her grandfather, her family's kinship with the Nightwatchmen down the decades. I see the pride in her face, at their passion for what is now her passion. At learning about them, that they were worthy of writing about, by every Nightwatchman.

The way she talks about the family programme collection, curated by hand, started by her great, great, great grandmother. How tactile they feel, those folds and imperfections. The indentations of autographs, grubby spots from long coach trips home in pockets and bags. A lifetime of club and family intertwined so deeply that you can no longer distinguish one from the other – the Marshes and the Town. As written in Mackie's book. The pride in her voice. It is quite something.

That feeling of belonging. Of having a place. Even if it is a perpetually trophyless lower-league football club. It is priceless to Stacey, like it is to so many others. Like it is to me.

And every now and then, after our rounds, we come back to discover a programme not yet taken home for the collection, team sheet up, and Stacey looks at me.

'Guh-grandad Frank?' she asks.

I shrug my shoulders. I do no more. Because I know no more. Then I stand. I watch her staring down at it. Fingers caressing the page. Reaching out.

Chapter Eight

When it came to a great many things, Bob Andrews was a bit of an innocent. By all accounts, not least his own, he was one of life's drifters, being taken with no great design from one thing to another.

He held no truck with money. It was a means to an end, to pay the rent. It had never been his motivation for anything he did. It had never stood in the way of his principles; he saw everyone as equal, deserving of respect, and had never had any problem standing up to perceived injustice.

When a foreman at a factory he had worked in bullied a young apprentice mercilessly, he confronted him. He had asked if he meant to reduce a young lad to tears, almost every day. And if he had, Bob asked what kind of a person would want to do that? He was sacked on the spot, which was a shame. He had enjoyed the simple pleasure of contributing at his little post along the production line – fixing the seats and fuel tanks to Triumph motorcycles that drifted toward him on a slow rolling conveyor belt.

After the factory, he worked in a nursery, planting out saplings. Then he worked as a steward on the Stranraer ferry, criss-crossing the Irish Sea over to Larne. And when he came back home, it was pure chance that he stumbled across the part-time job of being Stanley Peters' relief.

He took to it immediately, enjoying his rounds of Inchmery Road, and when Peters retired, it made sense all round for Andrews to take it on full time.

He liked all the people he mixed with in the offices, the ground staff, and he enjoyed the buzz of a match day. He also liked the calm and quiet, late at night, where it was just him and Inchmery Road. The rest of the world locked out.

He would often talk about one night in particular. In December 1984. A little before midnight. Snow falling heavily. Silently. Cascading out of the darkness. Laying deep across the pitch.

He stood out on the Inchmery Road terrace and looked up at the flurry drifting down, like static on a television set, resting on his face and eyelashes, that made him blink.

He sat with a cup of tea and watched it from the West Stand benches, all night, or so it seemed. Inchmery Road illuminated in the darkness: a dim, ghostly white. The East Stand roof smothered. Terraces lost beneath the snow. Their steps replaced with smooth slopes slanting down to drifts building in the goalmouths. Magical, he called it, among an eerie half-light, a thick snow flurry, faint charcoal strokes of stand and floodlight pylon among the white-out.

The most beautiful thing, he said, which would be turned so ugly in his mind a few days later.

How both could exist in the same scene, he would always say, only goes to show how confusing life can be at times.

But out of such ugliness, a friendship was made. A friendship for Mackie's ledger.

Dennis Lawrence came to the Town in the summer of 1983. He had been an apprentice at First Division Birmingham City, but while some of his youth team made the grade, and were offered their first professional contract, Dennis was one of the ones let go.

There followed a summer of going from one trial to another, up and down the country, desperately searching for a way back into the Football League, another chance. And it was only the Town, down toward the foot of the Fourth Division, who put their faith in him.

A one-year deal on a meagre wage with a lowly football club on the way to nowhere it may have been. But it also made him a professional footballer. And after so many years of hard work and dedication, a young dream had come true.

Lawrence had been born in Birmingham, the first of his family ever to be born outside of the Caribbean, his parents having moved from Antigua as children in the fifties as part of the Windrush generation. And after a first season in professional football flitting between the Town reserves and first team, scoring two goals in seventeen Fourth Division appearances (most coming as a substitute) he made a little piece of Town history in August 1984 by becoming the first ever player to earn full international honours.

Two 1986 World Cup pre-qualifying fixtures for Antigua & Barbuda against Haiti in Port au Prince saw a nineteen-year-old Dennis lead the line in a four-nil defeat on August the fourth, followed by a two-one win three days later.

Not enough for a national team that had been mothballed for years (and would be again for another four years after the fixtures in Haiti), a team that had only ever tried to qualify for the World Cup once before, and had been hastily assembled for these fixtures, to progress into the next round of qualifying. But it was enough for the local paper to run a piece on him and his exploits, celebrating the Town's first ever international player, and the pride both Lawrence and his parents had felt.

To this day he still is in a select group of one, and his achievement was duly cut out by Andrews and pasted into Mackie's ledger.

After the promise of his first season, Dennis was rewarded with a new two-year contract, and he set about repaying that faith with a protracted run in the first team.

To Bob Andrews, he was just another one of the team who he rooted for from his spot by the Nightwatchman's door on a match day. A young player full of raw talent, who could enthral and frustrate in equal measure – going on mazy runs, hitting inch-perfect passes, finding the top corner of the net from seemingly impossible angles, then missing an easy tap in, lobbing the ball into touch when a Town player was wide open, losing the ball in a dangerous part of the pitch.

A raw talent. But no more so than an entire squad of nearly men, who found themselves in the Fourth Division because they were still searching for the one thing needed to make it higher up the leagues: consistency. All working hard on the training pitch, on a Saturday afternoon to find that missing piece of the jigsaw, and that dream move up the ladder toward the big time. And unlike a good number of the team, Dennis had time on his side. He was a young lad, with plenty of seasons in which to grow.

In his dream to make it to the top, he was no different from the rest of the Town team. And at the same time, he was very different. Something Bob Andrews only fully comprehended the week of his beautiful snowstorm. Well into Dennis's second season.

In the eighties snow never stopped play. Pathways would simply be cleared, salt scattered, and groundsmen would sweep the lines on the pitch clear right up until kick off, then again during half time if there had been any further flurries. Game on.

The only concession to the conditions would be an orange ball rather than the usual white that would bobble across the bone hard pitch, kicking up puffs of snow behind it.

The Saturday after the first snow of 1984 had the Town at home to Torquay, and the Inchmery Road faithful skittered and tottered through drifts of snow to their usual spots.

Breath from clumps of support on the Inchmery Road terrace smoked up above them into low, expectant cloud readying itself to dispatch another heavy snowfall that would dissolve the far goal to the faintest of outlines.

It was a scene made for Christmas cards, not good football, and a dour nil-nil draw seemed the only possible result as both teams struggled with the conditions. A point doing neither side that much good at the foot of the league.

An entirely forgettable game of football.

Though not for Bob.

Whether he had ever heard such calls before, he could never be sure. Maybe he had, but he hadn't understood where they were aimed. But that day, from his spot behind the benches of the West Stand, there could be no doubt.

Dennis Lawrence was a tall lad. All arms and legs. That sometimes made him look ungainly. Almost out of control. But when it all came together, he would carry the ball down the wing, cut inside, and deliver a perfect cross, or a withering strike on goal that had people out of their seats.

But when it didn't come together, the grumbles would start. And even worse, and unlike any of the other Town players, the grumbles would start from the moment some looked down at the team sheet to see his name up at number ten. Lawrence having to prove himself every game to some, while the rest of team always seemed to have the benefit of the doubt. At least for the first twenty minutes or so, until they too had earned the frustration of the benches.

He wasn't the first black player to play for the Town. Mark Coleman had played two seasons in the seventies before a move up to Second Division Cardiff City. But Dennis was the first for a good few years, and he wasn't a fraction of the player Coleman had been.

Which seemed to signal fair game for a small minority.

It all came into focus for Bob Andrews that Torquay game, as Lawrence tried to control the ball on a bone hard pitch and run the flanks, just the other side of the grit track in front of the benches.

He heard in an American deep south impersonation someone call out: Run Boy, run,' as Lawrence sped past, followed by a few chuckles.

It felt sinister to Bob.

It didn't sound complimentary.

A few minutes later, after Dennis had been closed down and tackled, losing the ball, someone from that little huddle of bodies proclaimed that Lawrence playing in the snow was a disaster.

'He stands out like a sore thumb among all this. Like a nugget of coal in a snow drift. Their defence can see him coming a mile away. He should never have started, in weather like this.'

More chuckles.

'They are used to the heat, aren't they,' someone else said. 'I'll bet he never saw snow when he was in the jungle.'

More laughter.

Bob stepped forward and leant across to them, asked why they were saying things like that.

'Ah, give it a rest, mate,' one of them said. 'We're just having a bit of fun. It's nothing personal, is it?'

Bob stepped back and sipped at his tea.

It seemed personal, he told me when he retold the story. It was personal.

They weren't talking about any of the other players like that.

And when Lawrence was subbed off with twenty minutes to go, the huddle of bodies on the West Stand benches cheered, before a ripple of applause from the rest of the ground drowned them out.

Bob hadn't liked it and retreated into the Nightwatchman's office before the match ended, watching first the supporters, then the players drain away into the night at the final whistle.

Bob had never spoken to Dennis Lawrence before. He rarely spoke to any of the players. He would nod and smile to all of them as they came and went past the Nightwatchman's door. They always seemed in a rush to get somewhere. Were it not for Peter Wright's bicycle, and Gerald Mackie's ledger, the chances of Bob and Dennis ever striking up a conversation would have been virtually nil.

But there was Peter Wright's bicycle, Gerald Mackie's ledger. And they did.

Ten days or so after the Torquay game, the Town had a long Tuesday night away trip that had them home long after one in the morning. The players trudged off and slipped away after a chastening three-nil defeat, and Bob helped Colin with the kit, before waving both him and the bus off for home.

Despite the bitter cold of a December night, Bob had decided that he would brush down and polish what little of Peter Wright's bicycle remained on view. He had a treatment to stave off rust, and would rub it into the handlebars, the sections of frame and wheel still exposed.

The Wright-Mackie story had always touched him, and he enjoyed doing what he could to preserve it a little longer.

He had lost himself, as he often did, in the work, brushing away a fresh dusting of snow before crawling round to find the best position to get to every spot. He was marvelling at how the tree had absorbed the bicycle, wondering if it had preserved the paint inside, the frame stuck fast in the gnarled bark, when he heard a noise, away on the other side of the car park.

Standing by his car, the last in the car park – a cheap, small thing befitting the wages of a Fourth Division footballer – was Dennis Lawrence. Head down, both hands resting on the roof by the driver's door, he half-heartedly hit the roof again with a fist.

Bob clambered out from his spot and wandered across to him.

'Are you all right Dennis?' he said with a familiarity that all supporters had of the first team. They were never spoken to with surnames. It was first name terms, despite only knowing them from their endeavours out on the pitch. That intimacy of support always seemed to warrant a first name.

He turned, surprised that he wasn't alone and shrugged at Andrews.

'My car won't start,' he said with a softly spoken Birmingham accent. 'It's not even trying to turn over. I suppose it must be the alternator… I don't know.'

They stood for a time, looking at the exposed engine beneath the propped open bonnet, before Andrews, not knowing the first thing about car engines, motioned for Dennis to follow him.

'Well, I don't think there is anything we can do at such a late hour. I wouldn't know where to start, to be honest. Engines have never been my thing. And I doubt we can raise a mechanic at this time of night. Let's get you inside and warm, then we can see about getting you a taxi home. I will leave a note for the office to get a mechanic out first thing in the morning. How does that sound?'

Lawrence nodded meekly, closed the bonnet, followed Andrews into Inchmery Road.

He sat, tired, with sagging shoulders suggesting that the day had thoroughly defeated him, next to the bar fire in the Nightwatchman's office.

He looked into the orange glow of the heater, the twinkling lights of George Chester's Christmas tree, while Andrews did what all good Nightwatchmen did in a time of trouble – made a mug of tea.

'One day, I have a story for you about that tree,' Andrews said with a smile, handing Lawrence a mug 'But for now, let's get that taxi for you. I'll be right back,' and he headed upstairs to the office to find a telephone.

They sat quietly for a time, waiting, before Andrews pointed at the programme from that evening's game on the edge of his desk, and asked if it had been a tough one.

Dennis nodded, flicked through it, looking at his name on the back.

'Yeah,' he said quietly 'tough.'

After a few more moments of silence, Dennis looked across at Bob.

'They were making monkey noises. Some of the fans. Every time I touched the ball,' the hurt palpable in his eyes.

'Loud as day. It felt deafening to me, all I could hear, especially right against the touchline. Just a few feet away.'

'I suppose I should be grateful that no one threw a banana at me.'

He nodded when he saw Bob's look of incredulity.

'No, it happens. Believe me. And do you know what happens when it does? The linesman kicks them back out of play, and we get on with it. You just have to try to block it out. But I couldn't tonight. When it gets inside my head, it's like I play through a fog. I feel out of synch with the flow of the game. I feel out of synch with everything. With football – everything.'

'I am told to get on with it. To ignore it. It is easier said than done when you are the only player that it is happening to. Nights like tonight, I wonder whether it would just be better to pack this all in.' He paused.

'Sorry,' he said, 'you don't want to hear all this.'

Bob shook his head. On the contrary, he said, he did.

Dennis told him of a life that he had no idea existed. Of having to always watch your back when out and about. Never going certain places, especially on your own. Avoiding streets that National Front members lived on. Just because he was black.

'It doesn't matter if you are just a little boy. You are fair game. Being spat at. Punched. Kicked. And if you react, well, you get it ten times over. Those that hate you. That hate you being here, they let you know how they feel.'

'But football was always the escape. Playing – well, it can be such a blessed release. Where you can be yourself. Where you can express yourself, with all the shackles off. That is why it hurts so much, I think,' he said and shrugged. 'When nights like tonight happen.'

'Out there on the pitch, we are all equal. Free to play the game. Well, we are supposed to be. When we are not, when the outside gets in, when that joy gets ruined. I have nothing left. That's how it feels.'

'And my team-mates. They try to encourage me. They tell me to ignore it. They can hear it too. But it isn't aimed at them. It's not that easy. Some days I wish that one of them would just pick up the banana, throw it back at the crowd.'

Whenever Bob talked about this conversation, he did so with tears in his eyes.

Dennis Lawrence was a lovely person, he said, who became a good friend. He had a warm smile, and a chuckle that would make you want to chuckle too. He would always stop to talk to supporters, sign autographs, for as long as they wanted.

He never said a word out of place, even when he had reason to.

He was a gentle soul, with a good heart, who just wanted to play the game he loved, and not have his life filled with a bitterness and hate for those who hated him. Who tried to degrade and humiliate him.

Given the opportunity, he was a joyous person, who liked a good story over a cup of tea, who liked to laugh and smile, connect with people, make friends with people.

And in time he would become fascinated with all the characters in Gerald Mackie's ledger, and their stories. He would ask Andrews to show him Peter Wright's bicycle and tell him the tale of George Chester's tree. Of Danny Stokes, and his part in Jon 'Blitz' Sugg's life.

It was a ledger he first saw that cold December night, the night his car broke down.

Bob Andrews didn't know what to say, that first night with Dennis Lawrence, other than how sorry he was that Lawrence had had to experience such things.

That he thought it was abhorrent.

He told Dennis that he didn't know too much about football but knew enough to know that when he was on the ball, bearing down on goal, he found himself craning for a view at the back of the West Stand benches, willing him on. And when he jinked and swerved, turning defenders inside out, when he lashed the ball into the net, Bob's heart genuinely sang. It was enthralling. Intoxicating. Magical.

It was a gift, that he had. And people, people like Bob, loved him for it.

He had taken out Mackie's ledger. Told him that it contained the soul of the club. The stories that made it what it was. The people who made it special.

He turned to a page that Bob had made up, containing the newspaper article of Dennis's international debut for Antigua & Barbuda. A faint, grainy image of the Antigua team included.

Next to it, a postcard sized photograph of Dennis in his Town kit that he had bought from the club shop.

He would be remembered, celebrated, admired, he told Dennis, at least in this book. For his great achievement.

He would be in the company of some great people. And he deserved to be there.

Andrews told Dennis that he would add a page with what he had told him. Because it needed to be documented. In the hope that one day it would be looked back on with horror and shame.

That one day, some Nightwatchman who Andrews would probably never know, would tell the tale of the pioneer Dennis Lawrence, and how he achieved his dream of being a professional footballer, despite it all. He fished out a pen and offered it to Lawrence. Maybe he would sign beneath the article? For those on his side. Which he did. And as the lights from the taxi swept across the main entrance, a horn honking, he nodded, thanked Andrews for the tea, for his help, before turning and slipping out into the night.

The next evening as he headed into work, he noticed Dennis's car had gone. Alternator fixed. One less problem for the young man. And for that, Andrews felt glad.

The Friday before the next match, the last Friday before Christmas, Bob had a knock on the Nightwatchman's door as he was settling in for his shift. Lads and lasses from the office upstairs, the ticket office, would often knock and wave goodbye for the night, pause for a moment to look in on George Chester's Christmas tree.

It was the night of the office Christmas party, so he was prepared for multiple disturbances, and multiple retellings of the tale, as the wine began to loosen everyone up. But when he looked up at the door, it was Dennis Lawrence standing there, a bag clutched in both hands against his chest, smiling weakly.

Andrews ushered him in, shook his hand, told him to sit, that he would get the kettle on.

He couldn't stay too long. He always had an early night before a game, Lawrence said. But he had something for him. For his book. He pulled out a colour A5 photograph and handed it to Bob. Inscribed along the bottom:

"Antigua & Barbuda National Team. World Cup qualifier. 4 Aug 1984. Port au Prince, Haiti." Followed by the names of the players, who stood in two rows, one crouched down in front of the other in their yellow kits, Lawrence standing proudly at the end of the back line. Beneath a brilliant blue sky, a strange pitch in a strange land, lined with a distant sea of faces. A run of palm trees behind them, obscuring grand, old colonial era buildings with pillars and ornate balconies.

'Your picture from the paper was looking quite sorry for itself. I thought you could do with a better one.' He picked up a pen from Andrew's desk and wrote – 'To Bob, with best wishes, Dennis Lawrence' in the corner of the photograph.

Bob thanked him profusely. Told him he didn't know what to say. Dennis smiled, told him he had a few of them at home, it was really no bother, and he watched as Andrews carefully slipped it into the right page of the ledger.

'I have something else to show you,' he said, and pulled out a couple of shirts – his Antigua jersey from the match, with 'Lawrence – 9' printed on the back, and a blue Haiti shirt that he had swapped after the second game.

'I don't suppose there are too many of these in Britain, eh?'

Bob supposed not, feeling the fabric, tracing the national team badges with his fingers.

'What an adventure,' he said 'What was it like?'

Lawrence puffed out his cheeks and shook his head.

'It was crazy,' he said and smiled. 'A bit of a whirlwind. We only had a week of training as a team in Antigua before we went. We had never even met each other before then, and I had only ever been in Antigua once before, when I was about six or seven, on holiday. So even that was a bit overwhelming: the heat and everything.

'We only got to Port au Prince the day before the first game, trained on the pitch that night, then played the following afternoon. We gave a much better account of ourselves in the second game, once we had settled in a bit, though we didn't do enough to qualify.

'Port au Prince was bewildering and sweltering! We had a few days between the games to explore. It was a brilliant, chaotic place. Colourful, grand old buildings, churches, and markets. People coming at you from everywhere. Warrens of little narrow streets and shadowy shops. There were Voodoo markets selling potions, skulls, all sorts, for ceremonies that you could hear at night. Trumpets blaring around bonfires in the huge graveyards across town.

'We would head down to the port and drink coffee after training. It was a bit cooler down there, with a bit of breeze from off the sea, and we would sit in this park watching the world go by. Cargo ships bound for Cuba and beyond. The people were very friendly. Especially after they beat us by four goals in the first match!

'Then, as quickly as it all happened, it was back on a plane, back here, where I had two days before the first game of the season. It was as if it had never happened. A blur of a dream.

'The hot Caribbean sun definitely feels like a distant dream among all this snow.

'It was only four months ago. It feels a lifetime. Maybe, one day, I will get to go back. Though the national team doesn't play very much. The football association can't afford it. It might be another four years before we get to play again at the next World Cup qualifiers. That would be a shame. We had started to shape up nicely by that second game.' He shrugged his shoulders.

'I guess we will wait and see.'

'What an experience,' Andrews said. 'No matter what happens in the future, no one can take that away from you. What you achieved out there. You are an international footballer. Twice over. There's not many who can say that.'

Lawrence smiled, and they sat quietly for a while sipping at their tea.

'I also wanted to come by,' Lawrence said after a time, 'to apologise, and thank you. I shouldn't have sounded off the other night. That wasn't very fair. But I wanted to thank you for your kindness and understanding. It meant a lot.'

Andrews leant forward in his chair and shook his head.

'You have nothing to apologise for. It is me that should be apologising. It is sickening. Never apologise for feeling the way you do. After what they say. What they do. And if you need to vent, or talk it out, I would be honoured if you stopped by. I really would.' He put down his mug.

'Come with me. I need to show you something,' and Andrews ushered him down the corridor, pausing at pictures along the way, pointing at faces that were in the pages of the ledger alongside Dennis.

He opened the door at the far end out onto the West Stand, the low slanting roof of the upper tier looming over the sea of benches beyond. He pointed away to the benches where those insults about Dennis a few weeks earlier had come from. He told Dennis about confronting them. He also told Dennis of two letters he had received that week, from people who were also sat on the benches that game, who were equally offended by their racist nonsense.

'If you are having a tough time out there,' he said, pointing at the pitch. 'If things aren't going quite so well, then you look over this way. I will be stood right here. A friend. And so too, somewhere on these benches, are those two people who wrote in. Friends also. I will give you their letters, they are yours really, they were writing to support you.

'If you are having a tough time. Look this way. And know there are people cheering, willing you on.'

'And at away games, well, I don't know what to say. Just know that you have friends out there. It's not much. It does nothing to stop what is happening to you, but,' he said. 'It is something at least.'

Dennis put his hand on Bob's shoulder, tried to say something, but the words choked in his throat. Instead, he shook Andrews' hand, and they walked back up the corridor to their teas.

The next day, on another snowbound pitch beneath wintry skies, young Lawrence cut in off the wing, rode one tackle that lifted the ball up to chest height, and as it fell, he volleyed it over the keeper into the roof of the net. A three-one win secured, and three vital points a welcome Christmas present for all, he jogged back to the half-way line, looked across to the benches in the West Stand.

He stopped, smiled. The biggest grin. And nodded.

From then on Lawrence would be a regular visitor to the Nightwatchman's office.

After games he would duck out of the players' lounge early and spend some time chatting.

He would come by after training every now and then, hanging around until Bob came on shift.

And if the abuse had been particularly bad at an away game, he would help Bob and Terry carry the kit in, wait until everyone else had drained away, and then he would vent to Bob.

There were no soothing words to be given, other than what had already been said. Bob just sat, listened, shook his head. Said how sorry he was.

No matter how hurt he was for his friend, it could only ever be a fraction of the pain Dennis felt. A direct assault on who he was. His very being. All Bob could do was make tea, listen, shake his head, and be there for him, take him on his rounds of Inchmery Road, where, after a time of silent contemplation, Dennis would sometimes ask for a story from Mackie's ledger. And Bob would oblige.

He would talk, they would wander across the terraces, through corridors and passageways, before finishing up at a spot that had some relevance to the story he was telling. The past and the present overlapping as Dennis leant against a crush barrier, a pillar, headed out an exit gate to look at the row of poplars, pushed through the bushes to Peter Wright's bicycle, and listened to Andrews' stories.

He really enjoyed them, he would tell Andrews: all these hidden tales, hidden lives of Inchmery Road. And he would often find himself by Peter Wright's bicycle for a few moments after training, or a match, gently brushing away fallen leaves and the like. Looking down at it fused into that old oak. Still waiting for its old mate, all this time.

When Lawrence won the man of the match award a few weeks after Christmas, after photographs with the match sponsors, he brought the little bottle of Champagne he had been given and handed it to Bob with a grin.

'I can't stand the stuff,' he said. 'Best you have it. No. That's not right. I want you to have it.'

It sat proudly on Andrews' desk, until Dennis won another, then another – both being handed over to Bob like the first. For safety he transferred his little collection onto a shelf by the door to the West Stand, where they couldn't be knocked over by an errant elbow. Three becoming five in time. And there they have stayed, long after Bob Andrews' tenure had come to an end. Gathering dust. All this time.

When Dennis's parents and little sister came over to watch a game, it was Bob's office he took them to, slipping out early from the players' lounge, smiling as they poured over the pages of the ledger with Dennis's international exploits proudly displayed, looking at his "man of the match" champagne lined up in a row.

And so it was, this little friendship blossomed, for the four seasons that Lawrence stayed at the Town, with as many appearances from off the bench as starting. He helped the team keep its head above the bottom four every year, scoring the odd rocket from outside the box.

He endured racist bile. He wandered with Bob Andrews on his rounds. He helped to put up George Chester's Christmas tree every year, in exchange for a retelling of the story by the light of a string of colourful bulbs.

He sat with Bob in the Nightwatchman's office, and they looked through all the old programmes and postcards, newspaper clippings, letters, and other oddments that had come to find themselves in those desk drawers. At the very bottom a small pile of frail programmes and clippings from Peter Wright and Michael Trim's time at the club. Their names on the team sheets. Neatly folded newspaper reports detailing their endeavours. Both had played in Dennis's position, had seen the horrors of the trenches in World War I, had their lives as professionals ended as a consequence, Michael at least coming home with breath still in his body. Their descriptions in the ledger by Mackie's own hand were vivid, heartfelt, loving, mirroring the youthful excitement both had exuded at living out their dream.

Gerald Mackie's description of them moved Dennis, and he would turn the pages of their programmes with a gentle, measured care, tracing his finger across match reports detailing a swashbuckling raid down the same wings on which he now plied his trade. Peter's bicycle waiting for him to finish.

He would often find himself gently opening the envelope containing Danny Stokes programme from the day he died, tracing the folds and creases from a terrified hand that had clutched it tightly as the bombs fell. He would help Bob brush up the poplar leaves when they fell in autumn across the Victoria Road terrace. He would polish the little plaques by their trunks, feeling the indentations of each name beneath the cloth.

And in between he would play out his humble lower league career as best he could, glancing across into the shadows of the Lower West Stand whenever he needed a little boost, searching for that match-winning cross or goal.

A simple friendship over post-match mugs of tea, walks across the terraces, hours poring over Mackie's ledger, a friendship born out of the hate of others; Dennis Lawrence became another ghost of Inchmery Road in the summer of 1987 when a new one-year deal that had been promised never materialised.

Bob and Dennis had shaken hands warmly after the final match of the season, wishing each other well, until next season. Then, in the blink of an eye, and with barely a by-line in the local paper, Lawrence was released, then picked up by Scunthorpe United on a six-month contract.

And with that, Lawrence was gone. No opportunity for farewells, just a "see you later" that never came to pass.

He played eleven matches for Scunthorpe by early November, then didn't feature again. And when his contract was up at Christmas, he was let go. And with that, he would never play in the Football League again. Four and a half seasons the sum total of a young boy's dreams, if you only measure dreams by the Football League.

Because, as it turned out, Lawrence was far from done.

Life carries on. Whether you like it or not. Players, managers, coming and going. Fortunes fluctuating. There is always the next match, the one after that. Coming thick and fast, from August to May.

There is little time to ponder too long, though Bob would follow his friend Dennis and his Scunthorpe career via the vast results page in the Sunday paper. Down among the small print of the Fourth Division, his name in the Scunthorpe line-up, sometimes in brackets if he came on as a substitute, his one and only goal for them in front of thirteen hundred spectators at Crewe Alexandra on Halloween.

Then, after November, nothing.

He would scour the team line-ups of the rest of the Fourth Division in case he had been transferred.

But he hadn't. And his name would never return.

When it came, it was from out of the blue. An envelope with some strange looking stamps, left on his desk in the June of 1988.

It was from Dennis, sent from a town called Willemstad, capital of a collection of tiny Caribbean islands called Netherlands Antilles.

Inside was another team photograph of Antigua and Barbuda in their yellow kit, Dennis standing proudly in the middle of the back row. A hot sun bleaching the background to a faint haze, the pitch to a jaundiced yellow.

On the back he had written:

'A World Cup qualifier against the Netherlands Antilles, lost one-nil in the first leg. We will be back in late July for the second leg. We are about to sail for Martinique to play in the Caribbean Cup. It has been so good to get back out on the pitch. It has felt an age.

I'm really looking forward to the trip. A proper little adventure!
Will keep you posted! All the best to you Bob. Dennis.'

A month later and he received another little parcel with a Martinique post mark and stamps with brightly coloured parrots and other exotic birds on them. Inside was a little tournament programme for the Caribbean Cup 1988. On the cover was a picture of the trophy, and on the back the dates of all the fixtures. Inside were the names of the four squads, their dates of birth, their club team, and how many national team appearances they had amassed, all beneath a team photograph of each nation.

For Dennis, his listing was rather sparse – no club listed, and just the three international appearances. With no mention of his career in England, his name was easily overlooked for the more complete and colourful records of his team-mates playing for the likes of Lion Hill Spliff, Grenades, Five Islands and Aston Villa in the Antigua & Barbuda League.

On the back of the programme, Dennis had neatly written in the scores for each match: a two-all draw against the hosts on the fifth of July, a one-all draw against Trinidad & Tobago two days later, and a goalless draw against Guadeloupe on the ninth.

Tucked inside the programme was another team photograph, where there were all smiles out on the pitch. Medals round their necks. In the background, a steep mountain covered in lush tropical forest.

On the back:

'A runner's up medal! And undefeated! Now back to Willemstad for our World Cup match.'

Finally, in early August, an even larger parcel arrived, this time with Dennis's Antigua and Barbuda match shirt, and a photograph of the team stood on the waterfront at Willemstad. Crystal clear waters and a row of brightly coloured and ornate buildings – a hotel, a town hall, and a church, all lined with palm trees.

'Thank you for your kindness and friendship. A small token for you, Bob. To brighten up your office.

We lost three-one, so we haven't qualified for the next round. But I did score my first ever international goal! I am sad that our games have come to an end. It was such an adventure. On to the next one!'

He wrapped the photographs, the programme, inside the shirt, placed it next to Mackie's ledger in the desk, and he would often bring them out to inspect, losing himself in the pictures, the hot Caribbean sun.

After Willemstad, Bob would receive updates from Dennis, every month or two. Telling him all about a football career that would take him wherever there was a contract.

After his five games for Antigua and Barbuda, he saw out 1988 playing for Bodø/Glimt, a Norwegian Second Division team based in the Arctic Circle. Because of the harsh winters, the Norwegian season went from March to October, and Dennis played regularly over the last three months, doing enough to earn a contract for the following year.

He wrote of pre-season training beneath the Northern Lights, the sky lit up in supernatural greens – swirling and dancing like some celestial murmuration as they ran drills on a pitch surrounded by towering snow drifts, the shadow of great mountains.

He wrote of long coach journeys hugging steep mountains, with crystal clear fjords below. Hour after hour of beautiful scenery to reach the rest of the league away down to the south. And when they had been taken, Dennis included a team photograph, and one of him alone, arms behind his back, smiling proudly in his yellow kit that was littered with sponsorship logos. He wrapped them in letters detailing a season of struggle with a tiny squad. But he had been scoring goals, playing well, and enjoying himself tremendously.

He played well enough to earn a contract in the Icelandic First Division the following year with Þór Akeyuri, a team on the northern coast, and as far removed from the capital Reykjavík and the majority of the league as Bodø/Glimt had been from Oslo.

In time, a team photo of Dennis, all in red, accompanied letters full of exploits on the pitch – goals scored in front of a small, but close-knit and fiercely proud Akeyuri crowd, who would perch on the steep grassy banks that surrounded the home pitch.

He wrote of long, winding trips to away matches along the rugged coastline. Wild, tossed seas churning beneath dark skies, the odd sight of a pod of Minke Whales among the white-crested waves. Black volcanic landscapes of rock, steaming fissures, geysers spouting sulphurous streams. Great mountains lost beneath a blanket of snow, even during the long summer months when the sun never set.

Nineteen nighty-one saw him move to fellow Icelandic top-flight side IBV, located on the small island of Vestmannaeyjar some five miles south of the mainland.

A team photo with Dennis sporting smart black and white stripes arrived on Bob's desk a month or so into the season. A monstrous outcropping of rock loomed up behind the pitch and acted as a windbreak to the otherwise exposed playing surface, that was a great vantage point to look across the little town of Heimaey, the harbour beyond, and on a clear day, mainland Iceland in the distance.

He was happy, Dennis would write, he was playing well, enjoying his football. He had got a part-time job delivering post across the island. He would wait with his bicycle for the morning ferry, pick up the sack of post, and be on his way. He liked it when the farmstead out on the peninsula got post. Their sheep would jog alongside him, as if they themselves were expecting news, and he would stop and talk with Hannis the shepherd and feed his flock handfuls of grass picked from the verge.

It was a good life, Dennis wrote. Not quite the First Division back home, but it was a good standard of football all the same. The pay wasn't bad. He was playing well and having an adventure to boot, discovering some amazing places.

He was playing well enough for the club to invite him back the following season, just as soon as he had finished his international obligations in 1992.

Since Willemstad in 1988, Dennis had played just the one further game for Antigua and Barbuda, a two-all draw with Bermuda in Hamilton in 1990.

But 1992 saw him with a full schedule of international games for the first time ever, and he committed to them fully, moving to Antigua to prepare with the team.

In April he helped make a little piece of history with a three-two aggregate win over the Netherlands Antilles to progress to the second phase of World Cup qualifying matches for the first time ever.

In May he was in Saint Kitts and Nevis for Caribbean Cup qualifying, where he helped the team to a five-nil win over Montserrat, a two-nil victory against the British Virgin Islands, and a narrow one-nil win against the hosts in the beautiful capital of Basseterre.

Team photos, a red Saint Kitts shirt swapped with their left back "Charles," and descriptions of walks up into lush tropical forests in the hills above the town, watching monkeys swing from tree to tree, arrived on Bob Andrews' desk.

Then in June, in Trinidad, they drew with Suriname, lost four-one to Martinique, and seven-nil to the hosts in the Caribbean Cup finals, before heading across to Bermuda to lose three-nil and two-one in the second round of the World Cup qualifiers. A scribbled note from the airport detailing whitewashed buildings along Hamilton harbour that made you squint in the bright sun, and news that he had read a book on the Bermuda Triangle that had brought a tingle down his spine when he went for walks out to the pier head, looking out at a mystical sea. Stories of missing ships and airplanes. Gone in an instant. Something unknown claiming them, far out to sea, before so much as a mayday. His note wrapped around a little programme from the two matches.

By the time the letter arrived at Inchmery Road, Dennis was already back on Heimaey and playing for IBV, where he would stay for the rest of the season, before switching across to Malta to play for Hamrun Spartans through the winter and spring.

Photographs started to arrive of beautiful old medieval Maltese sandstone cities, as if they had simply grown up out of the rock beneath them to look out on the shimmering Mediterranean. Narrow alleyways, shuttered windows, lounging cats. Match programmes with Dennis sporting the red and black stripes of Hamrun.

He was torn, he would write. Both IBV and the Spartans wanted him back for the following seasons. He had enjoyed playing for both very much. He had enjoyed the cultures, the people, the places, and he didn't know what to do.

As it happened, fate took the decision out of his hands.

In the second to last match of the Maltese Premier League, Dennis twisted awkwardly and damaged his anterior cruciate ligament. He wouldn't know it then, but that would be the end of his professional career. The end of his international career.

After eight months out of the game, living with his sister in Birmingham, the injury had healed. But it had taken his speed, and his feints and jinks out on the wing. His professional career was over. No more international football. No more Iceland, Norway and Malta.

He was sad it was over, he wrote to Bob, but he had no regrets. The career he had had, the clubs he played for, the games he played in, the places he had been and the things he had seen, the people he had met; how could he possibly have any regrets? He wouldn't have his career any other way, if he had his time over.

He settled into a life as a postman, he had enjoyed it away in Iceland – he would try it again – while playing football for part-time Moor Green in the Southern League Midland Division as a sweeper, in behind the centre backs. He still loved to play, he would write to Bob, though he couldn't really run around any more. But experience and anticipation put him in the right place at the right time more often than not, which kept him in the side.

But even then. After all that, and in the very last throes of his playing days, Dennis wasn't quite done. And a beautiful little quirk of fate brought him back to Inchmery Road one last time on a cold, dank November afternoon, in the FA Cup first round.

An unlikely run through the qualifying rounds in 1995 saw Moor Green pulled out of the hat to play the Town at Inchmery Road in the first-round proper.

Their league form had been as off and on as the Town's, and they did well to keep the score down to three goals, a late consolation goal in the final minute had the away fans jumping in the paddock beneath the scoreboard.

Dennis Lawrence played seventy-five minutes as sweeper, and when he was taken off, the two thousand or so souls inside Inchmery Road rose to their feet to applaud him to the touchline. Recognition of the four seasons that he gave his all for the Town, doing everything in his power to make their Saturday afternoons that bit more enjoyable some ten years earlier.

Time and distance can solidify a reputation. And for most Town supporters, looking back at those lean few seasons at the foot of the Fourth Division, Lawrence's skill and goals had been a bright spot in an otherwise dreary spell spent scrabbling to avoid re-election.

Flashes of Dennis's brilliance cropped up among conversations between some of the older heads on the benches of the West Stand when they saw his name on the team sheet. It had made Bob Andrews smile. And as Lawrence jogged to the dugouts on the half-way line in front of the West Stand, he applauded the applause, waved warmly at all four sides of Inchmery Road.

And just before he ducked down and out of view into the Moor Green dugout, he looked up and across at the shadowy recesses beyond the rows of benches, at where the Nightwatchman's door would be. He smiled, waved, tears streaming down his face. And with that, he was gone.

He retired not long after, in the New Year of 1996. One last match at Inchmery Road bringing a career full circle. A standing ovation a fitting tribute. A perfect way to sign off thirteen years of endeavour:

one hundred and fifty appearances in the Football League, eighteen international games for Antigua and Barbuda across the Caribbean, and six years playing in Norway, Iceland, and Malta.

What any young boy or girl daring to dream wouldn't give for Dennis's playing history.

And the abuse he and his generation had to suffer – it became the beginning of a legacy aimed at stamping out such stains on humanity, in the hope that not too many more generations of young children would ever need to endure the like.

Still a work in progress, to this day.

After the cup match, Dennis ducked out of the players' lounge and made his way to the Nightwatchman's office, for one last mug of tea with Bob Andrews. He smiled as Bob brought out all the bits and bobs Dennis had sent over the years. Team photographs and programmes from all over the world. Postcards and letters. His Antigua shirt, and the swapped Saint Kitts and Nevis jersey.

Treasures safely stowed in the drawers beneath Gerald Mackie's ledger.

Andrews beckoned him to the corridor to the West Stand, at a framed picture of Dennis in his Antigua strip.

'You'll be there for all time,' he told him. 'Just like all the others.'

When Bob Andrews retired, he made copies of all the photographs and postcards and tucked them inside Mackie's ledger. Between the pages of Dennis Lawrence's story.

I would often stop by to visit him on the way to work, before he passed away in 2017, and he had all of Dennis's things in an old hat box beneath his armchair. He would get them out all the time, he would tell me. A bad hip kept him housebound in the main, but he would travel, see the world through those pictures and postcards. Through the pages of programmes from far away. Through Dennis's descriptions of far-flung lands in his letters, envelopes adorned with strange, colourful, exotic stamps.

He would lose himself, imagining the sights beyond the edges of the photographs, picturing mountain ranges, ruins of ancient temples, lush rainforest, bustling harbours, all the things Dennis had described. As if he were stepping into the pictures themselves, wandering off beyond the frame's end.

An adventure of his own. Shirts draped across his knees.

He had made a series of painful trips down to the little bookshop just off the seafront, where he ordered fold-out maps of the places

Dennis had played: Caribbean islands surrounded by a fathomless deep blue sea, the jagged, storm ravaged coastline of northern Norway, ominous volcanic mountain ranges of Iceland, the Maltese archipelago.

He would lean into them and study the topography: sandy beaches, steep, dormant volcanoes covered in lush forests, mountain ranges and fjords. Harbours and ancient sites. Crosses for churches.

Tiny sprawling town centres that Dennis had once called home, boxed off at the edges of each map. Little plans of intersecting streets around town squares and parks, harbours. Roads at the farthest edge trailing away to nothing, heading out into a mysterious interior of forests and hills. None more mysterious and captivating than Iceland's, where vast ruinous volcanoes and a mountainous wasteland of past eruptions looked more like a moonscape than anywhere on earth, stretching out across Bob's lap in a stunning, inhospitable, unreachable mystery.

He would look at his postcards and photographs, the programmes and newspaper clippings that Dennis had sent him, and with his finger he would plot them on his maps, imagining harbour fronts and stadiums as Dennis had described them. Exploring the crinkling folds of each map in his mind's eye.

The heat of Saint Kitts, rustling palm trees. The bustling chaos of Port au Prince. The eternal darkness of an arctic winter, the Northern Lights dancing in the sky. Dusty ruins of ancient Maltese civilisations. Dennis, playing his football among it all.

He took to tucking all the letters and photographs, everything pertaining to one particular country, within the folds of each map, like a living, working scrapbook. His adventures in a hat box, staving off the ever-shrinking world that had been closing in around him as his hip grew ever more painful.

And when he passed away, instructions in his will had the box returned to the Nightwatchman's office. Photographs and postcards replacing photocopies in the ledger. Maps, letters, match programmes and shirts safely returned to the drawer in the desk. With all the other treasures.

Dennis Lawrence came to the funeral and was invited back to the Nightwatchman's office for a small wake – tea and biscuits just as Bob had liked.

I had been a young man in my early twenties when Lawrence turned out for the Town. I told him how I loved to watch him play from behind the goal. He smiled, shook my hand, thanked me.

He slipped out unnoticed among the steady stream of people coming and going, and left Inchmery Road without ceremony, as he had done back in 1987.

The last time that I remember seeing him, he was stood away in a corner on his own, looking out into the room, but not *at* the wake. Lost, he was – absent. Away somewhere with Bob. Just the two of them, drinking tea in the office, or wandering about on their rounds, like it always used to be.

The next time I looked across, and Dennis had gone.

I don't know if he has ever returned.

Chapter Nine

I think the very best thing about my job, about Gerald Mackie's ledger, is being given the chance to explore a physical, tangible version of what swirls about us every day around Inchmery Road, unseen, unspoken. As elemental as the air we breathe, we just take it as read that it is there. This connection with others. This unbreakable bond of kinship, friendship through our mutual love for our little football club on the way to nowhere.

And I get to see it, feel it, curate it, from our desk in the Nightwatchman's office. It swirls around us, out of the pages of the book, the drawers stuffed with little treasures of football matches past.

People, some long gone. But still here, somehow, in the shadows, in the stories we tell.

And every now and then, someone new comes along, seeing old things for the first time. Making new connections, adding to a story we thought had already been told.

People like Stacey.

She has brought pictures of the bombs that fell as Mary Sugg was saved by Danny Stokes and Harry Bell. She finally put a face to Tanner Rowe, found a new picture he took of Inchmery Road. Another snippet of Town memory saved.

She has done so much more besides, as you will find out in time.

And in doing so, sometimes, like motes of dust in a sunbeam when a door is opened, these new moments, these reclaimed memories tumble, collide with something quite unexpected.

Points in time, often unconnected, meeting by pure accident and igniting something deep down, eliciting, so vividly, sounds, smells, colours from another time. Coming from nowhere. But overwhelming everything.

That picture Stacey discovered, of the local cinema on the seafront, taken by Tanner Rower for his exhibition in 1927. It took my breath away.

That usherette, her uniform, her hair pinned up. Her smile. It looked so much like Evie. So much.

It wasn't her, of course, But it looked so much like her. That uniform that hadn't changed in all those years. That smile, that sparkle in the eyes, knees bent slightly to let the children get a better look at the tray of ices and sweets.

That's what Evie used to do.

Though that picture and Evie, they existed decades apart. Nearly half a century. Different worlds. Collided. After all this time.

Worlds that brought me to where I am today.

My name is Charlie Truckle, and I have the best job in the world. I am Nightwatchman of Inchmery Road. Only the fifth full-time Nightwatchman in a century.

The job found me when I desperately needed finding, at the age of forty-two. After my world that had been perfect in its own simple, unremarkable way, fell away around me.

Before becoming Nightwatchman, I had worked in a little cinema along the seafront, that I had joined straight from leaving school.

I started off by selling tickets in the little booth at the entrance, where I got to watch the world go by. Elderly couples for the afternoon matinees of old musicals, young couples for the late-night monster movies on a Friday and Saturday. Lines of young children on a Saturday morning for their half-penny cartoons.

In between shows, along with keeping popcorn stands stocked up and tidying the foyer, I learnt how to make up and break down the 35mm prints up in the projection booth, working quietly to the soothing whir of the film running through projector, spooling back up on the spinning platters. Shadows and bursts of light across the walls as the action played itself out, transported down onto the screen by a flickering beam of swirling light. The satisfying sound of the print's tail flapping and chattering through the labyrinth of rollers, another screening successfully completed, the projector shutting down, to reveal an absolute hush for a moment, before the chief projectionist had me scampering between the rows to collect discarded ice cream tubs and cigarette butts.

Then it would be back into my little booth looking out at the seafront for the next show.

Thursday nights, and the chief projectionist and I would climb ladders to take down the titles of departing movies from the canopy, replacing them with the new ones for Friday.

We would cross the road and look back at it lit up to check for spelling mistakes. But also, just to look at it, timeless and beautiful as it was – illuminating another week's adventures that were waiting inside.

It was also a good spot to watch the usherettes, or rather, in my case, one usherette. Evie.

She started a couple of years after I did. First part-time on the weekends, then when a full-time position came up, she took it. Which was the best thing that has ever happened to me, as I got to spend nearly every day with her. Me in my ticket booth, her with her tray alongside.

She had light brown hair that would curl onto her shoulders after a shift, unpinning it and letting it cascade. She had a smile to light up the dreariest room. Hazel brown eyes that always seemed bright, full of life. She could see the good in everything, and everyone. And her laugh compelled you to laugh too.

And if it was blowing a gale, or raining, or cold, I would prop the little door to my booth open so as she could shelter in behind it when there were no customers to serve, getting the benefit of the little heater at my feet.

And after the last show had gone in, we would cash up our takings, get everything ready for the following day. We would chat and laugh, about anything, nothing. And quickly I fell in love.

But I was desperately shy. Too shy to do anything about how I felt. Instead, I would walk her to the bus after work, I would hang around her stop to walk in to work with her before a shift. I would make her teas to keep her warm. I would do everything I could to be close to her, other than ask her out.

I was mortified at my cowardice. Frozen by the fear. Until, one day, as we stood idly waiting for Evie's bus, she waited until it rounded the bend onto the seafront, then she turned to me.

'Well, she said, 'I think it's about time that you asked me out, don't you?'

I didn't know what to say. I felt my mouth drop open. And as the bus pulled up, she smiled.

'Well?' she said, stepping onto the foot plate at the back of the bus.

I panicked.

'Would you like to go out with me?' I blurted as the bus shuddered, sputtered, started to pull away.

Evie bit her lip, put her hand to her chin, a smile betraying her actions as she looked up to the sky as if deep in thought. Then she laughed, nodded.

'Yes,' she said, waved, and I stood and watched as the bus picked up speed and slipped away along past the promenade. I stood and watched while I thought I could still see her silhouette as she made her way up the stairs to the top deck and sat down.

I stood until there was nothing left to see, after the bus had turned back inland, and on into the town.

We were married after two years, during which time I left my little ticket booth behind and became a full-time projectionist, lacing up the movies and setting them on their way at the right time. I loved the sound of a correctly set movie running through the gate. If you made the loops of film between each spool too big or little the film would chatter and rattle as it ran – and the image would jog a little on-screen. But when you got it just right it would purr as it ran through. Smooth as silk. I took great pride in that. A job well done.

Evie had stepped up too, becoming the cinema's first female duty manager, and we lived our lives to the sounds of whirring film, sweeping soundtracks drifting out from the auditorium, the excited chatter from adventures experienced just the other side of those thick velvet curtains.

It was a blissful life, for ten years, until Evie passed, aged just thirty-three.

It happened suddenly. One day the world was walks along the seafront to work on summer's days, the fresh smell of cut grass from the parks clashing with the warm, salty breeze off the sea. Cups of tea left for one another around work with a biscuit. Evenings holding hands, waiting for the last film to play out, sometimes in the projection box, watching through the porthole at rows of attentive faces. Sometimes beneath the canopy, listening to lapping waves dragging across shingle on the beach.

The next, it was hospital corridors. Ashen-faced doctors who were very sorry. A squeeze of the hand from Evie, and with eyes that were slowly losing their sparkle, she would tell me that it would be all right. We would be all right.

We would hold each other, for the longest time. We would just sit, watching the world carrying on around us as if nothing was the matter. We kept each other close, and we waited.

And then it happened.

And Evie was gone.

After it was done, going back to work was both a blessing and a curse. At times it helped me to feel closer to her. I would linger about her usual spots, where it was so easy to imagine her, to believe that it really was her standing there, my Evie come back to me.

But that moment was always followed by a crushing void of emptiness, loneliness, when the illusion faded, and a cold reality set back in. Her usual spots, empty, a bitter reminder that the love of my life was gone. That some days, all hope was gone. Though Evie would have hated that, me feeling that way.

So, I did my best. For her.

I got up. I went to work. I did all the things that she loved about our life together. On my days off I went to see the Town, if they were playing, standing on the Victoria Road terrace beneath the row of poplars I would come to learn so much about in another life.

Evie had no interest in football, but she feigned it for my sake, always asking after the results, always taking the time to read about the matches in the local paper, scanning the league table, always knowing who were next to visit Inchmery Road.

I kept going to work, I kept going to the football. I would feel guilt, almost horror at getting lost in the match, caught up in the emotion of it for a time, the joy at a good goal rippling the net. These simple pleasures. It felt in bad taste, disrespectful, as if I had forgotten about my Evie.

But slowly, I came to learn that life and death had to exist in the same moment, at the same time. One couldn't extinguish the other. You just had to learn to live with both and forgive yourself for being human if one took over the other for a moment.

So, I did what I had always done. I went to work. Evie had loved that little cinema, so helping to maintain it, it seemed the right thing to do, for her, even though at times the memories of her would break my heart all over again.

I went to the football, I went to work, bereft, but knowing that it helped to keep her close.

As audiences filed in beneath the canopy, pausing at the ticket booth, the usherette, I would stand by and watch, losing myself in it all until it was time to start the film. Simple actions and interactions that Evie had been so good at, making all feel welcome. I would lose myself. Every now and then I would chat to regulars and the like, who would stop by with a kind word.

And that was how I came to know Bob Andrews.

He loved his classic matinee musicals about as much as I loved going to see the Town on my days off, and we would talk about both in the foyer of the old cinema that was held together with as much love and dedication as kept Inchmery Road ticking along.

He had been one of the first to give me his sincerest condolences, a hug, at Evie's passing.

'If there is anything I can do,' he had said, knowing that there could be nothing. But even so, every now and then, he would slip me a complementary ticket for the Town, in the good seats at the top of the West Stand. And, in return, as a thank you for his kindness, I would slip him through to see his film free of charge.

It had been a life indeed, with Evie lived inside my projection booth, beneath the canopy. Getting lost in snippets of film as I checked the image through my little porthole. Watching the excited chatter of folks as they came and went from a particularly good movie. Old-timers reliving days gone by after one of the classics, young couples on first dates setting off on a grand adventure together, courtesy of midnight monster classics like Quatermass and the Pitt, Horror Hotel, and The Trollenburg Terror.

And without Evie, it felt the best way to keep her close, keep my memories of her from fading away into the fog of time. So that is what I did.

I worked and watched our little, ornate old cinema grow ever older. I watched its loyal customers grow old too, Among the fading curtains and fittings, the velvet-backed seats up in the circle thinning and fraying while young dating couples evolved from Friday Fright Nights to Wednesday evening blockbusters, to married couples dropping off children at the Saturday morning cartoons.

And I would have watched them too on their journey, growing up, dating, enjoying the midnight monster movies like their parents once did. Time passing ever on, only Evie never ageing, forever sheltering behind the ticket booth door, smiling from the manager's office, looking up into the canopy of brilliant bulbs in the foyer. I would have done it, watch them grow, but the cinema was forced to shut down.

Dwindling admissions that preferred the newer cinema on the other side of town sealed its fate. And twenty-five years of service – nearly half of it tending to Evie's memory – came to an end suddenly one evening.

That was it. There would be no tomorrow. No time to say goodbye to Evie, to her special little spots about the place. The glittering lights of the canopy were snuffed out, the shutters were drawn across. And that was it.

It was a bereavement all over again.

In the weeks and months that followed its closure I would often take a walk down to the seafront while looking for other work and linger mournfully where the chief projectionist and I had stood across the road. Where I had first seen Evie. I would look at the canopy, dull and empty. Ticket booth shuttered. Out of bounds.

It re-opened a year later as a bingo hall, and I would sometimes go, just to be inside once more.

I would buy my bingo cards from the booth, but I wouldn't use them. Instead, I would just sit, and look about, at a place that was so familiar, and yet so different.

Fittings had changed, the rows of seats in the auditorium had been unbolted and replaced with round tables and chairs. The screen had come down. In its place a huge sheet with a tropical scene of palm trees, setting sun, a beach hung suspended behind the bingo caller up on the stage.

Doors that led away up towards the offices that Evie had once used, the projection box now out of bounds to me.

So familiar, but so very different. Askew. I don't know if it brought comfort or not. But I went anyway, and watched those doors, those corridors that had once been Evie's.

For a year or two I was rudderless, working as a hotel porter during the summer season, and in the local sorting office for the Royal Mail in the eight weeks up to Christmas.

It just about made ends meet, and when money became too tight, I would forgo watching the Town in the Fourth Division, instead plumping for the five pence reserve team fixtures in the Combination League.

And there, by chance, one cold February afternoon at the reserves, with all my work dried up, I bumped into Bob Andrews.

He had been up in the upper tier of the West Stand, chatting with a steward when he saw me. He shook my hand warmly, asked how I was, and how sorry he was that the cinema had closed.

'I loved that place,' he said wistfully. 'I loved the walk down, the fresh sea breeze, and I loved losing myself in the pictures. So sad.

Have you found anything else yet?'

I told him of my temp work, that it just about kept my head above water. But that things often got pretty lean – which was a politeness – without Evie, without our cinema.

He nodded, thought for a bit, then said the words that changed my life forever:

'What are you doing after the match? Do you have time for a cup of tea? I might just have something for you.'

We sat in his office after a forgettable ninety minutes and warmed ourselves by the heater, sipped at our tea.

He was in need of a relief Nightwatchman.

'Two nights a week to start with. Twenty hours in total. They have done interviews already, but I know you. If you want it, it is yours. It is maybe not as many hours as you want, but it is constant. Every week, all year round. And there will be holiday cover that will top things up. What do you think?'

I didn't think. I said yes.

'Excellent,' Bob said, 'When can you start?'

I started right away. Giving up my dinner. The earlier I learned how things were done, the earlier I would start getting paid.

For three nights I followed Bob on his rounds, learning what needed checking, and how to do it.

He took me all around Inchmery Road, and it felt like Christmas morning. Exploring the corridors beneath the main stand. The boardroom and manager's office, the players' lounge, and the main office. The windowless corridor beyond the Nightwatchman's door, just off the main entrance, that led to the changing rooms, the laundry, the groundsman's room that always smelled of wood stain and engine oil, the door into the little ticket office with its three portholes looking out onto the car park.

A door at the far end that opened out into a little stock room, another door on the far side taking you behind the counter of the club shop, its windows shuttered tight. Blank-faced mannequins in Town shirts lurking in the darkness.

It was a thrill to walk down the players' tunnel and out onto the red grit track that lined the pitch, looking up at the West Stand, my spot on the Victoria Road terrace, the floodlights looming beneath scudding rain cloud.

Bob showed me every gate, every turnstile shutter, every door and window. Every nook and cranny beneath the stands. The ladders up to the walkway on the lip of the East and West Stand roofs.

He would talk me through the set of keys that we had to carry as we wandered across the terraces. Each one unlocking another part of the club.

He walked me through the job, night after night, instilling in me through actions rather than words the pride and privilege he felt in being entrusted with this undertaking. Keeping the place so many found magical, spiritual, their everything, safe and sound.

I got it. I had been coming to see the Town play since I was a little boy. First with my grandfather in the early seventies, then with my Mum after he passed away.

Bob Andrews, and those that had gone before him had been keeping our little ground safe for me. For Granddad. For Mum. All those years. Quietly, anonymously, timelessly.

And now I got to do it too.

After so much struggle, it felt like a dream come true. It was a dream come true. A dream I never knew existed.

The job, the club, Bob Andrews, they saved me. Just like the club saves so many every day. A sense of belonging, meaning, a feeling of home that Inchmery Road provides. Making the lonely feel less so, the lost that little bit found. The bereft, comforted. A constant when little else in life is.

There will always be next Saturday. Next season. There will always be something to look towards.

Our little football club on the way to nowhere.

And as I close my door on the way to work, I look behind me, just as I used to before a match all those years ago.

I look at Evie, smiling at me, fingers crossed on both hands for good fortune and a home win.

I smile back. Nod. Close the door.

Over cups of tea in the long night hours, Bob showed me Gerald Mackie's ledger, and I would listen intently to the forgotten stories of Inchmery Road, to stories I had never heard of. Stories of those that used to call the Town home.

We would scrabble through the bushes in the car park to look at Peter Wright's bicycle. I had no idea that it existed, and had been there all this time, despite me having been to games at Inchmery Road as often as I could for more than thirty years by that point.

He told me the meaning of the five poplars behind the Victoria Road terrace, showed me the subtle changes in the construction of the East Stand, where it had been built back up after the bomb that claimed the lives of hero Danny Stokes, young Arthur Thompson, and Charles, Anne, and little Alice Manning in November nineteen forty.

And like the Nightwatchman before me, I took on the little rituals and acts of remembrance for those within the ledger, as if I had known them personally. The way Bob spoke of them, the way they had been written about by the varying hands that had contributed to the ledger during the past hundred years, it was easy to feel as if I had known them. Somehow. Through time and a common bond with the Town.

By means of the ledger I learned the hidden history of Inchmery Road. An anonymous history of the lives, and sometimes deaths, of people who lived and loved our little club, tucked away up among the tight knit weave of streets. Some stories just little snapshots of moments, captured in Mackie's book by either photograph, or a few words. Other tales more complete, stretching down yellowing pages, crinkled and brittle through time.

Theirs was a history that couldn't be captured through match reports or league tables. Or behind the glass of trophy cabinets. Theirs was a story of community and friendship, belonging and meaning found through our little club. More precious than cups and titles, but far harder to preserve.

And for every story captured in Mackie's ledger, Bob reasoned, there must be so many others that have simply faded away with time, drifting unheard, unknown on the winds that scatter the pages of discarded newspapers across the terraces.

How many had we missed, he wondered, us Nightwatchmen? How many had played out, and then slipped away once more?

Little stories and moments of love and belonging, meaning.

I suppose we will never know.

Though every now and again one surfaces, one that we hadn't known about. And when it does, like those that went before me, I dutifully capture it and paste it into the ledger.

A few years ago, an article appeared in a magazine about a Town player who vanished into thin air. Just disappeared. As if he had never been there.

Tom Maskell was his name, and he was an apprentice when Dennis Lawrence was at the club. He played five first team games at the end of a season when there had been an injury crisis. In fact, Dennis was one of the players this young reserve had tried to cover.

I had been at one of the games he played in, thought I don't remember too much about it.

But I know I had been there.

He had done well over his five games by all accounts, and the future was looking bright for him. But by the following season, he had vanished. He left his home for Inchmery Road and pre-season training, but he never arrived.

He had simply disappeared. Neither here nor there.

A journalist, who was a Town fan, wrote a piece about the Town left back who simply vanished, and his failed attempts to find him. Sarah spotted it and brought it in for me. For the ledger.

Then she brought in another little article, not too long ago, by the same journalist. Tom Maskell had re-appeared.

He wouldn't say where he had been, for more than thirty years, or what had happened to him.

He just wanted his old life back.

There was a little black and white photograph of Maskell with an elderly man, stood on a boat on what looked like a grand old lake.

Maskell wouldn't say any more. And the journalist respected that, despite there being so many questions left to ask.

A little Town mystery, of the missing left back, kind of solved.

Chapter Ten

I read somewhere, quite some time ago, about the Night Marchers of Hawaii. Where, on moonless nights every month, after the waning crescent of one cycle slips away, and before the next, the ghosts of ancient Hawaiian warriors rise from out of the ocean to march to ancient battle sites or sacred places. Battle drums can be heard above the rolling surf and conch shell horns as they march.

Any mortal that stumbles across the procession, sees the rows of apparitions approaching, must lay prostrate on the ground, face down, and not look up, for if they do, if they look upon the night marchers, they will meet a violent end.

There they must stay, listening to the sounds of the beating drums, the conches as they draw close, then pass. Only running home terrified once the sounds have faded away.

I like to think that we have a benign version of the night marchers, here at Inchmery Road. As I do my rounds in the dead of night, I imagine, I feel the souls that once called the terraces, the rows of creaking seats in the upper tier, the cheaper benches of the lower tier, a second home, materialising out of the shadows. Nameless faces from the past, countless souls lost to time, manifesting once more at their preferred spot.

I feel it most after a night game. The floodlights burning up into the sky, drawing in a few thousand souls from the town about them. After the bustle of anticipation outside, the chatter of turnstiles, the laughter of friends outside the pub. After the roar of encouragement as the teams jog out onto the pitch, a brilliant dazzling green. After the desperate endeavour of the players, stretching every sinew, throwing themselves into tackles, last ditch blocks, chasing balls down the wing, raking passes, thrashed shots on goal. After the final whistle and points celebrated or mourned as the crowds slip back away into town. After the players' warm-down on the pitch and complete their duties in the lounge with sponsors and visiting guests, Inchmery Road winds back down and the car park clears. After the visiting team coach pulls out through the gates and heads off back across the country, they have their moment.

Once all of that has been and gone for another game, in the seconds after the floodlights snap off, calling time on another match day. In the total darkness after losing such brilliance.

For the briefest of moments: faint, swaying crowds on the terraces, seas of faces in the stands, huddled bodies along the benches, looking on expectantly at long-gone players in oversized shirts and shorts, passing and running, chasing the ball across the pitch, for the slightest of moments, fading away almost as quickly as they had arrived. Maybe Peter Wright, Jon Blitz Sugg, Harry Bell.

Silent applause in the stands, enraptured faces dissolving away once more into darkness.

Passions, memories, devotions of long-gone supporters and players alike, charged by the electricity of a night game, for a heartbeat or two.

An echo. All those people, for whom it meant just as much as it does to us today.

And then, with that, they are gone. Dissolved back into the darkness. Lost to time once more. Or, at least maybe, until next time.

I stand there in the darkness for a while, where they had once been.

Then I start on my rounds.

If I had to describe my tenure as Nightwatchman, I would have to say that it has been one spent, quite unintentionally, collecting waifs and strays. The quiet, the hidden, the often overlooked.

I don't really know how. Or, indeed, why, but I seem to stumble across them. Or rather, when I do stumble across them, they leave such an impression that I can't forget them again.

Quite possibly I see a little bit too much of myself in them. I see isolation, seeming lost, within themselves or out in the world, and it chimes with me. Though I am much better now – time not so much healing the sadness of Evie's loss, rather, enabling me to normalise those feelings, their familiarity less jarring and spiky now – I see keenly those who don't appear to be quite so lucky yet.

People like Stacey Marsh.

For as long as there have been Nightwatchmen at Inchmery Road, there has been the Marsh family selling match programmes. Or match cards as they were before World War I, when Stacey's great, great, great grandmother Margery Marsh began selling them.

Marsh had been her maiden name, becoming Wyatt when she married in 1912 on the day the news broke of the sinking of the Titanic.

But she applied for the job of match card seller under her maiden name, to honour her father Albert, who had first taken her to a Town game in 1902 much to the annoyance of her mother Catherine – the football grounds being 'no place for a young girl' to her mother's mind.

When Margery gave birth to daughter Betty, she couldn't afford to give up her position as match card seller, so she would have baby in a sling across her chest and she would carry on in wind, rain, and snow.

Some of the more well-to-do gents would slip a farthing or half-penny into the sling for the baby, and that way she could sometimes more than double her wage – with little Betty rattling and jangling home after the game, with a match card tucked in beside her.

And when Betty was old enough to join her mother, in a practical capacity, taking a pitch on the corner of Victoria Road, she signed up willingly, proud to follow in her mother's footsteps.

Betty's son, Don, was equally eager to join the family tradition, as was his son Frank.

And when Frank passed, his daughter Layla took up the mantle. And when her daughter, Stacey, was old enough to count out change, she became the sixth generation of Marsh programme sellers at Inchmery Road. Though she was the first that struggled to take to it. Almost entirely down to her debilitating stutter.

I have mentioned already that the more nervous Stacey gets, the more stressed she finds herself, and the worse it becomes. And that on bad days she simply withdraws into herself, becoming mute. Shoulders drooped, red-faced and forlorn.

A childhood of teasing on the playground turned her into a shy, shrinking wallflower, living life on the periphery of things, quietly and friendless. Which is everyone else's loss, as she is a wonderful, warm soul, with a smile to brighten the darkest day, possessing the empathy and compassion of a genuinely unique human being.

I could tell from those early days, when she would come with me on my rounds delivering tea to the programme sellers on cold, wintry afternoons, that she was one of life's good ones.

I could tell when she would force herself to her pitch out by the poplars on Victoria Road when she was old enough, not wanting to disappoint her mum, or break family tradition. She would shrink away against the wall, or the trunk of a Poplar, her price rosette fastened to her coat. She would do it, though she didn't like it, for her mum. And for all those Marshes who had gone before her.

It went against every fibre of her, standing out there. Exposed. But she did it. For the sake of others.

And what she has brought to the stories in Mackie's ledger, things that had been missed, mislaid, lost – that comes from such a sincere connection with the people concerned. A desire to see them even more, every last bit that we can. It is the result of a love for life, for other people's lives, even if your own is mostly played out on the edges of things.

It is what you get when you give a good person the chance to prove herself, in her own way.

Relief Nightwatchmen come and go; two nights work often not enough to sustain oneself for long, and a chance at promotion in a job held by just five people over a century appearing slim to say the least.

They come. They go. Sometimes at just the right moment for someone else.

For people like me and, as it would turn out, for people like young Stacey too.

There seemed to be just the one thing that helped Stacey's stutter, other than being in the company of those that made her feel comfortable, and that was the Town.

A lifetime of reading and re-reading the Marsh programme collection had given her a near encyclopaedic knowledge of our little team on the road to nowhere. She would be able to recollect the statistics for even the most average, the most fleeting of Town players: loan recruits coming and going within a month. Journeymen physically breaking down, fading away before our eyes out on the Inchmery Road pitch – Stacey would be able to tell of their halcyon days elsewhere.

She used to scan the team sheet in our quieter moments programme selling on Victoria Road when she was a little girl, and she would be able to conjure up biographies of any opposition player who had once graced Inchmery Road for the Town:

'Duh-Davies played for us uh-uh-a couple of seasons ago. Wuh-went to Alt-Alt-Altrincham. His duh-dad played for Manchester City in the eighties.'

Her stutter receding a little the more she lost herself in the statistics of a lower league life that had long since passed through.

Her passion for the Town, her comfort in isolation, she would make a perfect Nightwatchman, and I told Layla so when the relief position came up.

With Stacey only being nineteen, I wanted to run the idea past her mum before I mentioned it.

I would make sure that the groundsman would see her safely locked inside, I said. And then it would be a case of her checking everything from the inside. And I would give her my telephone number, I said, with the instructions to call, for whatever reason, if she needed to.

Layla burst into tears. She said it was a wonderful idea, and she thanked me so much for thinking of Stacey. She was such a lovely, warm-hearted girl, she said. She just needed a chance, for someone to have faith in her, even though she had none in herself.

'She will be so made up to learn that that person is you,' Layla said.

I think this remains the most wonderful thing anyone has ever said to me.

And with that, young Stacey Marsh became a Nightwatchman of Inchmery Road.

She took to it with the wide-eyed enthusiasm that I expected. Even the most mundane elements. Walking corridors never seen by most in a lifetime of support for the Town. Peering into changing rooms, storerooms, offices and boardrooms a special thrill for someone who had always wondered what it might be like, deep within the hidden recesses of her club.

She would follow me on my rounds across lower tier seas of benches, upper tier lines of seats – stretching away beneath lofty rafters, learning the job. She would skip down the players' tunnel ahead of me, looking out at the Inchmery Road pitch. Stands, terraces, floodlights looming up above her. The scrunch of the grit track beneath her feet as she waited for me.

She felt the weight of privilege in having her precious club all to herself, in the quiet of night. She took on the honour of keeping it safe, of being its custodian, with a passion born out of a lifetime of love for the place. For the team.

She rattled gates, peered into the gloomy club shop, hung up new shipments of replica kit. She swept the terraces, sanded down rusty spots on peeling crush barriers, checked turnstile shutters and doorknobs, she tended to its safekeeping, its upkeep as diligently as she read Mackie's ledger, listened to my recounting of tales I had read, told others so many times that they had become my own – even though for some, I hadn't even been born.

She would gingerly turn the brittle and yellowing pages of the ledger, peer at the photographs, newspaper clippings, programmes, fixed on certain pages. Islands in a sea of handwriting that stretched from binding to edge, detailing the lives of those who once called Inchmery Road home, either spiritually or physically, often both.

Stacey loved it. The stories contained within, moved her, sometimes to tears, this patchwork of love, devotion, and fellowship that had, over more than a century, become the glue that helped bind the creaking bones of Inchmery Road together. Bodies through the turnstiles, in the club shop, assisting fundraising drives keeping the wolf from the door. Volunteers' painting, renovating, replacing, and rebuilding. Unseen time spent doing their little bit, willingly. Peter Wright, David Smith, Danny Stokes and Jon 'Blitz' Sugg. Her own grandfather, and all the other Marsh programme sellers before him. Dennis Lawrence.

Old black and white pictures of office parties, or a few people smiling in the sun outside the main doors on a cigarette break. Young lads standing proudly in a Town kit out on the pitch, hazy terracing in the distance. Untold lives lived. At Inchmery Road.

I once read about the Golden Temple in Amritsar, India. A Sikh temple that on high religious occasions never turned anyone away needing a place to sleep, or a meal. Hundreds would volunteer every day to prepare vats of daal and mounds of chapatis, wash up plates and bowls, serving more than fifteen thousand meals a day. All in the service of their religion.

There were no lists. No rotas. First thing in the morning there would be no volunteers. And then they would come. Hundreds of them. And the temple would keep its promise to feed and house those needing it. Day after day. For all time.

It is an honour to help. To wash dishes morning, noon, and night.

Inchmery Road, and those that tend to it: I see many similarities. Those of us employed are on barely a wage at all, and we never ask for a rise. And those that volunteer, they ask for nothing at all. All in the service of their beloved little football club that enraptures a few thousand souls living on the way to nowhere.

It moved Stacey greatly, Mackie's ledger of memories and ghosts, the people preserved within, and she would head on out to the car park at a little after one a.m. in the hope of hearing young Peter Wright's bicycle bell drifting out through the gates, on his way home to Gerald Mackie.

She would linger on the East Stand benches that saw Danny Stokes and Arthur Thompson lose their lives in the Blitz. She would peer into the box in the corner of the Nightwatchman's office at George Chester's Christmas tree neatly packed away, and on the first of December she would help me put it up. And she would stand listening to the story told at Christmas parties, or for the odd request in the weeks leading up to Christmas, as engrossed as she had been as a wide-eyed little girl with her mum, becoming lost once more in the shadows of twinkling lights frozen across the far wall.

She would sit and look at the latest away programme for the Marsh family collection on the corner of the desk, sometimes flipped over to the team sheet – somehow – and she would enjoy reading about her family, stretching back to the very first pages of this grand old book.

Sometimes she would falter a little on reading about her strong, female ancestors, who forged a Town institution in the service of the football programme. Who made that prime pitch by the main gates their own.

'Wuh-what wuh-would they muh-muh-make of muh-me?' she would ask mournfully.

I told her that bravery, courage, came in many guises. And the way she had taken to learning to be a Nightwatchwoman – the very first Nightwatchwoman at that – as well as sticking with the programme selling: they would be proud as punch.

She would nod her head when I told her that was what I believed, though I think she may have been nodding out of kindness for me. I don't think she believed it herself.

I hope that, in time, she will.

Stacey stuck with me for a few weeks, learning the ropes, until the night came for her to go it alone. She was tasked, as all reliefs do, with Sundays and Mondays.

She took her set of keys, my phone number on a slip of paper in her pocket, with the promise that she would call if she needed me, for anything at all, and waved me off weakly, before closing and locking the main doors. Her face at the window watching as I walked away.

I sometimes wonder if me giving her the job only helped to enable her isolation from the rest of the world. Whether it was doing her any good, simply entrenching her in a life of solitary confinement. But it is not for me, or anyone else to judge how someone lives their life. And, after all, I was a projectionist in a little dark room before I became a Nightwatchman in another little dark room. Each to their own.

And despite my fears, young Stacey found her way. She seemed genuinely happy in her work, fulfilled, content. Enjoying a vocation that gave her unfettered access to her one great passion. Where she could absorb every sight. Had time enough to truly see it all.

She became a great Nightwatchwoman, and only used the slip of paper in her pocket once, when a couple of lads, with a skinful of courage from the local pub scaled the Victoria Road End wall to fulfil an ambition to play out on the Inchmery Road pitch.

With a ball discovered in the Victoria Road goal, they swung and fell in fits of laughter at a missed cross – wheeled away to receive the applause from an imagined crowd at a scuffed shot bobbling into the back of the net. They even ran to embrace the local policeman who was called out after Stacey rang me from the office:

'Chu-chu-Charlie. Thuh-there's tuh-tuh-two muh-muh-men on thuh-the puh-pitch.'

A night in the cells, with a warning ringing in their ears, and the knowledge that they had scared a young girl half to death, they appeared at the main doors to Inchmery Road the following day. Apologies to Stacey, along with a bunch of flowers and a box of chocolates that were shared over a mug of tea in the Nightwatchman's office. If there was anything they could do, they said, by ways of saying sorry, Stacey was simply to say the word.

Which she did. In time.

But to start off with, she stuck to her chores.

She would do odd jobs in the club shop, restocking the carousel of Town players' photographs children would covet on match days. She would clean the floor and polish the counter. And when that was all done, she would walk her rounds and make a note of any doors or handrails that were faded or peeling, lugging a ground sheet and pots of paint and brushes back to the offending spot – and she would carefully and lovingly make them good as new.

She would sweep the terraces, rub down any rough, rusting spots on the crush barriers with some iron wool before treating it with a solution, painting over it.

With a large tin of varnish, and plenty of time and patience, she treated all the benches in the Lower West Stand.

Starting at the Victoria Road end beneath the old scoreboard, she sanded then varnished each and every one, to the point that the old-timers who frequented them made comment. She did the same for David's bench, where he had changed all that time ago. Though we couldn't be sure it was *the* bench. It certainly looked as if it could have been. It was an old and sturdy looking thing, that could have stood the test of time. Whether it was or wasn't, she tended to it like it was.

It was a painfully slow process, all those chores, but in between her rounds, and readings of Mackie's old ledger, she did it.

She enjoyed it, she would say, having the place all to herself as she worked. And when her back started to ache too much, she would stretch and rest, and sit quietly, taking in her surroundings as if for the first time.

It was a feeling I knew all too well. There was always something about that timeless old place that made you stop and wonder. That compelled you to pause, and look along the sea of seats, or out across the pitch, leaning up against the barriers on the terracing.

The magic of having it all to yourself, this special place that has meant so much to so many over the years. The privilege of having the time to feel the decades of memory about you. All those people who lived and died for this little football ground on the road to nowhere.

Like those Nightwatchmen that had gone before her, Stacey saw it – Inchmery Road – for what it was. More than simple brick and timbers. It was a living, working monument to the passion and devotion of a small town. It had absorbed her entire family, and it had absorbed her long before she became custodian of it.

She had been, ever since she was a little girl, sitting in the seats up in the East Stand that had once been her grandfathers, her great grandfathers, had been occupied by every generation of the Marsh family since its construction – Betty Marsh being present at its grand opening in the twenties, great grandfather Don accompanying her at its re-opening after it was built back up after the Blitz.

Her and her mum would rush round to the late turnstile once they had stowed away any excess programmes and the takings from their pitch in the club shop, and they would watch the Town, every game, without fail.

Tending to Inchmery Road, painstakingly restoring the West Stand benches, checking doors and shutters to keep the place safe and sound – it came naturally to her. It needed no explanation. She would have done it for free had there been no wage.

She gave herself to it, sometimes keeping me company two or three nights a week without any pay, falling in alongside me as we wandered about the place.

And in return, Inchmery Road gave to Stacey. Opportunity. Moments of self-belief to match that which Layla, myself, others had in her. Though they would be born out of a perceived failure of hers, and a missed opportunity.

It was a peculiar quirk of fate that one of Layla's all-time favourite Town players was Bob Andrews' good friend Dennis Lawrence.

Layla had been captivated by his expressive play; his electric dribbling down the wing, where the ball seemed stuck to his feet. His sweeping crosses to the far wing. Thunderbolt strikes on goal that always seemed to make for the top corner of the goal, when on target. She had adored it all, and never forgot his time playing for the Town. If anyone ever asked her for her all-time Town XI, Lawrence would always be one of the first names she quoted.

She hadn't known about Andrews' friendship with Lawrence until long after he had left for pastures new. But when it had come up in conversation one day after a match, when young Layla had taken over from her father as Head Programme seller, she became enthralled by all the photographs and letters Lawrence had sent, from all over the footballing world, when Andrews showed them to her. It was a comfort to her to see that he had gone on to experience great footballing adventures, and that his skill and endeavour had entertained others as much as it had her.

Layla Marsh would have stayed Head Programme Seller at Inchmery Road until the day she died, just like her father. She had loved it, every facet of it, from the moment she had first accompanied her dad as a young girl.

She had had no other ambition in life, other than to continue the long, proud family tradition of programme selling for the Town. And when Frank died suddenly, she took over the reins, despite her tender years. She would have it no other way.

It was only the onset of crippling arthritis, possibly brought on by decades of standing in bone-chilling temperatures outside the main gates of Inchmery Road, that ended her vocation in middle age.

She carried on for years, in terrible pain, labouring through the narrow streets to get to the ground.

Holding a pile of programmes in her hand caused searing spasms through her fingers and wrist, and fetching change from her apron became an arduous, withering ordeal.

Eventually she had to give it up but would still try to make it to the games themselves. But as her condition worsened, her spot on the East Stand benches would remain empty during the harsh winter months of the season.

She would make it to late autumn, scuffing gingerly through the last of the falling leaves to her seat, before experiencing most of the rest of the campaign in her armchair at home, listening to the games on local radio. And if there was an early spring, bringing warm spells of sunshine, she would see out the last of the season back at Inchmery Road. A blanket covering her legs, to try to ease the pain from the chill wind that accompanied the afternoon shadow across the Lower East Stand.

It had been too cold for Layla to attend Bob Andrews' funeral, which she had been upset about. But she had contented herself that young Stacey would be present, who by that point had become both Nightwatchwoman and Head Programme Seller for the Town, taking over from her mum.

It was a promotion taken out of obligation rather than desire, not wanting to be the Marsh that broke the chain of history all the way back to the earliest days of the Twentieth century.

She did it – head programme seller – with smiles and nods, the odd word to her regulars from beneath her bobble hat, updating her rosette that had become a little tattered with age whenever the price went up. She had refused the offer of a new one.

'I... buh-but you muh-made this one, chu-Charlie,' she would always say 'I like thu-this one.'

Those sparkling blue eyes of hers, they could generate more warmth than a thousand words.

It was hard for her, being head programme seller, but she did it, and she would end each day with a huge sigh of relief after every match, once all the money had been counted and deposited in the club shop.

After Bob Andrews' funeral, she had rushed back to Inchmery Road to prepare a large urn of hot water for the tea, spreading out biscuits on plates and dotting them about the office. And when the guests arrived, she blended into the walls as she always did when we had company, becoming as invisible as she could make herself.

With people wanting to talk about old times, I only saw Stacey twice. Once as she materialised by my side, pointing across the way at her mum's favourite: Dennis Lawrence.

'Uh-is thuh-that really huh-him, Charlie? Duh-Dennis Luh-Luh Lawrence?'

She beamed when I nodded that it really was, then dissolved away again into the crowd.

The second time I saw her was as the wake had wound down, and only a few stragglers remained, draining the last of the urn. She was stood outside the main doors, a pen in one hand, a piece of paper in the other. Tears streaming down her face.

I put my hand on her shoulder, asked her what was wrong. She held up the empty piece of paper, the pen.

'I wuh-wuh-wuh-wanted to guh-get duh-Dennis Lawrence's autograph for muh-Mum. He is one of huh-her favourites. I thought it wuh-would be a nuh-nice surprise. Chuh-cheer her up. Her huh-hands have really been huh-hurting luh-lately.

'Buh-but I couldn't duh-do it. I was too suh-scared. I juh-just stood and wuh-watched him leave.

'It wuh-would have really chuh-cheered her up, Chuh-Charlie,' and she started to cry again.

I took the pen and paper, hugged her, steered her back into the Nightwatchman's office and sat her down.

We sat quietly drinking tea, Stacey looking at the crumpled sheet from her notepad, the biro that I had dropped onto the desk.

I told her that her mum would be very proud of her for trying, in wanting to do it. I told her that she was a wonderful girl. Intelligent, caring. She was just shy that's all, I said.

'You have nothing to fear with people. Or, at least, with those worth your time. Those who will see what I see. What your mum sees. People will see you for *you*, not what you see in the mirror. You are not your stammer. It is just a tiny little part of you. You are so much more. You are so many wonderful things. And you can do anything.'

She nodded, though I knew that she didn't believe me. And we sat quietly for a while drinking tea. Which is when it came to me, and

I heard myself saying:

'Are you free tomorrow evening Stacey? Would you come in? Just for an hour or so, if you like. There is something that I want to show you. That you might be able to help me with. That might help us both.'

She nodded over the rim of her tea, smiled weakly, then we sat as the day began to fade outside, and watched the shadows lengthen.

Chapter Eleven

Stacey sat down at the Nightwatchman's desk when I beckoned her, pulling her bobble hat back onto her hairline like she always did, so as she didn't get hot. She watched me take out a little parcel of things from one of the drawers.

I placed them gently on the table and looked at her.

'This will all be for the ledger, what I am about to tell you. I just haven't got round to it yet. But I will. When I get the words right in my head. And maybe you can help me with it. Help young Poppy Hudson too.'

'Huh-who is Puh-Poppy Hudson?' she asked.

'Another little mate,' I said with a faint smile, unfolding the ragged check cloth that held the parcel of things together.

'It's a wonder you two never met. Though I imagine you may have walked past one another, many times, as you went round to your pitch on match days. If we could recollect memories as sharp and detailed as a photograph, I bet we might find you with your box of programmes, Poppy sat on the wall by the main entrance, just a few steps away. It wouldn't surprise me at all. She would have been maybe five, six years younger than you.'

'And now,' I said, '*this* is Poppy Hudson.'

Lying on the check cloth was a triangular Town pennant in the club colours, folded around a worn envelope, a few old season ticket voucher books, and two little notebooks.

But now, free from its bindings, the pennant slowly unfurled itself like a flower petal, stubby yellow tassels around the edges of it that had the club badge in the middle. An image of a football beneath the badge as the pennant tapered away to a point. Signatures of a Town squad littered across the face of it in a fine black marker. Smooth to the touch over the embroidered cotton surface.

'These are hers: Poppy's,' I said, and nodded at Stacey to take a closer look. She leant in to study the signatures, brushing a loose strand of her hair behind her ear, deciphering them one by one, helped along the way by the modern twist of the players incorporating their squad number into their script. Sometimes framed within the sweep of a capital D – beneath the angle of an A – sometimes an extension of the last letter. Others simply let their number linger close by, some encircling it, some letting it stand alone.

Stacey muttered to herself, the names of players as she worked them out, then she looked up.

'Fuh-from tuh-two thousand and tuh-twelve'?

She was on the money. It was the 12/13 squad that had signed Poppy's pennant. A thoroughly uninspiring collection of names that had helped the Town to a bottom four finish the season after being relegated out of the Football League.

Even for the Town, these players were a humbling collection of journeymen – and a part of the all-time low point in the club's history – being relegated down into the second tier of nonleague football at season's end.

But Poppy had loved them. Just as she had loved the team the season before that had lost the Town's precious Football League status.

They certainly weren't a team you could dislike. No matter how poor they had been.

They had clearly given their all for the Town. They just hadn't been good enough. And the club didn't have the money to bring in any better. They had collapsed down on the pitch devastated when relegation had been confirmed, mirroring the despair in the stands.

Their collective failure, it didn't matter to Poppy. She loved them. Everything about them. And she loved the Town.

I first spotted her, Poppy Hudson, in the autumn of 2010, as leaves from the grand oaks lining the Inchmery Road car park skittered here and there on the breeze before piling up in drifts against the railings. The Town were rock bottom of the Football League after an awful start to the season, which had thinned out the number of autograph hunters lingering about the main entrance on match days to just the odd soul. A damning indictment of the play witnessed that season.

And there, among this failing band, a little nine-year old girl in a faded and worn, old pink jacket, holding a programme of a League Cup match from that September in her hand, a pen in the other.

When a player arrived, she would look up in awe at them. Eyes wide. And she would wait her turn to be seen, handing up her programme and pen, watching as the signature was applied, before staring at it with a wonder that the author probably didn't deserve.

She stood out for two reasons. Firstly, her age. She was so young, possibly too young to be out on her own for such a long time. She looked tiny next to the players, and the other comings and goings on a match day, standing up against the far wall to keep out of everyone's way when there were no signatures to acquire. Her brown hair had been cropped clumsily, her fringe a little uneven, and she shivered a little in her threadbare coat and patched jeans.

Secondly, when everyone scurried away to their turnstile of choice as three o'clock drew near and the car park, the walls outside the pub cleared of people. As the programme sellers hurried to the club shop to drop off their stocks and money. As the odd latecomer jogged up Inchmery Road as the shutters came down on the club shop, fumbling for their money at the turnstile, young Poppy stayed put.

She would wander a little way along, opposite the ticket office windows, where a stretch of wall was low enough for her to perch herself on, and she would make herself as comfortable as she could. She looked up at the West Stand and craned her neck to the sounds of applause, the roaring of an expectant crowd barely two thousand in number. The shrill whistle of the referee.

She would look at her outdated programme that had the Town frozen in an unlikely seventh in the league table after only three fixtures, and she would check who the opposition were, and where they had been placed a month or so ago. Then she would interpret the match beyond, based on the groans and complaints, the ripples of encouragement, the oohs and aahs of near misses, the muted roar of a hundred or so away fans, should they score, drifting out over the stands and across the quiet streets beyond.

At a home goal, and the roar of the Inchmery Road faithful, Poppy would stand up on the wall. It didn't improve her view – the pitch still lost behind the frame of the West Stand – but she did it anyway, craning on tip-toe to feel just that little bit closer.

Every now and then a high clearance would crest the West Stand, and Poppy would follow it as it lurched and bobbled across the corrugated roof – sometimes dropping back down onto the pitch, other times falling down and into the car park, or onto the club shop roof. A second or two later, an old-timer would come out in a high-vis jacket and retrieve it, gingerly climbing a ladder if it had come to rest up on a high point. Then, ball under his arm, he would slip back away through a little door, and Poppy would wonder at the next high ball if it was the same one that she had seen being retrieved.

At the final whistle she would work out the score based on the expressions of those leaving the exit gates. But no matter the looks of thunder and despair at another home loss, the Town always remained seventh in Poppy's old programme.

And as the crowd filed away, somewhere amongst it, so too did Poppy, so as when the full-time rush had passed, her spot on the wall was empty too. Until the next game.

I started looking out for her once I had noticed her, this little girl all alone. She would collect her autographs in her programme, look longingly at the folks as they slipped inside, then sit on the wall and listen and crane as the match played itself out. Shrinking further beneath the canopy of a tree if it started to rain.

Then one cold, fog-bound November afternoon, she appeared, shivering out by the players' entrance in her jacket too thin to provide much warmth. A crumpled sheet of paper, no programme, proffered to the players as they came by. The freezing fog made the sheet limp and heavy, hard to write on as it got more and more damp, but she persevered – as did the players, who laboured to scribble something before her pen stopped writing or the paper snagged and ripped.

Poppy kept trying to smile as each player handed back the ever-shredding slip that hung loosely in her hands, losing its fight with the elements.

I found myself walking toward her before I had even thought of anything to say. I just found myself wandering over. I introduced myself, said I was the Nightwatchman, that I looked after the ground. I nodded down at the deteriorating sheet of paper.

'Where is your programme?' I asked, 'You usually have a programme.'

'I don't know,' she said meekly.

I said how it didn't look like the kind of thing she would lose. How she had held onto it so dearly. Like it was a treasure.

She shrugged her shoulders.

I smiled, nodded.

'Well, all right then,' I said. 'Good luck with the autograph hunting. I hope you don't get too wet.'

She smiled weakly.

I smiled back, turned, left her be.

A little later, after the match had started, as I locked the main entrance, I saw her sheltering from the drizzle beneath a tree. I watched her trying to fold her sodden sheet of paper, before tucking it into her pocket. Then she stood there, quietly, and listened to the sounds of the match.

The next home game, after the match had kicked off, I watched young Poppy from the main doors, sitting on her wall, looking up at the roof of the West Stand, listening.

I made a couple of mugs of tea, one with lots of sugar, and took them out to her.

She smiled and sipped at hers, the steam betraying how cold it must have been to be sat out in such a thin coat for so long.

We shared the packet of biscuits that I had stuffed in my coat pocket and listened to the muted sounds of the game, Poppy staring down at the biscuits with wide, hungry eyes, only taking one when I said for her to help herself. Time and again.

I learned her name. She learned mine.

She had never been to Inchmery Road before that season, or a game of football ever before, but then her name had been pulled out of a hat at school, that had been given some tickets for the Town's League Cup match against Accrington Stanley in early September.

They had got a bus from school. Had been handed a programme and a chocolate bar as they got off outside the main gates and had been herded up into the West Stand.

She had loved it. It had been so exciting, beneath the floodlights, the match going up and back with long passes and runs down the wing, even though the Town had lost.

They had been shepherded down onto the pitch at half time, where they blinked up into the lights and waved at the four corners of the ground as the school party was announced over the speakers. The pitch so green, she said, like it was magic or something. Then they had a few moments to get the autographs of the Town substitutes, who had been warming up behind them. Then it was back up into the stands for the second half, the night sky feeling electric with all the shouts and cheers from the crowd. The players roaring about, up and back. The brilliant floodlights shining down.

She only got two signatures that night, but she loved them. Actual football players! That played down on that magical glowing stretch of grass. In front of all those people. Their pictures in the programme she had been given, standing proudly in their Town kits, their statistics on the centre pages. Games played, goals scored, substitute appearances. A part of the exciting show.

And she had been trying to collect the autographs of the whole team ever since.

I asked her how she was doing, and she pulled out her folded piece of paper from her pocket, threadbare and falling apart.

'I've got quite a few,' she said, turning it gingerly, before folding it back away.

And still no programme?

She shook her head.

I asked her if her parents didn't mind her being out here all on her own. She shook her head again.

We sat quietly over a second mug of tea, Poppy warming her hands on hers, holding it close to her chest.

'So, why don't you go in,' I said, nodding at the turnstiles 'Why sit out here, if you love it?'

'I don't have any money,' she said.

'Could your Mum or Dad not take you?'

She shook her head.

'No pocket money you could save up?'

She shook her head again.

'It's all right,' she said. 'I can imagine it from all the noises. I've been inside, so I picture where the ball might be. I remember how all the stands look, so I can see it in my mind. I sometimes look at the dummies in the club shop window, wearing the kit, and I imagine them running about, as if they were playing… I hope to go back in, some day.'

She was a small, frail-looking thing, but there was a strength about her. A strength that suggested that she was used to being on her own, looking out for herself. That she had been doing so for some time. She wasn't afraid to be out there all on her own. Being bumped about in the crowd as it threaded its way into the stands. It was a price worth paying to be close to her new-found love for the Town.

She was a likeable kid. Polite. She liked to chat, as if it were a rarity for someone to take an interest in who she was, what she liked. And she enjoyed asking me about my job, looking after Inchmery Road. She thought it must be the best job in the world. I didn't disagree. She asked if I never got scared, late at night, all on my own. I said I never had, that it was nice to have the place all to myself.

She nodded, sat quietly imagining it.

And when our second mug of tea was up, she handed it back to me and smiled, thanked me, her eyes widening when I said to put the remainder of the packet of biscuits in her pocket.

'And you will be all right, out here?' I said.

She nodded.

I told her that if she ever needed anything, just to knock on the door. I pointed away to the players' entrance. She smiled, said thank you, waved as I walked away, then craned her neck up to the sky, listening to Inchmery Road.

It was only a small little thing, aimed at the pocket money market in the club shop. But it was very smart, with the club crest embossed on a navy-blue cover. Beneath it, the word "Autographs" printed in faux gold gave away what the little pocketbook was for.

Inside the front cover was a photograph of the team, the page opposite a list of that season's fixtures. Beyond, a tantalising sea of blank pages for the adventures and encounters that would be had with full-blown professional footballers. And professional footballers for the Town at that.

It came with a little pen that slipped through a loop of material sewn into the lip of the back cover.

Everything a young autograph hunter needed.

Poppy beamed when I gave it to her at the next home game. A smile that didn't look like ever ending, she stared down at it, brushing her fingers across the club badge on the cover. When I told her that I had been worried that her little slip of paper would dissolve away to nothing, she gingerly took it out of her pocket, and slipped it inside.

'Thank you,' she said. 'Thank you so much, Charlie.' Then she looked up as I told her to see if it worked properly, nodding at the Town centre back and goalkeeper who were walking across the car park toward us.

It did, and she stared at that first page in her book. Two sweeping signatures across pristine paper.

By kick-off she had collected seven, and she showed me as I brought her out a mug of tea, and we listened to the groans of the Town faithful as her magnificent seven failed to light up a dull November afternoon. A last-gasp equaliser at least giving a little cheer for the cold, dark walk home at the full-time whistle.

I didn't hear it at first. It took a little while, above the bustle of a football club winding down – a gentle tapping against the main doors.

The visiting team coach had pulled up outside, and their kit man was busy lugging boxes out to be stowed in the hold. Ticket office workers, the match sponsor's guests, came and went across the foyer. Canteen staff ferrying platters of sandwiches here and there – the little knocks had become lost among it all, until the visiting kit man waved me down.

'There is someone out here. Says she needs to speak to you.'

It was Poppy. She smiled. She held out her new autograph book to me.

'Would you be able to keep it here for me? It would be safer here.'

I shrugged and nodded, asked if she didn't want to have it to look at during the week.

She shook her head.

'It might go missing,' she said. 'Things always go missing at home. The nice things.'

I nodded, turned it over in my hands, paused.

'Poppy,' I said, 'are you all right? Is everything OK at home?'

She paused, then nodded. Smiled.

'Well, all right then,' I said. 'See you next week?'

'See you next week,' she said. 'Goodbye, Charlie.' She looked back and waved as she reached the main gates, then she slipped away into the night.

I took her autograph book back to my desk, flicking through it. Beneath her seven signatures she had written out the name of the player with a looping, determined nine-year-old script. Slow, deliberate, joined up strokes as neat as she could get them.

In time, and as her autograph collection grew, and players came and went, she would add the number of appearances each one made, and their goal tally.

At the foot of the Football League there was often a revolving door of short-term loan players to plug gaps in threadbare squads. There was no shortage of new signatures for Poppy to collect, and their time at Inchmery Road was dutifully recorded beneath their name: seven precious Town appearances here, four there. A couple of substitute outings for the more underwhelming loanees. Every slight contribution to her beloved Town captured for posterity in her little autograph book.

The care she had taken in writing in their names moved me. She had not wanted to make a mistake in her new book. Her little three-pound pocket money trinket.

And while her gratitude and thanks warmed my heart – a small thought seemingly going a long way – the fact that she didn't want to take it home bothered me. As did her spending pretty much an entire Saturday completely unattended, hanging around Inchmery Road until after dark.

The next home game she tapped at the main door, smiled as I

presented her with her book, all safe and sound. She thanked me, then took up her position to spot the players as they arrived – her little figure becoming lost as Inchmery Road became busier, match day winding up with countless timeless rituals. Old friends meeting at the same spot, by the same turnstile. Others heading for the pub. More just milling about, chatting. Most, if not all, completely unaware of their proximity to Peter Wright's bicycle, and its miraculous merger with an old Inchmery Road oak tree.

Hot dog and burger vans. The chiming of the bell on the club shop door, wide-eyed children peering into a bag holding a brand-new Town kit, parents bursting with pride at reliving a seminal memory from their own childhood. Handing it down to the next generation.

Stacey Marsh and her band of programme sellers trailed queues as eager collectors waited their turn. Dribs and drabs of Town's faithful support, wrapped up in coats and club scarves that had seen many a winter, turned the corner and made their way up Inchmery Road. As time crept on toward three, dribs and drabs turned into a steady stream, clogging the road.

Then, just in time for kick-off, the timeless scene contracts. Draining away through turnstiles, leaving a hush, a stillness outside. As if nothing had happened.

Leaving little Poppy Hudson, leaning up against her wall, gloomy shadows thickening about her as the floodlights began to strengthen up into the failing sky.

I watched her as she scanned her new acquisitions in her autograph book, glancing up at the odd latecomer jogging for the turnstiles.

Then I found myself doing something that I hadn't expected of myself. I am not an impulsive man. I never have been. I found myself wandering over to Poppy, beckoning her to me.

'Come with me,' I said, and held open the main door for her.

I ushered her through to the Nightwatchman's office, then down the corridor to the West Stand, and opened the door out onto the narrow concourse behind the lower tier benches – the sounds of a match in full swing breaking like a thunderclap.

'It's not much of a view,' I said to her as she looked out open-mouthed about her 'But I suppose it is better than nothing eh?'

She nodded eagerly, smiled from ear to ear.

'Well, just stay by my side and we will be fine,' I said

unconvinced. I had no idea if I had just broken some rule – letting someone in without a ticket – but I pushed it to the back of my mind, instead watching an enthralled Poppy standing on tiptoe to see over the heads of the rows of bodies in front of us. Peering up into the rafters of the upper tier as it obscured a high ball. Craning forward to follow the play as it headed toward the Victoria Road end. And as the odd soul hurried along past us to the toilets, or to beat the half-time queue at the tea kiosk, she would press herself against the wall, to keep out of the way.

At half time she sat dwarfed in my office chair cupping a mug of tea, watching people coming and going across the foyer. Then it was back out for the second half, where she got to jump and cheer at two Town goals in front of the Inchmery Road end, and an unobstructed view of the build-up and finishes of new loan striker, Calvin Russell.

She held up her book to me, to show me Russell's signature, then went back to jumping up and down, clapping till her hands were raw.

She had got the Town bug, that was for sure. Standing out in the cold all those games had proven that.

And now, back inside, she had tried to consume every moment – her eyes absorbing the play, the floodlights burning up into the night sky, the sounds of the crowd and the firecracker bursts as those in the upper tier rose to their feet in anticipation of a Town attack, their seats snapping upright as they vacated them. The shadowy mass of terracing littered with bundles of supporters, the East Stand rising up out of the camber of the pitch opposite bearing down on the vivid swathe of grass. Cheers and groans swirling with the wind.

She stood wide-eyed, as if she were too scared to blink, for fear of missing something.

And as the final whistle went, and the benches of the Lower Tier rose to applaud their team. Amid all the warm handshakes and back slapping between friends and football acquaintances as they shuffled along their bench and out toward the exit gates, Poppy craned at the doorway to watch the Town players on the pitch applauding the Inchmery Road terrace, before they strode away to the tunnel with a swagger of a professional job well done.

She stood there for as long as she could, watching the ground drain away of life. The beeping of horns and cheers outside while the stands grew still and hushed. Normally she would be locked out, listening in. Now, Poppy stood on the inside, in the quiet, listening to the bustle of a match day dissipating beyond.

She stood there, looking out at the empty stands until I beckoned her in, where she sat behind my desk and quietly, carefully, wrote the names of the players beneath her newly acquired signatures.

I made her a cup of tea, found a plate of biscuits, and told her to wait there for a moment.

The ticket office was all but empty, shutters pulled down on the outside world, one desk lamp in the corner the only illumination on another match day successfully serviced.

Sat at it was Sally, the ticket office manager at the time. She looked tired, overworked, but she smiled as I popped my head in, beckoned me over.

'I was wondering,' I said, 'if I could pay for a child ticket for today's game.'

She told me to sit, and I explained about Poppy, and not wanting to get in any trouble. I didn't want to stiff the club out of a ticket sale and wondered if I could still pay.

'You know,' she said, 'as a full-time employee at the club, Charlie, you are entitled to a free season ticket. You don't need to pay for anything. And you can use that season ticket on anyone you like,' she said. 'Bless you, Charlie. You can put your wallet away. If you come and see me next week sometime, I can sort that out for you. I think everything has been locked away for today.'

And that was how young Poppy Hudson became a season ticket holder at Inchmery Road.

She couldn't believe it the following home match when I presented her with a little booklet of tear-out vouchers for all the remaining games in the season. Her name, her season ticket number typed out on the inside cover, above her seat details: West Stand Lower, Bench B 3.

It was a little way down the concourse from the Nightwatchman's office, almost opposite the Inchmery Road penalty area. It was a sparsely populated area, so her bench one row back from the pitch only housed an elderly couple, who used to sit swaddled together beneath a large blanket the entire match. And with no one sitting in the front row, Poppy got a good view of the pitch, and the substitutes warming and stretching, jogging along the touchline right in front of her.

I ushered her along the back of the lower tier her first time, season ticket and autograph book clutched tightly in her hands, and pointed out her bench, watched her take the steps down to the right row. Then, with her finger she counted the benches down to number three, smiled at the old couple, and sat down.

She looked back at me and waved, then sat, and stared up and out at Inchmery Road all about her. Waiting for her heroes.

And that would become our little routine on match days: Poppy collecting her autograph book, hunting for signatures while I wandered round to keep Stacey company for a bit on Victoria Road. Then just before kick-off she would meet me at the main doors to pick up her season ticket.

We would then walk along to the turnstile, and I would watch her through, standing on tiptoes to reach up to the man in his booth, watching as he tore out the voucher, then she would push on the old iron bars and the turnstile would clatter – and she would be gone.

I would walk back around and through the Nightwatchman's office to make sure she was safely at her seat, and she would smile and wave when she saw me.

At half time, she would weave between the bodies coming and going along the concourse, and we would sit in the office and drink a mug of tea, share a chocolate bar. And then at full time, she would wait for the majority to pile out through the exit gates, before walking back up to meet me at the Nightwatchman's door.

She would sit and thaw out with a cup of tea, looking tiny in my office chair, and carefully write in the names of her new signatures in her autograph book.

Then, as the day died down outside, I would pull a note from my wallet, and Poppy would wander down to the chip shop just off Victoria Road, and we would have fish and chips and mushy peas for dinner; Poppy eating a full adult portion with an intensity that suggested she hadn't eaten for a week.

I would often ask her if her mum and dad wouldn't be missing her. She would always shake her head, they would more than likely be out, she would always say. They were always going out, she said.

'And what about you?' I would ask. She would shrug her shoulders.

'I stay in my room mostly, doing drawings.'

It would also be Poppy that got herself up in the mornings, made some breakfast, took herself off to school, which she enjoyed, spending lunchtimes in the library reading adventure books.

And some days, if her mum wasn't home, Poppy would fetch herself some dinner with whatever was in the house.

'Where do they go? Your mum and dad?' Poppy didn't know. But if they had had an argument, Dad could be away for days, weeks at a time. Sometimes even longer.

I didn't know what to say, and I think Poppy liked that I didn't try. We just sat and had our dinner, enjoyed our time on match days together. And I felt comforted a little that she had her beloved team, her match days, and at least one big, hearty meal to keep out the cold.

Though I hated it when she handed back her autograph book, her season ticket, for safe keeping, heading out into the night with a smile and a wave. Until next time.

Safe keeping from what? I didn't like to think about that. But at the same time, I couldn't stop.

She never complained. She just got on with things. I didn't like that either.

She cherished her autograph book, her season ticket. She wrapped them up in a piece of check cloth, handling them gingerly like they were fragile ancient artefacts. And most evenings I would bring them back out from their safe spot in my office desk drawer and leaf through them. Looking at young Poppy's concentrated writing, as neat as she could get it, translating each footballer flourish.

I would pause at her season ticket bench, sit for a while on my rounds and think about her. This resilient little nine-year-old girl. And I would worry, because nine-year-old girls shouldn't need to be so. I worried at how she would wolf down her fish and chip supper on a Saturday, like a hot meal was a rarity, a treat. But I never knew how to bring it up. She didn't like to talk about home. Her parents.

If ever I pushed that little bit too far, she would go quiet. Which would make me feel terrible.

Inchmery Road was a happy place. I didn't want to ruin that for her. She would talk if she wanted to, I would reconcile myself.

I would just do what I could in the meantime.

When it came to me, I scolded myself for not thinking of it sooner, the Combination League fixtures of the reserves.

Poppy would be at every first team game, she had checked the fixtures in her programme, before it went missing, then she would refer to the little list at the front of her autograph book.

She had read the page on the reserve team in her programme, their list of fixtures, their match reports, and line-ups of unfamiliar Town players names. But, beyond that, she knew nothing about the reserves. Where they played, and when. There was no mention of them in her season ticket booklet. No vouchers for their endeavours. But it stood to reason she would probably enjoy the reserves just as she enjoyed the first team. It was the Town, the same spectacle played out at Inchmery Road on the Saturdays that the first team were away.

It was the same ground, minus the crowds, the same red and yellow kit, minus the sponsors' logo, the same game, lacking only in a little intensity, the result having less meaning. But it would be another match, another Saturday for her to look forward to. And, after all, reserve team players had signatures too.

It would also be good to know that she had had at least one good meal every week, rather than every other. A fortnight felt a long time when I thought about young Poppy out there, fending for herself. It felt an age between her visits. It would be good to see her safe and well more often.

It would be good to see her smile, see her enjoying herself.

On those extra Saturdays with the reserves, everyone would win – at least off the pitch.

When I mentioned it to her, her eyes lit up. She would love to go to the reserve matches too, of course she would. Which is how she came to be up at Inchmery Road every Saturday.

They only opened the upper tier of the West Stand for reserve games, but Poppy would keep me company down on the lower tier, where she was free to wander up and back, from the Inchmery end away up to the Victoria Road end, where she would look up at the old scoreboard in the corner that updated the hundred or so souls present on the first team score.

She had the whole place to herself, and she would love to try out different benches, following the play from different perspectives. She liked to sit near the corner flag by the Inchmery end so as she could feel the thud of boot on ball as a corner was taken.

She liked to sit right behind the dugouts so as she could hear the managers barking out orders, the intoxicating smell of the liniment oil rubbed on the substitutes' legs, keeping them warm, making her eyes sting.

And she would gather up the reserve team players' autographs, compiling their statistics beneath their names in her book with the same reverence as the first team – anyone that wore the red and yellow of the Town was worthy in her eyes. The only concession at a career played out in empty stadiums being a little 'R' after their name to differentiate Combination League games from first team appearances.

And at the full-time whistle she would watch the players off the pitch, before heading up to the chip shop, and we would have dinner in the office, watching the skies drain of colour outside.

She loved the office. She loved being in the secret parts of Inchmery Road that so few ever saw. She loved looking at all the pictures on the walls. She would gingerly rummage through all the treasures in the desk drawers: piles of old programmes, photographs and newspaper cuttings, letters, Dennis Lawrence's international football shirts, Mackie's ledger.

The story of Peter Wright, his bicycle, captivated her, and we would often head out there for her to help brush away fallen leaves, rub down what frame hadn't been absorbed into the oak. She would attempt to ring the old-rusted bell, the mechanism heavy, unresponsive. A little give, maybe one flat, dull thud.

She would love to sit by the door in the office and watch the players leave, filing away into the darkness. And then, before long, she too would need to leave, wrapping up her autographs, her season ticket in her cloth, tucking them away in the desk, slipping away into the night with a smile and a wave. Until next time.

I discovered Poppy's birthday by accident in February, after she corrected me one day. I had commented on how I didn't think there was a more dedicated nine-year-old autograph hunter in the entire country, when she shook her head.

'Ten,' she said, 'I'm ten now.'

And had been for a couple of weeks, it turned out.

'Well, happy birthday for a couple of weeks ago Poppy.'

She smiled.

I went in to work early on my next shift and wandered around the club shop looking for a belated birthday present.

Tina behind the counter had been a fixture at Inchmery Road for more than fifty years.

In her time, she had worked in the ticket office, been secretary to the Chairman for nearly twenty years. She had arranged the lodgings for apprentices and had even taken a few in herself.

She organised coaches for away games for supporters – if there was a demand. And she ran stadium tours as and when they were required.

Her passion for the Town kept her spritely and eager, even though she had just turned eighty. She could often be seen striding with purpose up and down the stairs, to and from the club offices with a youthful vigour that put many people half her age to shame.

She was our very own Peter Pan of Inchmery Road – her beloved Town keeping her young at heart.

And it was her position as Junior Town Club co-ordinator that she mentioned when I told her of my mission.

'She would get a membership card, and a birthday card signed by her favourite players, and a chance to win prizes in our competitions. We do a newsletter every month, and activities during the holidays. We have lots lined up for half-term next week. I could get her membership card and everything else made up for you in a couple of days. What do you think?'

It sounded great, and I paid for the membership, the activity week right there and then.

'So,' she said, leaning forward over a notebook on the counter 'What's her name and address?'

I gave her name but suggested that everything should be sent to the Nightwatchman's office.

'I don't think things are too good at home, to be honest. It might be easier for her if they came here. Is that all right?'

Tina smiled and nodded.

'Of course,' she said.

She dropped it all off herself the following Friday, having a cup of tea and a chat before home.

She asked after Poppy, and I told her all I knew. She promised that she would look after her during half-term week.

'You know,' she said, 'of the twenty or so kids that come along to the holiday activities, three or four don't pay – come from troubled backgrounds. I just let them in, and they love it. They are always the ones to grasp everything with both hands. Throw themselves in headlong. Some are a bit rough around the edges, but they are so happy to be a part of things.

'I know one of the local care-workers, and he brings them along. We do what we can for them – though God knows what they have to go back home to at the end of the day,' she shook her head.

'And then there are another seven or eight who are sent because they get fed a good meal at lunch. They are the kids who get free school meals during term time and might go without otherwise.' She shook her head.

'Their parents work, but they barely get by. They save up for the activity weeks, often going without themselves, in the process. It is heartbreaking,' she said. 'How hard they work, but still struggle. But they make sure the kids can come here. Have fun. Feel a part of something, and most importantly, get fed.'

'It's because of those kids that we started "Lunch Club" during the longer holidays. Any child that needs something to eat can come along every weekday. I buy tins of beans and jacket potatoes, loaves of bread, tuna, cheese, ham, fruit, crisps and chocolate bars, and the chef in the canteen knocks them up something out of it.

'They sit in the canteen afterwards and draw and play together. And then the chef organises a little match out in the car park for them before they are sent on their way with a pocketful of apples and oranges.

'There are a few from the office and canteen who bring in food as well, donate an hour of their time to watch over them, help with the kickabout,' she shrugged her shoulders, sipped her tea.

'You know, I started this club back in the late seventies because I heard that other clubs did a junior membership. I thought it would be all badges and membership cards. I had no idea it would turn into what it has needed to become.

'I am glad to do it. It is just so sad that we need to,' she said, paused.

'I hope your Poppy enjoys it. We'll do our very best.'

I gave Poppy her belated present before Saturday's game, with a little cupcake sporting one lit candle on top. She wolfed it down, then opened her birthday card signed by player-coach Dom Jeffries, and the young Town right-back Eddie Rosicki.

Rosicki lodged with Jeffries and had to come in early with him every match day – kicking about in the canteen while Jeffries and the rest of the management team had their pre-match meetings.

They were always in long before young Poppy arrived and had been two of the most elusive signatures in her little book.

Her eyes looked as if they were going to pop out of her head as she read the card, handwritten by Jeffries:

'A very Happy Birthday Poppy. Best wishes'

Beneath it, Jeffries signature, Rosicki's added alongside.

She couldn't believe it – they knew her name, she kept saying. A young defender with barely a dozen Fourth Division appearances to his name, and a journeyman lower league player who had once made a handful of Second Division games for Millwall. Heroes to young Poppy, as they wore the red and yellow of the Town.

I watched her during that Saturday's match looking down at the card, opening it carefully to look inside time and again. As if she couldn't quite believe it and needed to check that it was real. That her message, the signatures were still safely inside.

After the match she pored over her Junior Town newsletter and membership card, studying the itinerary for the activity week ahead.

'Your parents won't mind?' I asked her. She shook her head, smiled up at me, a head full of anticipation at a whole week spent at Inchmery Road.

I went in to work early the following Friday to watch a final few games of Junior Town five-a-side in a coned-off area of the car park.

Mismatched games where five and six-year-olds played with and against children more than twice their age – their elders passing to them slowly and deliberately, letting them tackle them, or dribble past them, smiling knowingly as they wheeled away in celebration at a goal scored.

Poppy, rosy-cheeked in the biting cold, ran up and back with a broad grin, lost in the chaos of it all. And at the final whistle, as all the children followed Tina through the main doors to Inchmery Road, up toward the canteen and an awards ceremony to finish off the week, Poppy told me about a training session run by a couple of the apprentices, and how they had said she was a good passer of the ball. She told of a stadium tour by Tina, where she got to see the changing rooms and everything, and how they got to watch a first team training session out on the pitch, and then got to meet the team afterwards.

Scavenger hunts, art club, story club, and football games outside beneath the barren limbs of Peter Wright's oak tree. It had clearly been a good week.

At the awards ceremony, every child won a prize. Signed photographs, a football, little sets of colouring pencils and notepads. Poppy won a box of chocolates and a large pencil with the Town crest embossed on it for 'most improved player' over the week. And at the end, as children drained away home, Poppy showed me over to a table with lots of drawings on it.

'At art club we had to draw our favourite part of the ground,' she pointed out her picture. 'I did that one.'

It was a picture of the Nightwatchman's corridor, looking out onto the benches of the West Stand, the pitch beyond.

She had drawn a couple of the picture frames along the wall, the most detailed being the old photograph of Gerald Mackie, Peter

Wright, and Michael Trim by the open door – their silhouettes carefully replicated, their sizes next to each other spot on, so as there could be no doubt as to what photograph she had drawn.

The benches, the little, whitewashed wall in the front of the first row, the pitch, the East Stand in the distance – all had been carefully, meticulously drawn out in pencil. The sliver of Inchmery Road seen from the Nightwatchman's door lovingly re-created as best as a ten-year-old girl ever could.

I was touched. Of all the things she could have drawn, she drew our little view, where we first watched a game together.

She picked up the drawing.

'It's for you,' she said, handing it to me. 'To say thank you. For everything.' She hugged me.

'See you, Charlie,' she said and smiled, waved, then slipped away for home.

I bought a frame for Poppy's picture and hung it behind the Nightwatchman's desk. She didn't mention it on her next visit, but I caught her looking up at it on the wall, a broad grin on her face.

And so, with that, life went on. We would have our Saturdays – autographs and season tickets, ninety minutes and fish and chips.

At the end of another season of struggle I signed her up for the two weeks of activities with the Junior Town Club during the summer holidays. She would also be a regular at Lunch Club during the rest of the summer and had taken to helping Tina in the club shop afterwards – tidying racks of shirts, straightening out the postcards of last season's players in the little carousel next to the counter.

At least once a week I would come in to work early to try and catch her to say hello. One afternoon I found Poppy weaving and contorting herself around the mannequins behind the large plate glass club shop window – Tina directing her as she dressed them in different coloured polo-shirts with the club badge on the breast.

I made some tea, and brought it round to them, and we sat on the steps outside and listened as Poppy told me what she had helped with.

She seemed happy, and Tina enjoyed the extra help, and summer crept by lazily on Inchmery Road. Echoes of lawnmowers cutting backyards, drifting across the rooftops. Cars creeping along hushed streets. Seagulls coasting and crying out on warm currents.

And when the next season finally came around, I made my way to see Sally to sort out another season ticket for Poppy.

She hadn't expected it, or even mentioned it, and she arrived that first home match of the new season to pick up her little autograph book, ready to hunt down the Town's new signings.

She clutched it to her chest like she was meeting an old friend after a long absence, flicking through the pages of autographs, their order committed to memory.

She turned to a fresh page, and neatly wrote across the top "2011/12," then wandered across to the wall to scout out players cars pulling into the car park.

'Poppy,' I called after her, and she looked back. 'You forgot something.'

She wandered back and looked up at me, her jaw dropping as I pulled out a brand-new season ticket booklet stuffed with match vouchers.

'Thank you, Charlie,' she barely whispered as she flicked through the booklet, at the new season laid out ahead of her.

'Well,' I told her, 'it would be lonely having fish and chips all by myself. So, I thought you had better tag along.'

She smiled. And smiled throughout the season.

No matter her situation at home, where she couldn't take nice things, she came to life at Inchmery Road. She collected autographs, watched the matches from her bench, and ate fish and chips for her tea.

During school holidays I made sure she was signed up for all the activities, and I would donate a bag of food for the lunch clubs. And on her birthday, she received a card, from the players, that she cherished, keeping it safe with her other things in the Nightwatchman's office even though it was signed by the squad that finally relinquished the Town's proud Football League status. A terrible season seeing the club relegated down into non-league football for the first time ever.

It didn't matter to her. It was her beloved Town. They were heroes in her eyes, and her birthday card was a precious treasure. And no matter what league they found themselves in, she would be ready with her little book, asking very politely for an autograph.

But despite Poppy's unswerving devotion and faith, her excitement at a new season, it was a tough time for the club.

Relegation into non-league had staff being laid off, positions mothballed. The relief Nightwatchman position disappeared, and I agreed to being paid for just three and a half days a week, though I would work the five. It was even touch and go at one point as to whether the position would be lost altogether, after more than one hundred years.

I think it would have been, had I not taken a pay cut. And it was a struggle, financially. But it was worth it, to keep my job. It is the best job in the world.

And, thankfully, after three seasons, the Town were promoted back into the Fourth Division as champions – and I got my full pay back.

It was a bittersweet moment – that promotion of 2015. The Town were back where they belonged, and with a championship trophy to boot.

But Poppy had not been there to see it.

She had been as surprised as before with her third season ticket at the start of the 12/13 season. And like the previous two, she never missed a Saturday game. Though, as with the previous two, the late finish of mid-week games meant she had to sit them out.

We had our match routines. Our little rituals. And to be honest, I have never been able to fathom who got the most out of them, out of our friendship.

Poppy had been enthralled, completely consumed by the drama of the games – collecting the signatures of those protagonists in her book. She loved being in the Nightwatchman's office, looking at all the pictures and football treasures stored in those desk drawers. She loved being able to have Inchmery Road all to herself for a time, stood at the Nightwatchman's door, looking out across the benches of the Lower West Stand as the ground became still again after a match. She loved fish and chips, her Junior Town membership card, Lunch Club and activity weeks.

And me?

I loved seeing how much she loved it all.

She never asked for anything. Never expected anything.

And her gratitude, the way in which she grasped these little opportunities with both hands, it was just beautiful to watch. And I cherished every single moment spent with such a little gem. She made me smile. She made me happy. Her company was a gift – quiet evenings, just the rustling of chip wrappers and the smell of vinegar. Poppy pulling the ring on a can of pop.

Undiluted contentment.

If Evie and I had ever been blessed with a child, I would have hoped that he or she would have turned out like Poppy, or Stacey for that matter. Beautiful souls. That lift mine. They would have Evie's too.

I say that Poppy never missed a game. That isn't true. She never missed a game, until she did.

The first match after autumn half-term 2012 against Kidderminster Harriers came and went without Poppy. I kept wandering past the doors with her autograph book in hand, waiting for her to appear. But she never did.

The players arrived, the crowd came, watched, and went again, passing her empty spot by the far wall. All unaware at the significance of her absence.

She never missed a game.

She had had such a good half-term week as well, leading up to the Kidderminster match. At the awards ceremony she won a Town pennant signed by the whole squad, for helping the younger children throughout the week. She was only eleven herself.

When Tina handed it to her, she held it as if she had just been presented with the Holy Grail, staring down into the sea of signatures – the club badge beneath. She brushed the tassels gently with her fingers, then looked up at me stood at the end of the room and held it up to show me.

A smile like no other.

She had carefully wrapped it up in her checked cloth, folding it around her autograph book, her two birthday cards, her season tickets, gently placing it all into her spot in the bottom drawer in the Nightwatchman's desk. She had not been able to stop smiling, and she glanced back at the desk as she left – already excited about looking at, holding her new pennant once more.

But she never did.

The Town were at home the following Saturday against Grimsby Town – another fallen Football League side – and again Poppy didn't turn up.

I stood with her book, and waited, peering through the crowd, thinking I had spotted her, for it only to have been wishful thinking. Another young child, or a flash of pink that wasn't Poppy's jacket among the throng, thinning out to nothing as kick-off approached.

I didn't know what to do. I found myself on the steps of the club shop, knocking at the door. Tina, coat already on, shop locked, about to make the dash to her seat up in the West Stand, opened the door and ushered me inside. A look of concern on her face, clearly mirroring what she saw in me.

I told her about Poppy.

She nodded seriously. Told me that she would make a call to her social-worker friend.

See if he knew anything. To leave it with her.

And on my next shift that Tuesday, I found Tina waiting for me outside the Nightwatchman's office.

She had been taken.

Social services.

Put into foster care.

Her whereabouts Tina's care-worker friend neither knew, nor would say even if he did.

'They can be moved anywhere in the country. Wherever there is an available space,' Tina said, ashen faced. 'Often far enough away from the problems that brought them there. To keep them safe. That's what he said.

'Her Dad has just been sent to prison. For years, not months. And it turns out that Poppy's mother has been absent for months and months. No one knows where. She just left, apparently.

They picked her up after she got home from the awards ceremony. Took her away. It looks like she had been fending for herself in that house for a good long while. Poor little thing.'

She had never said a word.

Though, looking back, she had also never lied.

She had been open about not wanting to take nice things home. And she had been honest when asked if her parents weren't worried about her.

She had been treading a fine line between shouting her anguish and heartbreak from the rooftops, but not doing so to protect those who didn't protect her. They were her mum and dad after all. Things could get better, maybe, some day. And a fractured, volatile, dysfunctional family was better than no family at all.

Better in her eyes than the uncertain life she now faced. The echoes of nicer moments, fragments of happiness and laughter, inspiration enough to try and hold everything together, somehow.

A little girl trying through silence, tolerance, and an enforced maturity beyond her years to protect her Mum, who she loved, to protect her dad, who she loved – her love for those who didn't deserve it, trying to hold the whole sorry mess in place.

We both sat in silence for a time, there was nothing we could do, it was out of our hands, Poppy was out of our reach, Tina wiping a tear from her eye before she left me to my shift.

Unable to look at her little bundle of belongings that night, I wandered the ground instead, pausing to look down at the spot she had made her own on the benches.

I took a mug of tea and sat there, closed my eyes, and tried to picture where she might be. In the hope that she might manifest in front of me, so I could grab her. Not let her go again. Bring her back to Inchmery Road.

Every game I would look out for her, hoping beyond hope that she would materialise out of the bustle of match day.

But she never came.

And the only thing that kept me from breaking down into floods of tears at her absence was knowing that she was still out there, somewhere.

That one day she might come back. Be sat on her spot on the wall. All pink jackets and smiles.

And if she did, her autograph collection would be in order.

I would keep it going for her.

I thought that she would like that.

And so, with every new Town player, I would take her autograph book and hunt them down, get them to sign. I would write their names beneath as neatly as I could, and when they left the club, I would jot their statistics down for her, as she had done to those that had gone before them.

Over time, her little book filled up, so I bought her another one, and started in on that. I kept it with all her other bits, and a new season ticket every year, that sat waiting for her.

It helped keep me busy, and kept young Poppy close, even if only in spirit.

I would flick through the new signatures on a Saturday night, and I would wonder about her, hope for her.

Her loss hurt as much as Evie's. Both were such wonderful, beautiful people. With spirits so similar, so caring, so special it was easy to imagine that they could have been, in another life, mother and daughter. At the very least the best of friends.

At least with Poppy there was one thing – hope.

And I would sit, and I would hope. I would think of young Poppy, wherever she might be.

That maybe she got to go and watch a football match where she was?

Or maybe she found out the Town result, and imagined it all, just like she used to. Craning her neck, looking off into the middle-distance, the game coming to life in her mind. Inchmery Road sharpening into focus about her.

I hoped. For her, for me, that that was the case

That she was all right.

I sometimes wonder where I will be when I die. Where will the ghost of Charlie Truckle find its home about Inchmery Road? In amongst all the others that have loved and lived this place above all other.

I have wondered about all the Nightwatchmen, and I think I know where they might be.

Gerald Mackie must be out by Peter Wright's bicycle, patiently waiting for him to materialize out of the darkness at a little after one. Re-united, finally. Tanner Rowe, I see by the main doors, camera poised, waiting patiently for a little slice of Inchmery Road life to present itself.

Stanley Peters I can't quite decide. Will he be over with Danny Stokes in the bombed out East Stand, holding his hand tenderly, right to the very last? Or is he to be found in the office, looking into the shadows of George Chester's Christmas tree? Different days I feel different ways. Maybe he does both.

Bob Andrews, I see in the office for sure, unaware of the overlapping of generations. Unable to see his predecessor. The tree. Andrews, oblivious to it, is drinking tea, reliving stories and jokes shared with Dennis Lawrence. Peering into photographs from faraway lands, those precious international shirts.

A friendship undiluted by time. Echoing on despite lives fading into the fog of history.

Snippets of a Bob Andrews' life joining the other ghosts of Inchmery Road, illuminated for the briefest of moments as the floodlights are snuffed out.

I thought for a good time that my ghost would be found at the main doors, looking out for Poppy. Or maybe at her bench, looking back to see if she pushed through the turnstiles on a match day.

I thought that that will be where my ghost will linger, above all the other meaningful spots to me.

That is where I thought.

Now, well now, I'm not too sure. Things change. Things happen. I guess I will just have to wait and see.

Poppy would have been fifteen at the time of Bob Andrews' funeral, Stacey almost six years her senior.

It came to me out of nowhere, the thought of one being able to maybe help the other.

So, when Stacey came to see me the day after Bob Andrews' funeral, I showed Stacey Poppy's little parcel of belongings.

I told her Poppy's story.

I told Stacey a little white lie, that trying to hunt down all the player autographs was getting a bit too much for me. That my dodgy knee was slowing me down somewhat. That it hurt as the cold weather hit.

It was true that my knee hurt. But not so much as to hinder me. And I always found the time, either before or after a match, to seek out whichever members of the squad I hadn't already got to sign Poppy's book.

But I saw it as an opportunity for Stacey. To reach out to people. For a greater good. So, I lied a little.

Stacey sat, flicking through Poppy's crammed autograph books, each page holding two, sometimes three signatures. A tattered, weather damaged sheet of paper tucked in the front. Fused together as rain-soaked folds had dried, the tantalising glimpse of black pen within. Signatures entombed, that would fall apart if anyone tried to prise the sheet apart.

'So,' I said 'Do you think you could help me out. For Poppy?'

She looked up at me, nodded.

'Yuh-yes, Charlie. I cuh-can help. Puh-poor girl. Do yuh-you think she will ever cuh-come back?'

'I don't know,' I said. 'But if she does, imagine how happy we will have made her, keeping her autograph collection all together.

She nodded.

'I wuh-will do my best, chu-Charlie. For yuh-you. And fuh-for Poppy.'

'I know you will, mate. Thank you.'

Chapter Twelve

It was not plain sailing from the start, for Stacey on her mission. It took time for her to build up a little confidence.

On match days I would see her look up from her work, getting all the programme sellers' aprons ready with change on the club shop floor when one of the players' cars pulled in.

I saw her edge out the door, Poppy's book clutched to her chest, then falter on the steps, watch the player across the car park and in through the main doors. Gone.

She would sigh, turn back inside. Though it wouldn't be just me that encouraged her.

When Tina from the club shop, who had been so kind to Poppy, to everyone, passed away a month or two before Bob Andrews, a young lad called Marcus had taken her place.

He had once played for the youth team, had even made the reserve team bench a couple of times before a terrible training ground injury ended his dreams of making it as a professional footballer.

It was not much in the way of compensation for a lifetime's dreams thrown on the scrapheap, but the club offered him the job of club shop manager, Junior Town co-ordinator, and Lunch Club organiser, as well as supporting him through an evening course in business management.

He took the opportunity with both hands, maintaining Tina's legacy as if it were his own, and he would help Stacey spot players as they came in on match days.

'Armstrong, Stacey. Do you need Armstrong?' he would ask.

'Guh-got,' she would reply if Armstrong had already made it into Poppy's book.

'What about McMahon?'

'Nuh-need,' and she would look up at Marcus nodding across the way, taking up the book, heading outside.

If she faltered, watched him go, Marcus would nod as she went back inside.

'Next time,' he would say. Smile kindly.

And over time, next time came. First McMahon, then a couple of loan players – Standing and Forsell.

She had jogged over to intercept Dennis McMahon, holding out the book.

'Cuh-cuh-could I guh-get yuh-your autograph, duh-Dennis?'

'Of course,' he said with a smile, and with a flourish he was done, and carried on across the car park. She turned and walked straight into Standing and Forsell. She stood there, frozen, then watched as they took Poppy's book, signed it, handed it back, smiled, then carried on to the players' entrance.

She saw me standing by the door. She held the book up, smiled from ear to ear, then looked across at Marcus grinning in the window of the club shop.

She had done it.

And in time she would do it again and again.

Not at every opportunity. There would still be moments frozen on the club shop steps. But slowly she started to get the autographs for Poppy's book.

Filling up page after page as players came and went.

Sometimes she would even find herself engaging in unnecessary conversation.

'I-it's nuh-not for muh-me. I-it's fuh-for a luh-little girl cuh-called puh-Poppy.'

Players would smile, nod, sometimes they would add 'To Poppy,' which would thrill her just as much as it did me.

The pride I felt in Stacey facing her fears was only matched by the sadness I felt in the necessity of the task, and Poppy's absence.

But they were an unwitting little team – Stacey and Poppy, though they had never met. One inspired the other to push herself. And in doing so, she did a nice thing for the other.

I have always thought that they would make good friends. I hope that one day they might be. That would be wonderful.

I would daydream that Stacey takes the job as Nightwatchwoman full-time when I retired. And that they met, somehow.

And Stacey shows Poppy the ledger, her story laid out in my handwriting.

And she sees just how much she meant to me, and how much her absence had been felt. Proof that she had been cherished and loved, and never forgotten.

Her little bundle of things, and an ever-growing pile of autograph books, unused season tickets kept together, waiting for her, new season tickets collected for her, even after I have gone.

More rituals for Mackie's ledger, to honour the humble folk who have made Inchmery Road the precious little place it is.

Folk like Poppy Hudson.

It would be nice to think of them as friends. Poppy and Stacey.

It would be everything.

Stacey pushed herself out of her comfort zone for Poppy and her autograph book. She made herself speak to players, all in the name of a little girl she had never known. Humble steps for most, but for Stacey it was enormous, interacting rather than just observing. And from it came an unintentional side-effect.

Eddie Hamer was a first-year professional, who had signed his first pro contract after a successful spell as a non-contract player for the reserves.

He was 21, and had travelled down from Otterburn on the Scottish border to take what appeared to be his last chance at making it as a pro.

He had been a youth player for Hibernian, then Partick Thistle, but had been released from both. He had then played a bit of part-time football away at Stranraer on the west coast in the Scottish fourth tier, before the travelling got too much. There wasn't much left of his meagre wage after petrol to get him to games and training twice a week.

Instead, he dropped down into Junior football, got a maintenance job in the Northumberland National Park, and started to save up. And while he did, he wrote a letter to every professional team in Scotland and England, asking for a trial. For one more chance.

Few wrote back – many clubs receiving hundreds of requests a month from young hopefuls. And of those that did, it was just the Town who offered a two-week trial. And that is how he came to pack his bags, make his way down to Inchmery Road.

He did well. Well enough for the club to offer to put him up for the remainder of the season, give him a chance in the reserves, which he took with both hands. He put in some strong displays in midfield, chipped in with assists and the odd goal, and did enough to be offered a low-end professional deal for the following season.

He may well have earned more money playing in Junior football in Scotland and working his maintenance job, but he had always dreamed of being a professional footballer. And through his perseverance, sacrifice, and dedication, he had made it. Wages be damned, he had become a pro.

He had made five appearances off the bench for the first team in the league and started a League Cup game in the opening weeks of the season by the time Stacey found the courage to chase after him across the car park in late October.

'Cuh-could I guh-get yuh-your autograph, Eddie? It's nuh-not fuh-for me, it fuh-for a luh-little girl called Poppy.'

Eddie smiled, took up the book and signed it – a new thrill he hadn't experienced before, part of the dream. Becoming one of the players that he had once queued up to meet as a young boy outside St. James' Park, Newcastle, when his dad had taken him on the train to see United play.

'So, what about you?' he said playfully. 'Poppy has hers. You don't want an autograph?'

Stacey felt her cheeks flushing bright red beneath her bobble hat.

'Nuh-no. I-I mean yuh-yes. Oh-oh-of cuh-course.' She scrabbled in her pockets for paper she knew wouldn't be there. Then she pointed back at the shop.

'I cuh-can guh-guh-get some puh-paper.'

He smiled.

'I'm just joking with you,' he said, handing back the autograph book 'You have made my day already. It is not often I get asked. Thank you. And thank you to Poppy.' He smiled, turned, and was gone.

Marcus looked up as she came back to the shop.

'Get it?' he asked.

'Guh-got it,' she said, face still flustered.

'Good,' he said. 'Are you all right?' She nodded, smiled weakly, got on with preparing her aprons.

It had been a dour goalless draw, and Eddie Hamer had remained on the bench for the duration, jogging down to the corner flag every twenty minutes or so with a few of the other substitutes to do some stretches.

Stacey had sat up in the East Stand with her mother, the weather not yet turned bad enough to prevent her from coming. And she waved her off as she always did after the game, watching her hobble on her walking stick away down Inchmery Road, turning the corner, slipping away into the weave of streets beyond.

With her mum safely away, Stacey hurried into the club shop, and began counting out the money from the returned seller's aprons – bagging up the little floats for each – tallying up the rest for Marcus to ring through the till.

It was rare for Marcus to get many customers after the game – pocket money normally being spent beforehand, with most wanting to head straight for home for their tea, or the pub for a pint at the final whistle.

The car park had mostly emptied, and the crowds had drained away by the time the bell chimed above the shop door. Both Marcus and Stacey looked up from their work, surprised. Becoming even more so when they saw Eddie Hamer step in from the dark. Hair still wet from a post-match shower, though it always felt a sham, undeserved if he had remained on the bench all game. An action carried out more from instinct than any necessity.

He was a handsome young lad, fair hair, cheek bones and jawline sculpted from a young life dedicated to training and keeping in top condition.

Though he didn't carry the confidence he had pre-match, possibly borne out of the fact that he had been surplus to requirements to a Fourth Division team skirting dangerously close to the relegation places. Dreams of another professional appearance dashed for another week – shoulders drooped a little in personal defeat, he gently placed his bag on the floor and stepped forward toward Stacey.

'I just wanted to pop in and apologise,' he said. 'I didn't mean to tease you earlier. I didn't mean to fluster you. I was just being silly.

'I'm sorry if I made you feel uncomfortable. Like I am doing now,' he said, watching as Stacey blushed redder and redder.

'I'm sorry,' he said. 'I just wanted to pop in to apologise. And I wondered if I could maybe buy you a cup of tea somewhen? Or coffee? Or whatever? To make it up to you.'

Stacey didn't know what to do. But found herself nodding. Nodding again when he suggested Tuesday afternoon. The coffee shop on the seafront.

'Ok then,' he said, smiling, picking up his bag. 'See you Tuesday. And sorry again.'

And he stepped out into the night, lost behind the sheet glass shop frontage reflecting its contents back in on itself. A wide-eyed Stacey wondering what had just happened. Marcus smiling to himself as he carried on with his cashing up, winking at Stacey when she looked over at him.

Mannequins unmoved, staring wistfully out into the distance, out into the night.

They sat by the window and watched seagulls coasting into the wind above a slate grey sea while Eddie talked for the both of them.

About life back home, working in the Northumberland National Park, how they sometimes wouldn't see another soul all day during the winter. How Saturdays at St. James' Park watching the Toon with 40,000 others seemed more deafening than usual after a week of solitude clearing pathways and cutting back gorse.

He told her that the afternoons could drag after training. He had never been used to so much spare time. He would sometimes meet up here with a couple of the players for a coffee. Sometimes he would walk along the seafront, and up over the cliffs beyond, watching sheep being buffeted by the winds in the fields. He had shared a sheltered spot in the ruins of the old fort built for World War II with a couple of them as a rainy squall swept in off the ocean – Eddie looking down at them as they looked warily up at him.

He would go to the cinema to catch a matinee every week, picking a film at random, sitting with barely a handful of other customers. He liked being caught up in a good story, with good characters, coming out blinking into the day afterwards, letting the emotion and adventure, the music over the end credits merge with the mundane outside – epic struggles dissolving into popcorn stalls and the sound of cars outside, piped elevator music drifting across the foyer.

He talked until Stacey had relaxed enough to join in, then he sat patiently, intently as she told of her family legacy at Inchmery Road. Her job as Nightwatchwoman on Sundays and Mondays. Who Poppy was, and why she wanted his autograph.

He bought them both a second coffee. Stacey had never drunk coffee before, but when Eddie ordered one when they first arrived, she did too. She didn't know why, other than it seemed a sophisticated thing to do. It was quite nice, with a cube of sugar.

'So, who have you got left to find, for Poppy's book?'

'Ruh-Remi Sommer. I uh-always suh-seem to muh-miss him. Jan Lindstrom. Mallick wuh-Wilkes. Fuh-Forsyth and Suh-Stones, nuh-now they are wuh-with the ruh-ruh-reserves I've nuh-not got them.'

'Yeah,' he said. 'I'm not surprised. The foreign guys all live together in a flat just along the seafront here. They always turn up on match days early. Something they are used to doing abroad. They come in for breakfast, then they make a pot of strong coffee. Too strong for me. And they sit about in the canteen, drinking it, thinking about the game ahead.

'Let me see what I can do for you eh? Let's see if we can't help young Poppy out.'

He dropped her off with a warm handshake, said that he had really enjoyed himself. That they should do it again, and he would be in on Saturday to pick up Poppy's book, see if he couldn't get those elusive autographs for her.

I watched him off from the players' entrance, a weak horn from his juddery old car tooting as he drove away. She saw him trundle off, then turned and waved when she spotted me.

'Chu-Charlie?' she said as she reached me, 'Wuh-wuh-was that a duh-date?'

It didn't matter, it had been a massive undertaking for such a shy, introverted girl, no matter what it was, and I listened as she described drinking coffee, sitting right out at the front of the shop, where anyone could have seen.

It wasn't a date. It was the beginning of a friendship, forged over alien hot drinks and a promise kept.

That Saturday, after another afternoon as an unused substitute, Eddie Hamer brought back Poppy's book, complete with all three signatures. Tucked inside were two slips of paper – Forsyth and Stones' autographs picked up during training that week.

'I'm sorry they aren't in the book. But maybe you could stick them in, or something?' he had said hopefully. And she did just that that evening, having asked me if I thought Poppy would mind – carefully cutting strips of Sellotape, placing them gently over the slips, fixing them in. The static between tape and paper had one leap up into the other, joining together slightly askew, but they looked perfectly fine in place.

From then on, they would meet up every Tuesday afternoon, unless the Town were playing away, and they would go to the cinema for a matinee before a coffee on the seafront.

Stacey would be all wide-eyed and full of smiles whenever their afternoon had been confirmed.

'Wuh-we're going to the puh-pictures, chu-Charlie,' she would always say, which I found adorable. An old-time excitement that Evie and I used to love to see in the children heading into Saturday morning screenings in our little old cinema by the sea. Hands held tightly in their parent's, craning necks to see past the curtain, and into the gloomy auditorium, imagining the adventures about to light up across the screen.

It was an everyday occurrence: friends going to the cinema. But for Stacey, as withdrawn as she was, it was a massive event. The little girl with her rosette, face hidden as best she could with bobble hats and hair, face flushed, frozen in fear, she was going to the cinema. With a friend, who just so happened to be a professional footballer. Albeit a struggling one.

With only the one start to his name there was never much chance of him being recognised as such as they queued for popcorn. He was met with familiarity by the ushers, the ticket seller, but only as one of their matinee regulars – who were in the main single old people, who enjoyed any transactional conversations in the queue ahead of Eddie and Stacey with a gusto that suggested it may be their only human interaction of the day.

Stacey came to enjoy this little rag-tag line of matinee misfits – all taking from their trip something far greater than simply the quality of the film they were about to see. Loneliness defeated for a short while. Isolation beaten back, whether a young footballer, or Nightwatchwoman, or an elderly gent with a stooped back who would always spend a minute or two chatting to Anneka the usher, talking about whether the weather was any good for the oyster boats trawling off the coast. Little dots on the horizon from the cinema doors.

'I worked them boats longer than you've been alive, your parents too I'd dare say.'

Anneka would smile and nod, make up small talk and act interested at these facts she had possibly heard a hundred times before. All a part of the job, humouring these matinee loners.

And after a couple of hours being whisked off to far flung lands, Stacey would enjoy watching the animation on their faces as they filed away into the foyer – hopefully insulating them from whatever loneliness awaited them for at least a little while.

It was special, and she enjoyed seeing it, celebrating their little win. After all, it was her win too, that got to be extended over coffee on the seafront. Chatting about the film, anything, watching the sky drain of colour above the sea, their reflections growing stronger in the window as the light failed. The old man's oyster boats trailing gulls back to shore after a long day's fishing.

It was a simple, social friendship with someone her own age. Something she had never had before. And she loved it. Someone wanting to be with her because they liked it, liked her. Meeting up, talking nonsense, but in each other's company. Which is why she was so sad when it had to come to an end.

Hamer got the news in early April. He wouldn't be getting another contract. He had only managed a couple of starts in the FA Cup, and a further three substitute appearances in the league since signing his autograph for Poppy. He would be moving on.

He sat glumly over his coffee that Tuesday afternoon and pondered his Town career of three starts and eight sub appearances. He liked it here, he said. He had wanted to stay. He had wanted to make a name for himself, become a Town favourite. He shrugged his shoulders.

'Buh-but you duh-did muh-make it Eddie. Yuh-you have lived yuh-your dream. Yuh-you are a professional fuh-footballer. Eleven guh-games are eleven muh-more than most can cuh-claim? You duh-did it.' She smiled at him, trying to hide the sadness she felt knowing she was losing her friend.

'You can duh-do it again. Wuh-where will you guh-go next?'

'I've had no offers from anyone else. I don't know. I guess I will have to go home, start writing letters again asking for trials. It's that or take up Remi's offer.'

'Wuh-what offer is thu-that?'

Frenchman Remi Sommer, one of the elusive signatures in Poppy's book had also been told he was being released. He had fared slightly better than Hamer, making nineteen appearances. But had blown hot and cold – one strong performance followed by an anonymous one. He kept getting knocked off the ball before he could get into his flow, and never adapted to the more physical side of Fourth Division football.

'Remi said that an old coach of his back in France has lined him up some trials over in Morocco, for some of the teams over there. Some play in front of huge crowds, win leagues and cups, challenge in the African Champions League. He thinks it is a good opportunity. He asked me to go with him. But I don't know.'

'Duh-don't know wuh-what?' Stacey asked.

'Morocco,' he said. 'It's not exactly what I imagined. It is a long way away. It's hardly Easter Road, Firhill, or St James' Park, like I dreamed when I was younger.'

Just as Stacey and Eddie got into their Tuesday afternoon routine, so did I.

I would find myself hanging around by the main doors, watering the potted yucca plants that stood either side of them that never needed watering, looking across the car park like a nervous parent for the lights of Hamer's old car to appear – smiling at Stacey's silhouette as it waved him away.

It's not like I was ever worried for her. She had been right, Eddie was a lovely lad, and a good friend to her. I just liked seeing her back safely, wandering across the car park as Eddie slipped away.

So, I wasn't sure what to make of it when the car pulled up, lights and engine cutting out, two silhouettes making their way across the car park toward me.

'Chu-Charlie,' she said with a serious look on her face when they reached me. 'Cuh-can I show Eddie suh-something. From the book?'

I ushered them in and watched as Stacey leafed through Mackie's ledger to Bob Andrews' handwriting, the postcards and photographs sent to him by Dennis Lawrence from all over the place.

'Huh-here,' she said and slid the book toward Eddie, 'Ruh-read this.'

As he did, she took out the Antigua shirt, the St Kitts and Nevis jersey and laid them carefully out across the table.

'Duh-Dennis Lawrence didn't suh-see his career going luh-like this. He wuh-wanted to play ruh-right at the tuh-top. But it duh-didn't happen for him, and he would wuh-walk a different path.

And he had an amazing career. Puh-playing abroad. Luh-look at all these adventures. All thu-these things he achieved. All the puh-people he met. Puh-places he saw. Games he played. For guh-great teams with fuh-fans who loved him,' she looked from Eddie studying the shirts, the programmes and photographs, postcards detailing his travels, and looked at me.

'Eddie has the chance to go to Muh-Morocco, chu-Charlie. For a tuh-trial. Cuh-can you imagine?'

I shook my head and said that I couldn't. That it sounded like a wonderful opportunity. I reasoned that the worst that could happen would be that if Eddie didn't like it, he could come home again. No better or worse off than he was before.

Stacey nodded her head in agreement, though I could see in her eyes how much it hurt her to do it.

She didn't want to give up the only friend her age that she had. And a Town player to boot. But she also didn't want her friend to give up on his dream. To lose faith and maybe pass up on a chance of a lifetime.

'You-you have puh-played in the Sco-Scottish Football League for struh-Stranraer. Yuh-you have puh-played in the English Football League fuh-for the Town. Eleven times.

'You huh-have achieved so muh-much already, hasn't he, Chu-Charlie?

'Wuh-once you puh-play for Town, you are always a tuh-Town player. No muh-matter wuh-where you go. Thu-that's what I thu-think,' she told him, pointing to his name in Poppy's book.

'You will always be a puh-part of it. You wuh-will have always puh-played for the tuh-Town.

'Buh-but now it's tuh-time for the nuh-next chu-chapter. To tuh-take a chu-chance. To explore. Ruh-right, chu-Charlie? Juh-just like duh-Dennis did. And luh-look at the wuh-wonderful times he had.'

We stood quietly, watched Eddie read – Stacey's bobble hat pulled back on her head, eyes glassy with tears at this selfless self-sabotage.

I did what all good Nightwatchmen do in situations like that – I made us all some tea.

The final game of the season Eddie watched from the stands, as did Remi and all the other players who had been told they were being let go. Those with contracts down on the pitch played with an intensity unbecoming an end of season Fourth Division fixture that had nothing riding on it. Envious eyes from the stands, and the knowledge that it could so easily have been them sitting it out inspired them on to a two-nil win. Impressing the management for the following campaign started here.

He stopped by the club shop afterwards to say his goodbyes, his 'Hamer – 23' shirt draped over his shoulder. A souvenir of his season as a professional footballer for the Town.

He gave Stacey a big warm bear hug like over-protective brothers gave younger sisters. He told her to take care of herself, that he would be in touch, then he was off; his little car shuddering out the main gates on the long drive north to who knew what; Stacey cutting a subdued figure as she joined me on my last post-match wander of the season about shuttered turnstiles and locked exit gates. The melancholy of a long summer without football exacerbated by the loss of her friend.

But to her great credit, Stacey kept up what had been gained in her friendship with Eddie Hamer, going to the pictures on her own every Tuesday matinee, standing in line with her little band of pensioners. Safety in numbers, even though she didn't know their names. Smiling, nodding, familiar faces. Welcoming, wordless companions every Tuesday, who lost themselves in the stories up on the big screen along with Stacey before waving each other off for the week.

Afterwards she would sip a coffee on the seafront at her and Eddie's usual table, sometimes watching the oyster boats trailing in from the waning light on the horizon, thinking of the old man from the cinema, before wandering up to Inchmery Road to keep me company for a couple of hours.

And one Tuesday in late summer there was a postcard from Morocco waiting for her when she arrived.

It was divided into four pictures, with a line of text across the middle – half in the exotic swirls and flourishes of Arabic, half in English. It read 'Rabat, Gateway to Morocco.'

The four pictures offered a similarly tantalising hint of the country: towering walls of a kasbah sun-kissed a deep sunset red, minarets captured in a sky of brilliant blue, a souk marketplace teeming with life beneath makeshift canopies shading baskets of brilliantly coloured spices, and an image of the old town: a tangle of ancient, narrow cobbled streets, shuttered sandstone buildings, ornate wooden doors.

Stacey looked at it, then me, eyes wide, flipped it over and studied the line of strange-looking stamps, her name above the Inchmery Road address. To the left a bank of tiny handwriting, crammed into every possible inch of space:

'Well, I did it, thanks to you! Arrived two days ago. It is so busy here. All you can hear is honking of car horns from the hotel. They only die down when the call to prayer comes. Huge speakers everywhere broadcast it, a song, or a chant, and everything else falls silent.

It is so hot too! Me and Remi stick to the shade when we go walking. He seems to know a lot about all the old buildings, the old town. It is beautiful, ancient, dusty and crumbling. We just wander through the markets, the streets.

Had our first trial last evening. There were scouts from all the clubs there. I think I did all right. Another one tonight. Will let you know how I do.

Thank you for convincing me to come. No matter what happens, it has been such an adventure.

Thank you. Eddie x'

'Huh-he did it, chu-Charlie! He really did it.' She sat down, flipping the postcard over in her hands from text to pictures, peering into every little nook and cranny of the old town, the souk.

She smiled, looked up at me.

In no small part, it was down to her, and I told her so. She had done a good thing for her friend. Set him on the right road.

'You ruh-really think so, chu-Charlie?' she said, smiling as I nodded back at her.

'Wuh-well imagine thu-that.'

She tucked her postcard inside Mackie's ledger, and in time it would be joined by letters and photographs, newspaper articles, more postcards – sometimes with Arabic on the front, sometimes an even stranger script of alien symbols that made up the Berber language of Eastern Morocco, where Eddie would ultimately find himself.

His letters and postcards to Stacey would detail a nervous wait after the second trial, especially when Remi was picked up by Kawkab Marrakesh in the top-flight. He had to hurriedly pack his bags and jump on a train with a couple of other successful trialists and was gone. And Eddie wouldn't see Remi again for a year.

It had been a nervous wait for Eddie, sitting about in the foyer of his hotel, watching the revolving doors spit people into the cool air-conditioning with a blast of dust and hot air from outside, hoping that one of them might be looking for him.

Finally, one was, the manager of second division Chabab Atlas Khénifra, offering him a one-year deal. The money was bad, he told him with his limited English that had been picked up from six months playing in Ireland for Galway United, and he laughed at his own honesty, but, he said, he would play. He would be leaving in an hour for Khénifra. He would come by the hotel in his car. If he wanted the contract, he should be outside waiting.

And that is what Eddie Hamer found himself doing, blinking into the sunlight, not knowing where Khénifra was, or what the Moroccan Second Division looked like.

He and Remi had only ever talked about the big clubs from Casablanca and Rabat. Huge derby days and championships, playing in the African Champions League. There had been no mention of the Second Division, and sleepy towns far from anywhere else.

A four-hour drive into the remote interior of Morocco, mile after mile of flat road through what looked like challenging farmland, grazing cattle, great stretches of inhospitable, arid scrub that slowly gave way to spiky foothills of rock and cliff did nothing to ease his sense of foreboding.

No mention that, yet again, he had found himself traveling way out to the very edge of the professional footballing world.

He had felt the same foreboding on the long, interminable drive out west to Stranraer that first time. And down to the Town across vast flatlands and stretches of fields as far as the eye could see.

Both had turned out to be great experiences. And as he sat in the back of the Khénifra manager's old car, bouncing over pothole after pothole through the dust and heat, he thought of the ledger Stacey had shown him, of Dennis Lawrence's journey, and he reconciled himself to keep an open mind. For the time being. That this would be his lot, and it was up to him to make the most of it.

It turned out to be a lot that he would love.

And would have missed out on, had young Stacey not shown him Mackie's ledger and Dennis Lawrence's adventures, had not encouraged him to take the chance. And he would be forever grateful, he would say in his letters.

Khénifra was a small town nestled at the foot of the great Atlas Mountains. Beyond them, the Sahara.

Eddie bought a little camera in the local souk and supplemented his descriptions of life in Khénifra in his letters with handfuls of Polaroid sized black and white photographs. Pretty squares lined by palm trees and Atlas cedars; old men in kaftans drinking coffee, watching the world go by. Small, lush courtyard gardens: an oasis in the sun-blanched landscape of dusty riads and buildings that rose up seamlessly out of the arid reds and oranges of the land beneath them. Seeming as ancient, timeless as the earth itself.

He sent pictures from up in the hazy mountains in the national park. Swathes of great cedars, grand shimmering lakes, thrilling white water rapids coursing between bouldered banks – the Oum Er-Rbia River on its vast, winding journey all the way to the coast far, far away.

He sent photographs of endless dunes snaking on the winds deep into the continent of Africa. Shadowy slopes of the Sahara Desert, sun-blanched skies as far as the eye could see.

He sent a newspaper cutting, a picture of him holding up a football shirt, smiling on an arid pitch in a modest looking stadium lined with low banks of terracing. A sea of beautiful, intoxicating Arabic text surrounding the photograph. Its meaning unknown, but enchanting.

'I hope it says that they are happy to have me. I guess we will find out soon enough!'

Chabab Atlas Khénifra played at the Stade Municipal de Khénifra, a small, compact little ground that could hold five thousand, though rarely did. Open terracing lined three sides – a swathe of exposed, green seats ran down the fourth.

'They don't need covering. It never rains. Though some shade from the sun would be nice. It can be brutal in the afternoon.'

The coach had been as good as his word, Eddie started nearly every game, mainly playing at right back. His Galway inspired pidgin English, complete with the odd Irish lilt to his vowels was the only language he understood. The rest of the team only knowing Arabic, Berber, and a bit of French.

"Up, Up, Up, energy attack attack," he shouts, then, "back, back, back energy defence." I do as I'm told. He seems happy enough. Most of the games are played in the evening, when it is still really hot, but it is OK. When we play in the afternoon, he puts me in the centre of midfield. I wouldn't last ten minutes at right back in that heat. It makes it hard to breath. He just tells me to hold the ball, pass, control, slow. It is about all I can do in that heat.'

Indecipherable newspaper articles and match reports arrived every couple of weeks on the "Inchmery Road – Khénifra hotline" as he called his letters.

Pictures of the team in action, league tables in Arabic that he would mark with an asterisk to show where Khénifra were – almost always mid-table.

He would write about long away trips by coach to play the wonderfully sounding Jeunesse Massina, Ittihad Khemisset, Chabab Ben Guerir, Racing Casablanca.

Hour after hour across an alien landscape of scorched, parched earth, rising mountains, villages and towns huddled beneath kasbahs and minarets, or behind the gates and fortified walls of a ksour, blinking and wincing as the shimmering ocean came into view.

He wrote of games played beneath darkening skies, the rhythmic beating of Darbuka drums in the stands casting an intoxicating, relentless spell over the play. Floodlights above, choked by swarms of bugs and mosquitos. Goals celebrated as if their lives depended on it, hands and eyes raised to the skies. Just like home.

In Khénifra, as winter drew on, the days would be hot, the nights plummeting, and Eddie would describe playing beneath the floodlights, black silhouettes of the mountains beyond, the drums forever accompanying play. Snow up on the high passes of the national park – a strange sight to be standing next to snow covered trees, drifts, looking out at the desert in the distance.

One day a parcel arrived for Stacey, littered with a line of strange stamps. It sat on the desk for a couple of days before her next shift, this bundle of brown paper taped together and fastened with string.

Inside were a couple of his football shirts – a red and white striped one both Stacey and I had seen before in newspaper clippings, and a blue shirt – both sporting the Chabab Atlas badge: red and white stripes beneath a slanting line of Arabic. An Atlas tree a brilliant green. 'C.A.K 1943' and a football above the line of text.

On the back of both shirts the number 2. Above the number on the red and white home shirt a line of Arabic:

يدديي هامير

'Believe it or not, but that is my name in Arabic! It is so beautiful. So much so that I doubt it could really say Eddie Hamer! We wear shirts with our names in Arabic for league matches, but they are printed in the local Berber language when we play in a regional cup competition. I love the look of Arabic, but the Berber language is just so wonderful. It is more than 2,500 years old. Imagine that!'

Stacey turned the blue shirt over to reveal his name in this little known, ancient language:

ⵣ/\Σⴳ ⵯoⵛⴳⵔ

'There is a little coffee shop just off the main square here in Khénifra, where an old man works. He is one of the few people who can speak English here, and he is also an Atlas fan! We sit and drink coffee like you and I used to, and he writes things in Berber to show me. I'm picking up what each little symbol means, though it is really hard. I have a notebook that I write them in and practice. It is something to do, and it makes me feel closer to the place, learning little pieces of their language that has been around for more than two and a half thousand years!

Stacey put down the letter, moved the shirts to one side, and rummaged through the parcel wrapping until she found a slip of parchment paper, thick and grainy to the touch, like it had been around as long as the language written on it in slow deliberate strokes:

ⵜⵎⵓⵍⵕ ⵢⵓⴱ ⵙⵜⵓⵛⴱⵙ ⵍⵓⵙⵙⵎ

'It says "Thank you, Stacey Marsh." I wouldn't be here if it wasn't for you. If you hadn't shown me all of Dennis's adventures in your book. I would never have come if you hadn't convinced me to try it.

It has been an amazing experience. The people are friendly. The football is a really good standard, and I am playing. I couldn't ask for much more.

I wanted you to have these shirts, for your collection in your office. To say thank you, Stacey. For everything you have done for me. I can never thank you enough.'

We sat quietly and pored over the shirts, Eddie's little note in Berber, at the couple of newspaper clippings and photographs, one of which was an elderly man in a Kaftan, sitting smiling at a table in his little coffee shop – Mahmoud. A beautiful ornate rug hanging on the wall behind him.

'It's fuh-funny, how life wuh-works, don't you think,' she said after a time.

'If Bob Andrews duh-didn't go to the cinema, your cinema, he wuh-would have never met you. He would have nuh-never given you the nuh-Nightwatchman job. And then you would have never muh-met me. You would have never seen Poppy and helped her out. Meaning you wuh-would have never asked me to fetch her autographs for her buh-book. And if you hadn't done that, then I wuh-would have never become friends with Eddie. And I guh-guess he wouldn't have been persuaded to guh-go to Morocco.

'I wuh-wonder where we all might be if you hadn't buh-befriended Bob. If he huh-hadn't got the nuh-nightwatchman job from Stanley Puh-Peters. I wonder what we might be doing instead?'

'I don't think it could be any better than this, where we are right now, don't yuh-you think, chu-Charlie?'

I couldn't disagree.

It is funny how things work out. How one little thing can lead to so many more. Little connections in life. Unexpected. Precious. If only you go with them when they come along.

Stacey carefully fastened Eddie's photographs into Mackie's ledger with little sticky corners, carefully sliding behind them their envelopes, letters and newspaper clippings stored within.

His shirts neatly folded and placed in the drawer with those of Dennis. The story of young Eddie preserved. His time at Inchmery Road chronicled, and his subsequent adventures in Morocco with another ex-Town player. There for anyone that would read it.

Season done, a mid-table finish secured, and a new two-year contract signed, Eddie and Remi set off on a two-week holiday across Morocco. Despite his team being relegated, Remi had played well, and was looking forward to the second year of his deal, where he would come up against Eddie.

Remi showed Eddie round Marrakesh, while Eddie took Remi up into the Atlas Mountains, then beyond to the edge of the Sahara. After that they took buses up the coast from Agadir to Casablanca, Rabat, Fes and Tangier, exploring Morocco's grand cities before flying home for a few weeks before pre-season.

Eddie appeared out of the blue one afternoon at Inchmery Road – a still, lazy, hushed summer's day as far from the next season as it was from the last. Breathless, motionless, the distant drone of a car, faint echoes of children playing in the streets somewhere about. And a scruffy looking traveller, dusty duffel bag slung over one shoulder, looking up wistfully at the West Stand.

Both Stacey and I had been in early, helping Marcus out with lunch club, setting up cones and the like for a game of football in the car park afterwards.

He hugged young Stacey, gave me a warm handshake, plopped a couple of cheap fezzes he had picked up from the airport on our heads, which had Stacey giggling, and we stood and watched the children play while he told us of his travels. How he was going home for a few weeks, before heading back for pre-season.

'I just wanted to come by and say hello,' he said. 'I've missed this place. I've missed you. It was such a happy year for me. Among good people. And if I hadn't come here, met you, then I would never have made it to Khénifra. I owe you so much.'

'And I've been thinking, Stacey. Why don't you come over, to Morocco, for a week or so? I'd love to show you the mountains, the souks, everything? You could catch a game, as my guest. I could sort it all out for you. My way of saying thank you properly. Pictures and postcards are one thing but seeing it with your own eyes is another thing completely. A little adventure together. Have a think.'

Stacey had stared wide-eyed up at me as Eddie had talked, a beaming grin. And as we watched him off for the train station and home, she had promised to think about it. Very hard.

'Cuh-could you imagine, chuh-Charlie – me in muh-Morocco?'

A few years earlier I couldn't have imagined it, not for one bit: the Stacey selling programmes at the Victoria Road End. Who would barely say a word to anyone, even me.

That Stacey, who could barely countenance leaving her room. For that Stacey, Morocco was just a place in an atlas.

But the Nightwatchwoman Stacey, the Stacey who had taken to helping Marcus out with lunch club and the Junior Town activities in the holidays, who was so good with all the kids, who was so kind and patient, playing and laughing with them, helping them with their drawings, holding their hands around stadium tours, nudging them forward to get player autographs after open day training. The Stacey who kept up her Tuesday matinee ritual, all by herself. That Stacey I could believe stepping out into the brilliant sunshine and hubbub of Marrakesh or Casablanca. Just as soon as she believed it herself.

It might take a little time for her to get to that point. To summon up the courage. But there is no rush. And I think she will get there. In her own time. And when she does, I will be so proud of her. Because bravery appears in many guises. And for Stacey to be living the life she is, doing all the things that she does, giving all that she gives, despite her sometimes-crippling self-doubt and shyness, that is bravery defined.

Things like her "Town Preservation Club."

Chapter Thirteen

I am getting old. I am starting to feel it. My bones ache terribly in the sharp cold of winter. They ache when the weather is on the turn. When it is going to rain. I am nearly seventy-three after all.

Any other job and I would have stamped my final timecard some years ago.

But the Nightwatchman tends to only give up their post when they absolutely have to.

So desperate have my predecessors been to stay in post, they have only relinquished the job they loved when it was painfully obvious that they had no other choice. When they were on the verge of becoming a burden rather than an asset.

It is a privilege to be the custodian of our little club, to have it all to oneself, night after night.

It would be the ultimate prize for any lover of the Town, to have the time to explore every single inch, to learn and take on the histories and traditions of more than a century of devotion, the stories in Gerald Mackie's ledger with all its characters and ghosts.

To be the one tasked with preserving them, tending to Peter Wright's bicycle. To be on the lookout for others, like young Poppy Hudson. Nurturing, remembering tales of sadness and tragedy, warmth and humour. To make sense of what this little football team means to the extraordinary people that follow it – a sea of nameless faces, every other Saturday. One generation fading away on the terraces behind the next, like layer upon layer of faint shadows on tracing paper. To be the custodian of this humble little institution that gave them meaning, belief, hope – it is an honour. And who would want to give that up?

Who would want to lose their voice on the pages of Mackie's ledger? To pass up the opportunity to quietly leaf through its brittle and crinkling pages, precious stories of love and loss, friendship, tragedy, mystery and grand humour. The drawers of the Nightwatchman's office stuffed with photographs and old programmes, newspaper cuttings, letters, books and football shirts – a chaotic encyclopaedia of time and place, people, their hopes and dreams.

If that has been your life for so long, how do you simply decide to up and walk away from such a task? To accept that you too are about to become just another memory, though in fine company.

In truth Nightwatchmen never truly leave, they just fade away. They reduce their hours, letting the job slip between their fingers as slowly as they can manage.

And then, when they are finally done, they still find themselves up at Inchmery Road, keeping the new Nightwatchman company every now and then, for a few hours into the night, for old times' sake.

It is not something that you can just stop. Because it isn't really a job at all. It is more a vocation, a calling. And leaving it is painful. I am starting to feel that now – the thought of it.

But it is time for me to start letting go. I will speak with the club, with Stacey, see about reducing my days down to three, and Stacey's up to four. She is more than ready, and the extra day's work will help her save up for Morocco. It is time.

It is easier when you know that who you will be handing over to has the job under their skin already. Has taken on the stories, the little rituals of remembrance and preservation. Sees what you see. Feels what you feel. Reveres this little club just as you do. And Stacey does. Always has.

And with it, she has found her voice in Mackie's ledger.

Beautiful, flowing, lyrical writing, imbued with a freedom and energy, liberated as it is from her stammer. Telling the tale of Eddie Hamer, and a man called Ray Carver, and the rest of the Town Preservation Club – she has become a fully-fledged Nightwatchwoman.

She had been inspired to bring up the idea of the preservation club by her little queue of matinee pensioners on a Tuesday afternoon at the cinema.

She would stand in line and watch the animation, the anticipation on their faces, waiting to slip behind the curtain, off to who-knew-where this week.

She watched the adventure, the romance, the far-flung places linger in the sparkle in their eyes as they made their way back across the cinema foyer as the credits rolled, looking for Anneka the kindly usher to chat to, to prolong the experience, to fend off the loneliness waiting for them outside.

And if she wasn't free, if she was inside readying the screens for the early evening shows, the swish of the automatic doors beckoned, and the sparkle in their eyes began to fade as they slowly made their way out into the cold light of day. Until next time.

And then she had an idea.

Stacey spent part of her shifts tending to some of the little maintenance jobs that always seemed to be pushed back by bigger, more urgent jobs that kept the groundsman and his apprentice more than rushed off their feet.

Treating the benches on the lower tier of the West Stand, protecting them from the weather had been as relaxing as it had been rewarding to her. Feeling like she was contributing to the preservation of our little ground, helping with its upkeep, gave her a pride and satisfaction akin to a good Town win on a Saturday. It was an act of devotion to the institution that was a major part of her life, had been a major part of her family for more than a century.

Preserving the tradition of a Marsh programme seller outside the main gates on match days, being a Nightwatchwoman of Inchmery Road and all that entailed, and now having the opportunity to physically tend to the girders and terraces, the steps and seats, the turnstile shutters and a million other little tasks thrilled her beyond words – it filled her with a sense of pride and purpose, just as tending to Mackie's ledger and Poppy's autograph books did. And she thought it might others too. Those that might need it.

'It could be cuh-called the tuh-Town Preservation Club. Suh-something like that,' she said as we sat next to one another in General Manager Sarah's office.

'We could advertise in the puh-programme or something. And if people who are lonely, or juh-just wanted to take puh-part came along, they could paint, or sweep, or whatever they cuh-could do, and they wuh-wouldn't be so lonely. They muh-might make friends, or something.

'We could give them buh-biscuits and tea. And they cuh-could feel like they were a puh-part of something. And some of the jobs that need doing could get done as wuh-well?'

It was a good idea, and Sarah liked it. And between the two of them they settled on a plan of action. The Town would open their doors to any willing volunteers on Wednesday and Thursday afternoons, and if that proved successful, they would think about more.

Sarah arranged for an article to go in the local paper, as well as in the programme, and the local radio station ran a piece every day for a week leading up to its start.

Stacey had been mortified at the thought of being interviewed for any of them and was happy for Sarah to be the public face of it, the one who coerced a couple of players to pose with her holding paintbrushes and brooms for the programme and the paper. Sarah even had little flyers printed up, and Stacey dropped some off at the coffee shop on the seafront, and the cinema, in the hope that some of her matinee comrades might see. She called in her favour with Tom and Sean, the two drunk pitch invaders, who volunteered to drive the club minibus to pick up those who were interested but couldn't easily get up to Inchmery Road.

And with that the Town Preservation Club began.

It was a ragtag band of people, usually around fifteen or so. Ranging from the very elderly, who would shuffle along with a broom across the Inchmery Road End, or slowly dust and oil the seats in the upper tiers, to young unemployed men and women who wanted to volunteer to show their worth. They would replace advertising hoardings, take up rotten boards and change them out for new ones, patch holes in the corrugated roofs of the stands, mix up concrete and level out crumbling walkways, and make sure all the old-timers were OK, stocked up with tea and biscuits.

And everyone in between would take up brushes and pots of paint, sprucing up turnstile shutters, doors, seats and benches. Anything that needed doing.

Breaks would be often, and people would mingle and chat. Old-timers telling the youngsters stories of games long gone, capers behind the goals with absent friends. Stacey's stooped oyster boat veteran of the cinema even came along and would paint crush barriers and chat to anyone that would listen. He would tell anyone, more than once, how he used to work the boats, back when there was a full fleet that put out to sea.

'We used to tow the gulls back to shore, who would sweep and shriek, looking for easy pickings. When we unloaded the crates, they would dive down and grab an oyster shell, scarper before we could swipe at them with our brooms.

'Some brought their plunder up here to Inchmery Road and used the roofs of the stands as a safe place to drop and prise open the oysters. They would drop them, pick them back up again, rise-up and drop them again. Over and over until they broke them open, and they had their dinner.

'When a ball clattered up onto the roof during a game, it would sometimes bounce and rattle the corrugated sheets up there and propel old shells back over the edge and down onto the top of the away team's dugout. They would look about them confused, holding up these old shells, stare up into the sky, and we would cackle back here behind the goal as they sat back down none the wiser.'

Stacey loved the story and wrote it down in Mackie's ledger.

She would watch a couple of old ladies sat on the benches having a chat. Over time they had gravitated towards each other, and would sweep, paint, whatever, as a little team. Cups of tea and biscuits on the benches accompanied by a wicked cackle of a laugh from one of them. And when the day was done, they would carefully place their brooms and paint pots on the pile by the players' tunnel, and, leaning on one another, arm in arm, they would make their way out to wait for Tom and Sean with the minibus to take them home.

It was a sight to see, these little pockets of endeavour about the place. Concentrating faces lost in the task they had found for themselves, broad smiles as Stacey brought round a tray of tea. Absent moments looking about Inchmery Road, chatting to neighbours, lending a hand to someone that needed it. Watching the groundsman and his apprentice, up and back with their mowers across the pitch.

In time, little jobs got done. Though it was just a by-product of a greater good: purpose, meaning, something to look forward to, someone to talk to. And it was all Stacey's doing, though no one but me and Sarah knew it. That suited Stacey down to the ground.

Lonely people being a little less so, withdrawn people a little less distant, the lost, a little closer to finding whatever they needed to find, it was what Inchmery Road had always done for the community. And Stacey had found another way for the Town, our little ground, to do it again.

She had seen, like all good Nightwatchmen do, what many people do not – the quiet people. Those that aren't remembered when the fortunes of the Town are recorded in a season's statistics.

The little, anonymous acts of humanity, friendship, belonging on the terraces and in the stands, in the pub, the queue for a programme, along bustling pavements. Acts that keep little clubs like ours vital and pertinent. The be all and end all, to a precious few, even if our scores rarely make it above the fold of the results page in the Sunday paper. A tiny entry in a sea of tiny entries – each club with their own sets of mythologies and tales. Maybe even their own version of Mackie's ledger.

Stacey had seen them, the lost, the lonely. And she tried to fix them, as best she could.

People like Ray Carver.

What a thing to do.

Ray Carver (only ever Raymond when he was being scolded by his late wife) joined the preservation club a month or two after it started. A large man with rosy cheeks, a bald head almost always obscured by a tweed flat cap, he did what he could on painful joints.

He would struggle on the steps up into the upper tiers unless assisted by one of the young lads and lasses, but he was a dab hand at fixing broken seats. Give him a bucket of spare parts and a wrench and he could make what seemed beyond repair not quite good as new, but, at the very least good for a few more seasons.

He had large hands and pudgy fingers that you thought would be a hindrance to intricate, dextrous endeavours, but you would see him slowly work his way along the rows of the upper tiers. And with his array of spare parts, there wasn't a sorry state that he couldn't resurrect, somehow.

He would often find himself isolated, away up among the seats, lost in his work, so as Stacey would make a special trip up to him with a mug of tea and a few biscuits.

'Uh-are you all right up huh-here all buh-by yourself, ruh-Ray?' she would ask, and he would always smile, nod. He could hear all the bustle below he would always say. And that kept him company. Plus, the girl painting the girders would often stop by and say hello. And a couple of starlings liked to skitter across the seatbacks after him, pouncing down on biscuit crumbs he scattered for them.

Ray had lost his wife a year earlier. And the silence in the house had been deafening. She had always had some plan or idea up her sleeve. Moving things about, wanting shelves put up, or taken down. Fairy lights along the hall so as it looked pretty at night. And when the ideas stopped, when she had gone, the silence was overwhelming. A great, never-ending void. Time dragging. It was unbearable. Every quiet moment highlighting all that had been lost, his beautiful Penny.

One fairy light bulb after another blowing, the string thinning out, the hall growing darker once more.

There for the grace of God go I.

The club had been a godsend. He was a little shy, and still a little shell-shocked, so working up on the seats had suited him. He could see and hear people about him, have little conversations in passing. The noise of others, watching them come and go across the terraces, wandering up and out onto the benches of the East Stand was a real tonic, without being too much too soon.

It would happen, he would say and smile to Stacey, all in good time.

As the Preservation Club days wound down, and tools were collected up to be stowed away, Ray would linger – moving pots of paint so as they were all stacked neatly together, taking up, then placing back a line of brooms, gently picking up, then putting back hammers, wrenches, all manner of bits used around the place.

He would sit on the benches of the West Stand and watch the people come and go, wave as they headed out to the minibus, others drifting out onto Inchmery Road.

Ray lived nearby, he liked to walk.

He would linger as the day wound down, looking out across the pitch, toward the goal in front of the Inchmery Road terrace.

Stacey would leave him be, for as long as she could. Slowly collecting empty mugs, washing them up, stacking them back in the canteen kitchen. Then she would sit next to him, watching the groundsman and his apprentice put everything away in their storeroom.

And as they said good evening, headed out, Ray would smile weakly, stand, and follow them away.

'Goodbye, Stacey. See you next time.'

'Suh-see you nuh-next time, Ray.'

Some days when the heavens would open and many of the meaningful tasks had to be postponed. Brooms would be taken up, and after a little bit of sweeping along concourses, the day would settle down into tea-drinking and biscuit-eating across the benches by the Nightwatchman's door.

A few would gather round a crossword puzzle in the paper, while others sat and chatted. Others still would take the time to sit quietly and look out at Inchmery Road beneath looming swathes of black cloud, that were so low that they seemed to have become snagged on the dissolving floodlights. Rain drumming on the West

Stand roof, falling in sheets down onto the grit track, pitchside, like you were inside a waterfall. And if you got too close to the pitch, a faint spray from the deluge would drift and tickle your face.

Most would choose to stay, even though there wasn't much restoration to be done. The company, the fresh air, the feeling of being somewhere that mattered would not be easily relinquished. Especially not for a little rain.

Ray would stay too, sitting quietly, looking out across the pitch, lost in his thoughts, sipping slowly at his tea. And one day, Stacey sat down next to him, offered him the biscuit tin, smiled, before looking out at the driving rain, the thickening shadows about the East Stand opposite.

'Huh-how are you, Ruh-Ray? Are yuh-you all right over huh-here on your own?'

He smiled back, nodded.

'I'm fine, love. Just letting my mind wander, out there,' he said, looking at the net in the Inchmery Road goal, sagging beneath the deluge.

Stacey took up a biscuit from the tin.

'Wuh-what do you suh-see?'

He shrugged his shoulders.

'I don't know. What could have been. Another life. I don't know. It's silly.'

Stacey shook her head.

'I duh-doubt it, ruh-Ray.'

He looked down at her, bobble hat pushed back to her hairline, taking a bite of her biscuit.

'No, maybe not. Just one of those moments that get away from you,' he sighed.

'I was thinking about when I was offered a trial for the Town. Back when I was a young man. I was thinking what may have happened if things had gone differently. The life me and Penny might have had instead. Maybe a life where she might still be here with me.'

He took another sip of tea, watched the rain falling from the roof above.

'When we were courting, I would always go on about how I would be a professional footballer one day. And that we would travel, to all different places. Have a nice car, expensive holidays in the summer. Want for nothing.

'I was playing for the works' team. I worked up at the refinery just up the way, and we had a decent little team. I was a goalkeeper, and we won the County League, two seasons running, where we would play the Town's third team, or 'A' team as they were known.

'We used to beat them, home and away, and it was how one of the club's scouts spotted me. He liked what he saw, and the club offered me a trial.

'I was to play in a Combination League match for the reserves a week on Tuesday, right here,' he said, pointing out at the pitch.

'I still have the letter, with the club's badge embossed at the top. Penny and I kept reading it, over and over. We were married by then, and she was so excited for me. So were the works' team. ENI Sports we were called, and they arranged for a stand-in keeper to take my place the Saturday before my trial, to keep me fresh.

'I couldn't stop thinking about what it would feel like, to be stood out there in the goal, looking up at the stands, the terraces about me. I had always stood behind the Inchmery Road goal as a boy, dreaming of one day being out there. And here I was, it was about to happen. My big chance.

'Anyway, I went along to watch the lads that Saturday. To cheer them on. But when I got there the gaffer was in a state. The replacement hadn't arrived, and the reserves had already left for their away game. The club's only other keeper was halfway up the county.

'I said I'd play. How could I leave them in the lurch like that? I didn't think that it would have been right. So, I got changed.

'We were defending a corner, and I knew I was in trouble right away. I had been trying to take it easy, play safe, so as I wouldn't get hurt before Tuesday. And where I would have normally come out to claim the cross, I hesitated. Then when I went up for it, half a second too late – that is all – their centre forward, and our centre back clattered into me.

'I fell awkwardly, and then they landed on top of me. Busted my collar bone in two places. And that was me done. There was no way I could play on the Tuesday. And, it turned out, I wouldn't play again all season. And never again in goal.

'The Town were very good about it when I telephoned them to say what had happened. The reserve team manager said they would look at me again when I was back fit. But I was never the same player again.

'My collar bone never healed properly. I couldn't extend my arm up above my head fully. It only goes a little way to this day,' he tried, raising his arm up flush with his shoulder.

'That's as good as it gets,' he said and shrugged.

'My goalkeeping days were over, though I played on for a few years with ENI reserves as a defender in the County League third division. But it wasn't quite the same. I enjoyed it, but not as much as before, not being able to express myself properly like I once had, and my collar bone would ache terribly in the cold.

'Better forwards would have the edge on me when jumping for the ball, because I couldn't use my arm for momentum. Even so, we did all right, and in my final season before packing it in, we earned ourselves a runner's up medal in the league. And then, after that, I would come on up to Inchmery Road and stand behind the goal and watch the Town, like I did as a boy. And I would wonder at what might have been.

'I put on a brave face for Penny. Always. But I was devastated inside. My dreams dashed. I had promised her a life I could no longer provide. I don't know, maybe I never could. Maybe the trial wouldn't have led to anything. But it was the not knowing for sure, either way, that weighed heavily on me.

'Penny used to read the travel supplement in the Sunday paper. She would love to look at the illustrated adverts for the cruise liners. A vast ship sailing into a sunset, lined with colourful drawings of palm trees and pyramids, the Acropolis in Athens, those grand heads on Easter Island, volcanoes, cathedrals and castles, all sorts, and beneath it all a list of exotic, far away destinations. There would also often be an article about a cruise, with photographs of some of the places that they went, a paragraph or two about the sights and sounds.

'I remember one about the Queen Mary, and a transatlantic cruise to New York City. There was a photograph of the skyline all lit up at night. Vast Manhattan skyscrapers towering up, twinkling on the water of the Hudson River. Penny loved it. She kept the magazine down the side of her armchair and would often bring it out to look at it. Lose herself for a time in the neon of Times Square, the Empire State Building, the bright lights of Broadway.

'On the bus to the refinery for a late shift, it turns a corner to reveal the refinery in the distance. Flare stacks, vast chimneys and towers, huge storage tanks, great spiderwebs of fractionating columns hugging platforms of scaffolding. All lit up at night. From afar it reminded me of Penny's magazine, her pictures of New York.

'If you squinted it would all blur a little, turn into something it wasn't. The vast skyscrapers of New York City. The twinkling lights of Manhattan. And I would scrunch my eyes up and dream, that one day we would get there. On a footballer's salary.

'After the injury it became a cruel twist, this mirage of a place we could never hope to reach on my wage as a maintenance man. I would fix toilets, light fixtures, fences, anything that needed doing. And as the flare stacks lit up with a roar, great plumes of flame lighting up the sky, it would burn away my little daydream back into the grand tangle of pipes and chimneys, the dull, never-ending thrum of industry. Like an underwhelming earthquake that never stopped, rumbling on and on.

'I had wanted so badly to get her on that boat, so she didn't need her magazine any more. But those trips were so expensive. It never happened. I regret it terribly,' he smiled weakly, looked down at Stacey.

'But do you know what, Penny never did: regret it. She never looked at the world and saw what we didn't have, what we'd never see. She only ever saw what we did have, me and her. What we did see. She was something else,' he said and shook his head.

'Why she settled for me I will never know. But I am so glad that she did.

'Instead of thinking about the trial that never was, she only cared about my two league winners' medals, my runners up one for the reserves. She insisted on them being on the mantlepiece above the fire, and she would polish and dust them every week. She would tell me how proud she was of me, for doing what I had done.

' "There's not too many that have such a pretty haul," she would tell me. And on days where I was feeling particularly down on myself, she would bring out this old shoebox from behind her chair.

'She used to come to watch me play, and unbeknownst to me, she had kept many of the programmes, tucked them in her old shoebox.

'She would bring them out, and leaf through them. Remembering crowds close to a thousand for some games. Great saves that I had made, remembering the roar of appreciation all about her, and how she had felt so proud, that it was her Raymond that had made them that way.

'Bless her heart. She could only ever see the good. In me. In anything. She was happy, with me, with our life. We would cherish the odd week away on the Isle of Netton, exploring it, devouring it like it was one of her far-flung places.

'She was the kind of girl who loved where she was, not where she wasn't.

'And she helped me find my way. And the look on her face when we finally saved up to go on a cruise, albeit just a short one across to the Mediterranean, you would have thought she were on the Queen Mary itself, gliding past the Statue of Liberty. She was so thrilled.

'In time I could even come up here to watch a match, stand behind the goal, and not beat myself up about what might have been. But I would still find myself wondering. Wondering what it would have been like to stand out there in between the sticks with the Inchmery Road terrace at my back. Looking up at the East and West Stands. Stood right where my goalkeeping heroes as a young lad had stood. I couldn't help but think what a beautiful thing that would have been.

'And now, here I am,' he said and looked out into the rain. 'An old man. And still, I sit here and wonder what it would be like, to stand there. Though now I know that whatever life that trial may have brought, I wouldn't swap it for the life me and Penny had. Not for all the money in the world, and all the cruises it would have bought.

'She was right. She was always right. And I often find myself sifting through her old shoebox, flicking through programmes of old games. And I see her, clear as day in my mind. My Penny stood in the crowd on the touchline. Smiling that wonderful smile of hers at me. Waving.

'I keep the box on her armchair, next to that old magazine tucked down the arm. It helps me to feel a little closer to her. For a short while. I can lose myself in it, completely.'

He looked down at Stacey, then hurriedly scrabbled about his pocket for his handkerchief when he saw tears rolling down her face.

'Oh, love, I'm sorry. I didn't mean to make you cry,' he said and handed it to her. 'What a silly old fool I am. You shouldn't have to sit here and listen to me babble on. I'm sorry, love.'

Stacey dabbed at her eyes.

'Suh-sorry, Ray,' she said, offered the handkerchief back.

'You keep it,' he said and smiled.

They sat quietly for a time, the rain drumming on the West Stand roof, then she gave Ray a hug, kissed him softly on the cheek, and stood up. She took up the biscuit tin, put her hand on his shoulder, before turning away for the Nightwatchman's door.

The following week had brought an end to the rain, and the bustle of the Preservation Club began in earnest once more. Conversations and laughter echoing across the terracing. Old-timers with new-found friends painting as the sun broke out above. Gulls wheeling aimlessly across blue skies.

From the upper tier of the West Stand, the clunking of the metal bucket of spare parts against Ray's leg as he carried it from one seat in need of repair to the next. This most unorthodox of social clubs in full swing.

A little after three, Stacey climbed the steps to find Ray ensconced in a flip up seat that had lost its flip.

'Ruh-Ray. Have you got a muh-minute? Thu-there's someone I'd like you to muh-meet.'

He got up awkwardly and slowly, then took Stacey's arm to help himself tackle the stairs down onto the concourse by the Nightwatchman's door.

Standing there, decked out in his club tracksuit, was the Town's goalkeeper, Simon Parks.

Ray was taken aback.

'What – what's going on here?'

'Stacey here says you'd like a little tour of my office,' he said nodding out at the pitch. 'That you were a mean keeper in your day.' He smelled of after shave, his hair still wet from a post training shower. A warm smile that suggested he was rarely called upon, as a jobbing Fourth Division keeper, to make someone's day.

He held out his arm for Ray to take, and he led them down between the rows of benches to a small gate that opened out by the players' tunnel. Up a slight incline and out onto the pitch, the turf soft but manageable beneath their feet, too early in the season for muddy patches to have made it slick and treacherous underfoot, that would dry and turn to dustbowls for the last matches in May.

They walked out to the Inchmery Road goal, chatting as they went, before standing beneath the crossbar, Ray using his good arm to reach up to it, nodding as Simon said something – pointing to the stanchions.

They walked out to the penalty spot, and Ray followed Simon's gaze up at the floodlights, watched him mimic jumping up for the ball – claiming an imaginary cross into the box.

They wandered the white paint lines of the penalty box, looking and waving at a few old-timers leant against a crush barrier, before Simon stood patiently and watched Ray as he wandered back toward the goal, looking out at Inchmery Road before him.

He closed his eyes, raised his head to the skies, craned his neck a little, as if listening to the roar of a crowd in his mind's eye.

He turned and looked at the terracing behind him, up at the stands, before making his way back to Simon. Head down, concentrating on where he placed his feet, they made their way back to the touchline, and Ray shook Simon's hand warmly by the gate that led back into the benches of the West Stand.

A laugh, a wave, then Simon Parks turned, slipped away down the players' tunnel, and was gone.

Ray watched him go, shook his head, then gingerly stepped down to where Stacey was waiting for him.

'Thank you,' he said quietly, his voice faltering. 'You arranged all that? For me?'

She smiled, shrugged.

And as tears began welling in his eyes, he bent down and hugged her, with a bear hug that almost completely swallowed Stacey up.

Hug done she motioned for him to sit.

'I thu-think you wuh-will need a cup of tea after that,' she said, put her hand on Ray's shoulder, and smiled.

It was a beautiful little moment to witness, which I did from the door to the Nightwatchman's office, before turning, making my way down our little corridor, past Gerald Mackie, Peter Wright, David Smith, Thomas Coneelly, Dennis Lawrence, and the rest.

Stacey had done it all. She had waited for Simon Parks one afternoon after the team had trained out on Inchmery Road. Slowly and carefully, she had explained about Ray, and if he would take him out onto the pitch.

For Stacey, it was enormous. To expose herself like that. To keep on going even when her stammer started to get the better of her. But she did it. And he did it. And Ray Carver finally got to step out onto Inchmery Road.

And with that I finally knew. It was time.

Stacey was ready. She had found her voice. She was the Nightwatchwoman of Inchmery Road.

And it was time for me to start letting go.

But not before one final surprise from Stacey.

Chapter Fourteen

In the one hundred plus years of its existence, different people have brought different things to the job of Nightwatchman, and the Nightwatchman's ledger.

Gerald Mackie brought about the book's genesis, inspired by the tale of Peter Wright.

Tanner Rowe added his camera, and an eye for capturing priceless little moments of life around Inchmery Road.

Stanley Peters and Bob Andrews brought their humanity, their compassion towards others. Seeing what maybe others might not. Taking the time to really *see* the lives and loves about them, and then documenting them so carefully, lovingly.

And me? Well, I have tried to play my part. For better or for worse.

But Stacey, Stacey has brought something altogether different, over and above her empathy and kindness towards others, to the history of the place. Something that has enabled her to see further, deeper into the stories of Gerald Mackie's ledger. Into the people. The ghosts of Inchmery Road.

She has brought modernity, the gadgets of now to see back through time. A little Inchmery Road version of the Hubble Telescope, finding new layers to old stories. Snapshots thought long since lost. She found Tanner Rowe's photographs from his exhibition. She found Tanner Rowe himself, and that solitary image of the man.

She discovered pictures of the Blitz through her research at the library, a terrifying image of the bombing of the town at the time of Jon Suggs' birth beneath the rafters of the West Stand. She found a picture of what was left of the East Stand, the Victoria Road terrace after the direct hit that claimed the lives of Danny Stokes, Arthur Thompson, and the Manning's. Photocopies of grainy microfiche adding a visceral edge to Stanley Peters' moving testimony.

From her laptop she has shown me pictures of places that Dennis Lawrence wrote to Bob Andrews about. And Eddie Hamer's adventures too. Town squares, markets, football grounds. Even newspaper clippings on matches in languages unfathomable to me, translated – again by Stacey's computer – detailing endeavours on the pitch by the both of them in Arabic, Maltese, Icelandic, Berber.

She used the internet to let people know about her Preservation Club. And she used the internet to do something I thought impossible.

She had been a little strange for a few days. Distracted, anxious. Her mind elsewhere as we wandered about on our rounds. She would smile and say that she was fine when I asked if anything was the matter.

I didn't press the point. I knew she would have said if anything was wrong. I just let her be with her thoughts.

Until finally…

The Preservation Club had been in full swing all day. Little clusters of activity beneath a warm spring sun. I would always come in to work a couple of hours early to watch Stacey's invention in action. Friends discovered through the club, chatting, laughing, sitting together drinking tea. The clatter of a wrench echoing out from some hidden point – Ray Carver working his miracles somewhere unseen – for an hour or so longer before it was time to down tools for another day.

That day, like every Preservation Club-day, I dropped my things in the office, and headed straight down the corridor to enjoy the pockets of endeavour across the terraces, a few figures away up in the East Stand. Familiar faces smiling, waving as I passed.

Among it all, down by the pitch, was Stacey, doing a strange thing. She had her laptop in her hands, but the screen and keyboard were the wrong way round, facing away from her, and she was panning it slowly around, from one terrace all the way across to the other, then round and across the West Stand.

When she saw me, she quickly turned the laptop back round, said something: what I couldn't tell, then she lowered the lid a little, walked towards me.

'You nuh-need to come with muh-me, Charlie,' she said. 'I huh-have something for yuh-you.'

She ushered me along the corridor back into the Nightwatchman's office and had me sit down in the chair behind the desk.

She took a deep breath.

'Thu-there is someone who wuh-would like to say hello, chu-Charlie,' and she carefully placed the laptop in front of me, opened up the lid.

For a second, I couldn't comprehend anything. Nothing seemed to make any sense. My head went into a fog, and I just stared at the young woman on the screen with tears rolling down her cheeks, hands clasped to her chest, a smile breaking out despite a sob making her shoulders hitch.

'Hello, Charlie,' she said, wiping away her tears. And then everything seemed to catch up with me in a heartbeat, on hearing that voice. Despite having a North American twang, it was the soft, fragile voice of a little girl I used to know.

'Poppy?' I said. 'Poppy, is that you?'

I looked up at Stacey who stood beaming, tears streaking her face, then back at the screen.

'Yes, Charlie,' she said. 'It's Poppy.'

It took a while to compose myself, Stacey giving me a hug while I wept. Then, after a minute or so I sat, shocked, looking at the screen at Poppy.

And while I did that, Stacey did what all good Nightwatchmen would do in a situation like that, she made some tea.

I cupped my mug to try and help my shaking hands, and stared at the screen, and Poppy held up a cup of tea of her own and laughed, and smiled, and cried.

She had changed so much… but not at all… at the same time.

Her hair was still the same, though cut with far more care and attention than before, her fringe not as haphazard as it used to be.

Her eyes, her smile, they were all grown up, but so familiar, lighting up this young woman's face with a warmth so beautiful I could never hope to describe it adequately.

After a stunned silence, she began to talk.

She had been in foster care for a year, moving around from place to place, all over, before being adopted by a family, and they had moved to Calgary in Canada when she was fourteen for her new dad's work. And, so far, neither they nor her had come back.

She was in her second year at university, studying English Literature, and she had learned to ski! They would go up into the mountains most weekends, at least the weekends the Calgary Flames were playing away.

'They knew I loved football, but there wasn't much of it in Canada. So, they took me to the ice hockey instead, which is their version of football. It is a religion. It's good fun, and I love it. But it's not football.

'They didn't know anything about soccer as they call it over here, but they tried, for me. We flew to Vancouver a couple of times, which was only a couple of hours away by plane, to watch the national football team play, against Honduras and El Salvador, which was so kind of them.'

'We stayed at the same hotel as the visiting teams were staying, and I pleaded to stay up, to wait in the lobby for them to come back after the games. Dad sat in the bar with a cup of coffee to try and stay awake while I waited patiently, pen in one hand, my programme from the game in the other. And as their coaches pulled up, and the teams got off, I tried to get all their autographs, beneath each of their little profiles, their picture. And I got most of them.'

'Their pictures in the programmes, they reminded me so much of all the treasures you had shown me, all down the years, safely stored in those drawers of yours.

'And it hit me right away, why I had been so adamant to stay up, to get these exotic autographs from faraway places. I had been doing it for you, Charlie.'

A tear began to roll down her cheek.

'I had wanted them all for you, more treasures for those drawers. But when I had them, I couldn't send them,' she wiped at her face.

'I had just gone. Vanished. I didn't even get to say goodbye. That must have been upsetting. I thought that you might have been angry with me. So, I didn't send them. Though I had wanted to, so many times. I just kept them safe, just in case. I couldn't bear the thought that you might be angry with me, for going away like that.'

'I always thought of you, Charlie, every Saturday,' she said. 'I would sit by the television in my foster homes and wait for the Town result to come in, and I would imagine myself back there, at Inchmery Road.

'Sometimes I would find myself outside, on my wall, sometimes on my bench in the stand. But I would often find myself next to you, standing at the back of the benches by the Nightwatchman's door.

'The sights, the sounds, they would flood back. As clear as if I were there. Every single little thing. I just had to close my eyes and I would be back there.

'Your kindness, Charlie, your friendship, it has been with me. Always. I never forgot about you, and what you did for me. And then, out of the blue, on one of the Town websites I look at, there popped up a message from someone, passing on a message they had seen from Stacey on another website, asking if anyone knew anything about a Town fan called Poppy Hudson.

'I messaged her and…' she shrugged, smiled '…here we are.'

'And now, a little late, here you are.'

Stacey pulled out a little parcel from her bag, handed it to me. Inside were two dog-eared programmes – tiny profile pictures of players with snippets of strange, faraway football grounds behind them, autographs everywhere about blocks of statistics detailing footballing lives lived in every far-flung corner of the world.

'A little thank you, for everything you did for me. Everything you still do for me, Charlie, every day. It's so good to see you again.'

'And I got you something else,' she said, and Stacey rustled about in her bag once more, pulling out a Calgary Flames ice hockey shirt – all red apart from a couple of yellow and white hoops on each sleeve, and down around the hem. A large 'C' across the middle.

I put it on, and it dwarfed me, Stacey giggling at the sight of me battling with the sleeves, Poppy beaming, clapping her hands in delight.

'It's a little big, because they have to get all their pads in underneath, Charlie, but you look very smart. C for Charlie,' she said.

I showed her all her things, kept safe in the Nightwatchman's drawer. Her pennant she had only held the once, her birthday cards, her autograph books. I held them all up to show her – her autograph book full to bursting, another one started. I told her how first me, then Stacey had been keeping them up to date with new Town players for her, just in case.

I showed her all her season ticket booklets, and a stack of unused ones, from every season since she had gone. Again, just in case. Waiting for her.

I told her how much I missed her, how much I thought about her. That I had never been angry. There was nothing to be angry about. None of what happened to her had been her fault. That I had been heartbroken at everything that she had been forced to endure.

And that now I knew she was all right, I felt like my heart was going to burst.

Mended, finally.

She promised that when she had finished her studies next year, she would come over and visit. And she could get some autographs for her book, and use that season ticket, though she couldn't decide if she would sit on her bench again, or by my side at the Nightwatchman's door. And then after, she promised, she would go and get us fish and chips, like how it used to be, and maybe she could come with me on my rounds.

We sat, sometimes talking, sometimes quietly, soaking in being in each other's company again, until it was time to finish up.

She waved, and grinned, and wiped away tears, and I did the same, even for a few moments after the screen had gone dark, in case it came alive again.

I sat in a daze for a moment, looking at Poppy's programmes, then I felt a hand on my shoulder. Stacey's hand.

'Cuh-come on, Charlie. I thu-think you could do with some fuh-fresh air.'

I took up Poppy's programmes, her other things, and carefully slipped them back into their spot in the desk drawer. Then Stacey slipped her arm through mine, and we walked down the corridor. Out into the light.

Chapter Fifteen

I think you know, for sure – that you have truly become a Nightwatchman – when it feels right to add your handwriting to Mackie's ledger.

When the stories you have discovered sit comfortably alongside those that have gone before. Different coloured pens, different sweeps and curves, flourishes adding to the kaleidoscope of humanity within. Your passages becoming a voice for the voiceless, the timid, the lost. No matter how blunt a tool you feel your writing might be.

Stacey writes with a passion and fluidity, a poetry that leaves her faltering stammer behind. Eddie Hamer, Ray Carver, her oyster boat matinee movie gent – she has added their stories to the ledger. And by doing so, she has added a little piece of herself too. Her interactions and interventions in their lives unwittingly describing a compassionate, intelligent, and brilliant young woman.

Her handwriting fits with the generations that have gone before, whose love and vision has infused Mackie's ledger with the humanity of each precious soul that once captivated them.

It was meant to be, Stacey and this job.

Her entries capture what it truly means to see Inchmery Road, and the people that have come to love it. Who have made it what it is.

She sees it. She understands.

It is easier to let go when you know that everything is to be left in safe hands. That the person taking over cherishes the stories of Inchmery Road and will protect and preserve them with the same reverence as you have done.

It is easier.

But it is far from easy.

Day after day. Season after season. Year after year – having this precious little place all to yourself – a place you have cherished since childhood. Revered with a near-religious fervour ever since. That lifts your spirits every time you turn the corner into Inchmery Road – that first sight of the floodlights, the West Stand raising the hairs on the back of your neck, even after more than fifty, sixty, seventy years of looking upon them – It is so hard to think about letting it all go.

Because you can't walk its terraces night after night, drift between rows of seats, tread silently along deserted corridors and passageways. You can't sit and listen, night after night, to the world outside, watch constellations pirouette, storm clouds gather, snow flurries fall, without becoming more than a little dependent on this special place.

You can't stand and watch season after season from the Nightwatchman's door, witnessing moments of greatness, moments of sporting tragedy, moments of grand humour and stupefying tedium. The cut and thrust of a game in motion. The poetry of twenty-two players feinting and jumping, running and passing, tricking and thwarting, finding one another with a near telepathic ability – passing the ball to where they know their team-mate will be in a few seconds' time.

You can't talk to those same players and managers – know them and be known by them on a first name basis. Have access to everything and everyone. Be cherished. Valued. Respected. You can't have that without this little club of ours on the road to nowhere fusing with the very fibre of who you are, so that it becomes hard to discern one from the other – in body and soul.

You can't come to know of Mackie's ledger, and the stories, the people within – who have become so familiar to you that it seems almost inconceivable that you never knew them in person. Their triumph and tragedy becoming your own, so that you would diligently wipe down and preserve a bicycle that wasn't your own. Listen out for its bell, the rattling of chains fused deep within a grand old oak tree.

Or place a programme face up on your desk, for the simple joy it will bring to someone else in turning it over, discovering the signatures captured on the team sheet.

Or put up an old Christmas tree, to let its legend stretch across the shadows on the wall. Colourful strings of fairy lights in the darkness drawing in wide eyes from the foyer, hoping for another retelling, shivers up their spines.

You can't take these people on, preserve their memory, raise them up with every reading of their story, every moment spent thinking of them, imagining them, looking out for them, without finding more than a little bit of yourself becoming invested in them, in Mackie's ledger.

Your acts of custodianship bind you to them. They become a part of your life.

They become familiar in a way that is hard to explain. You feel their pain, their pride, their joy.

All from the dusty drawers of the Nightwatchman's desk, and Mackie's ledger.

This encyclopaedia of the Town.

Photographs, passages of handwriting, piles of programmes and news clippings. Postcards, Christmas cards. Old football shirts, books with personalised messages. Anecdotes of long nights tending to the memories of others. It is easy to lose yourself within. And it is easy to want to stay lost. And, in time, I think that you do. Or, at least, that I have. Preferring this life to any other.

And it is scary to give everything up. To hand it over. To hand yourself over. To put all you have worked so hard to preserve at the mercy of another. All those ghosts of Inchmery Road. Your ghost.

But for more than a century, each new Nightwatchman has taken on that burden, and cared for them as if they were their own family. Which, in time, they always seem to become.

And with Stacey, I know that all us ghosts will be well looked after. Kept safe.

But even so, I still don't want to let go.

It will be a slow process.

I will go down to three days a week. Then two. Then I will eventually be reduced to stopping by, for old times' sake. Making up some nonsense like: 'I just happened to be passing, so I thought I'd pop in and say hello.' Even though we all know that Inchmery Road is on the way to nowhere.

But Stacey will humour me with a warmth and friendship, with open arms, just as I did Bob Andrews, and he did Stanley Peters. And we will wander the terraces together, watch games from the Nightwatchman's door, drink tea in the office and pore through all the treasures safely stored there. We will leaf through Mackie's ledger, with so few empty pages left that Stacey will soon have to find another suitable book to continue in before too long.

It may be a book that I will never get to see.

I might never know if Stacey ever gets out to Morocco. Or if she falls in love with Marcus from the club shop. He is waiting patiently. Diligently. I hope that one day she sees how much he dotes on her.

I hope that one day she sees that she can be anything she wants to be, do anything she wants to do.

That she is wonderful. Intelligent. Caring. Strong. She has done so much already.

And that all that have gone before her would be so proud of her. Are so proud of her.

I wonder if I will know that I have gone?

That I have become yet another ghost of Inchmery Road?

I wonder if you are aware of it, conscious of the fact that your actions are different? In walking your familiar route to the game. Your rounds late at night – always the car park first, leaning up against the gates, listening to the night, then up past the shuttered turnstiles of the Inchmery Road terrace, down Lepe Road, out onto Victoria Road past the poplars, checking gates and shutters, and back to the main doors. Then up onto the Inchmery Road terrace, across the East Stand, the paddocks of the Victoria Road terrace, finally along the benches of the West Stand, to Poppy's spot. And then back into the office. I wonder if it will feel very different. Will it feel anything at all?

Or will I be just an echo? A faint ripple from a pebble tossed long before, from some distant shore. And I won't know that I am doing it, as such. Energy from a lifetime playing itself out in ever decreasing circles. Until I fade, like all those that have gone before me, into the faintest of outlines.

A fragile shading of pencil among an intricate sketch? Caught between the pages of Mackie's ledger. Among the shadows.

Or will I be just a memory? In someone else's journey? A smile, a moment, a word or two, materialising whenever needed. A beacon for another finding their way as best they can?

Whichever it is, I will be happy with that. Because I will be in good company. The best. And as such, I am not scared.

I will have Stacey looking out for me. And whoever comes after her. And whoever comes after them.

People I will never know, but who may, in time, come to know me.

Whether I will know Stacey is looking out for me. Whether I will see her across time, on her rounds, I do not know.

I am comforted, however, that someone will be thinking of me, just like we have thought of Gerald Mackie and young Peter Wright, and all the rest that have made Inchmery Road the wonderful place that it is.

I am comforted that there is no other place I would have rather lived my life, once my beautiful Evie had left me.

The people I have met, the people I feel that I have met – through Mackie's ledger – the sense of belonging and meaning that I have felt. The sense of purpose driving me on through rain and snow and long, long cold, dark nights that were never truly spent alone – I have been truly blessed.

My name is Charlie Truckle, and, with the exception of losing my Evie much too soon, I have had the best life I could have ever hoped for, in the service of our little club, on the road to nowhere.

And I have my cup of tea, and a little while yet to wander Inchmery Road.

I have a few more games to enjoy. A few more retellings of George Chester's ghost story. A few more nights listening out for a bicycle bell just past one a.m. A few more programmes to be left on the corner of the Nightwatchman's desk.

Plenty of time for Poppy to find her way back home.

Plenty of time for quiet nights with my old mate Stacey.

Time enough for so much.

I intend to make the very most of every second. Listening to the creaking and groaning of old boards and beams up in the rafters of the West Stand in high winds. The drumming of the rain on the corrugated rooftops. Enjoying the excited murmur of match day, the scattergun chatter of turnstiles spinning. The thrill of the Town running out onto the pitch in their wonderful red and yellow – being propelled to your feet in anticipation. Cheers at a goal, applause at a neat pass, groans at a simple action performed badly.

Three points. One point. No points. A few thousand loyal souls filing out at the final whistle. The buzz of conversation dissecting the play, coming to terms with a collective fate, until next Saturday.

I intend to enjoy the hush that descends afterwards. Voices fading. Shutters snapped to. Floodlights turned off. Cars pulling out through the gates. The silence. And those who materialise out of it.

Jon 'Blitz' Sugg, Danny Stokes, Arthur Thompson, the Mannings, Betty Marsh – generations of nameless faces – huddled together on the benches, in the shadows of the stands, leant up against crush barriers on the terraces.

At the place that had meaning to them. For a second or two. For all time. In the quiet. In the dark.

I will enjoy my rounds, Inchmery Road all to myself. I will enjoy my time with my old mate Stacey. With Sarah, the general manager. With everyone.

I will enjoy leafing through all the Town treasures in the Nightwatchman's desk, as well as football shirts from faraway places thanks to Dennis Lawrence and Eddie Hamer. Postcards and programmes, clippings from around the world.

I will enjoy smiling at photographs from another time – happy faces at Christmas parties, at work, chatting in the sun outside the main doors. David Smith looking up at one of his heroes, awestruck. Harry Bell and Danny Stokes with Mary Sugg, her new-born, out on the pitch. Gerald Mackie with his friends Peter Wright and Michael Trim. Bob Andrews and Frank Marsh.

I will enjoy remembering fog-bound November nights, thick pea-soupers reducing the East Stand to the faintest of silhouettes.

Snow flurries falling from heavy cloud onto a sea of deep white. Silence. Just me, the tumbling skies, Inchmery Road fading behind a blanket of static.

Stifling pre-season summers, the rich smell of cut grass and promise at a fresh set of fixtures. Hot air ruffling open shirts. Warm sun soothing all ails. Sweltering nights littered with clouds of mosquitos. Ripples of applause across sparse, breathless crowds at pre-season goals that didn't matter, save for the satisfaction of a flowing piece of play, the ball nestling in the back of the net.

Shooting stars on clear nights. Just for you.

The thrill of a frozen, colourless winter day, but with a game on where so many others had fallen foul. People huddled in thick winter coats walking up to check, asking expectantly "is it on?" A nod of the head. Broad grins. A day saved, where so many others had been lain waste.

The magic of Boxing Day, an excitement, an event greater than a simple three points. We are a part of something special. That has happened for all-time. A holiday like no other.

Little Poppy Hudson with another autograph for her book. Staring down at the fresh ink with an unfathomable wonder.

I will enjoy them. Those memories. Then, I will join them. Another ghost rattling around Inchmery Road. For all time.

And, for what it means to me, for what it means to so many, what better place to be.

I couldn't ask for more.

So, I won't.

Good luck to you.

God bless.

And 'Up the Town.'

Dear Reader

If you enjoyed reading this it would be great if you could do a quick review on Amazon, Goodreads or whatever book review sites you use: just a line or two would be great. Reviews and personal recommendations are really appreciated by authors and small publishers and help us to keep doing what we do. Thanks.

Also from Mat Guy:

The Stanley B is a boat built before WW2. A survivor itself it escapes the scrapyard twice and is the thread that links the mystery behind up-and-coming footballer Tom Maskell, an old Rangers nearly-man and his estranged daughter, and a woman who sails to Dunkirk with the small boats before departing on a journey of rediscovery. They also share a love of the game and its power as a diversion from the harsher realities of life. This is one of the best novels with a football theme you'll read. Mat really gets to the heart of why football matters.

"Life is indeed a journey and Guy uses football as the metaphor in *Stanley B* to wonderfully travel it."   – *footballbookreviews.com*

Mat is also the author of *Barcelona to Buckie Thistle, Minnows United: Adventures at the Fringes of the Beautiful Game,* and *Another Bloody Saturday. More at: https://dreamsofvictoriapark.wordpress.com/about/*